To Woo A Troublesome Spy

Book 3 in The Seductive Spies Series

By
Cheri Champagne

Jacket design and illustrations by Deana Holmes
Editing by Jen Graybeal, Dayna Reidenouer, and Amanda Bidnall

ISBN: 978-1-7777443-4-2

Dedication

For everyone that takes on too much.

To Woo A

Troublesome Spy

Chapter 1

The shuffling of paper whispered faintly in Christian Samuels, Viscount Leeds' study. It was nearing the midnight hour, but Christian could not put his work aside. He had to decipher the encrypted letter that had been assigned to him and return the coded translation to Sir Charles Bradley—Hydra, as their band of spies called him—as soon as may be.

It wasn't a particularly difficult code to crack, but its contents were direly significant and possibly detrimental to their mission to keep England secure…and to keep British soldiers safe from Bonaparte's armies.

Christian took a sip of the brandy resting at his elbow before he bent over his work once more. The firelight lent a wavering, warm orange glow to every surface. To the average gentleman, the room could very well be considered a library, with its walls of wood bookshelves, naturally dark colours, and masculine ambiance. *Chris* was not an ordinary gentleman, however, and his estate was already in possession of a library. The other space was, unfortunately, overflowing with books; they adorned every surface: the shelves, the tables, the chairs. Books had even been stacked upon the floor.

A faint scraping vibrated along the walls of the room, and Christian sat upright, alert, as he listened. His household staff had already retired for the night and would not be expected to rise until the morning hours.

Hydra had warned him several months ago that his identity had been compromised…but as time went on, he had come to think that perhaps their adversaries had forgotten about him. Whether they attacked or not, Christian remained vigilant in his readiness.

He tightened the sash about his cerulean banyan as he stood. He wore naught beneath, but that would not stop him from killing his enemy promptly and ruthlessly, should the need arise. He swiftly retrieved the throwing daggers from his desk's top drawer and slid them into his pocket, the weight settling heavily there, pulling the material of his banyan crookedly to one side.

Christian rounded the large desk and strode decisively through the halls of his familial estate toward the source of the noise. His limp was less pronounced this evening, but the ache in his leg told him that rain would soon be upon them.

He descended the stairs to his foyer before he trod down another corridor to his parlour. The halls were dark, as the servants had extinguished the sconces before they retired for the evening. The gloom suited Christian just fine.

The parlour would have been black as pitch if not for the faint moonlight shining through the glass panes and opened curtains. He halted in the middle of the corridor and observed as the silhouette of a man broke the lock on one of the large windows gracing the far wall.

Pulse speeding, Christian leaned his shoulder against the wood panelling in the corridor, watching the man bumble about the room, dodging the strategically placed furniture. He was spoiling for a fight, and this man could be the ideal opponent.

Then the intruder's scent wafted toward Chris, and he had to roll his eyes. *Coffee and sandalwood.* Could a man be more predictable in his scent? He instantly knew who it was, and his alarm faded into faint disappointment.

The man paused in the doorway, likely becoming cognizant of Christian's presence.

With the precision and ease that came from years of practice, Christian removed one of the throwing daggers from his banyan pocket and threw it. *Thud.* The blade dug itself into the door's frame, just missing the skin of the intruder's cheek.

"Bloody hell, Samuels," Sir Bramwell Stevens cursed.

"Your entrance lacked subtlety," Christian drawled.

Bram Stevens had been recruited by Christian's own father and had trained with Chris since he was seventeen and Stevens was sixteen. The man knew how to quietly infiltrate a person's home and should have been able to succeed admirably. He was losing his touch.

"I thought you ought to know," Christian continued.

Stevens crossed his thick arms over his broad chest and leaned his shoulder against the doorframe beneath the deeply lodged dagger. His intriguing golden eyes glittered at him through the darkness. "Yes, well, I could have managed far better if I had not been in this state of urgency."

Christian watched Stevens' expression. Could the man be anxious? It hardly seemed possible. Bram played up his customary grin, but it failed to reach his eyes. Whatever it was that had brought Bram into Christian's home, it must be serious.

"Come along, then," Chris grunted.

He turned and led the way down the corridor, the uneven tread of his bared feet silent against the hall's thick runner.

Sir Bramwell Stevens, under the pseudonym of Bramwell Smithe, had been given the assignment of infiltrating the Marquess of Hale's estate—the property that neighboured Christian's—with the intent of uncovering any nefarious or traitorous activity and bringing evidence back to Hydra in London. Christian could only assume that his friend and fellow spy *had* found something…and it was not good.

They entered his study, the brightly lit room nearly blinding in comparison to the darkness of the halls. Chris strode to his desk and resumed his seat.

He caught Bram's lifted eyebrow and crooked grin as the man eyed Christian's banyan. Chris pulled back a frown. He could bloody well wear what he wished in his own home. He was a viscount, damn it!

"Have a seat, Stevens, and tell me what this *urgency* is about." He crossed his fingers over his middle and leaned against the back of his chair, waiting for his comrade to speak.

Bram sat hard in the chair facing Christian's desk, his grin abruptly gone. "You are in danger, friend."

Christian inclined his head. "I have been informed as much by Hydra. He says my identity has been compromised, thus my need for increased protection." Not that his efforts had come to much, for in these many months he had not seen anything untoward or out of the common way on his estate.

Stevens shook his head and pulled a bit of parchment from his pocket. He reached across the desk, and Christian accepted the roll.

"They know where you live and aim to pursue the lead directly."

Christian scanned the document and laughed, his voice gruff and hard like gravel under a boot. It was a rubbing of a dreadfully coded letter from one of Bonaparte's spies to another, outlining their intent to attack Christian on the morrow.

"It was a fool who wrote this." He tossed the parchment upon his desk. "The code is so simple a babe could figure it out."

Stevens gazed earnestly at him, his golden eyes uneasy. "Yes, but the message is clear."

Quite so. Christian raked a hand through his short, silver hair. He had hoped it would not come to this. But it would seem that his time for hiding in plain sight had come to its end.

He was no longer a fighter despite his ability and the occasional desire to engage. After his injury, Chris had taken leave of active duty and had focused his activities on deciphering codes and teaching cryptology at the school to those learning the trades of the Secret Service in Brampton. He continued to practise, and aided his fellows when they had need of him, but taking assignments in the field no longer appealed to him.

"Indeed," he conceded. "I imagine I shall make myself scarce for a short time. I will report to Hydra on the matter. Thank you, Stevens; you have done me a kindness."

His friend brushed off his thanks with a shrug. "I begin the return journey to London before dawn. The Misses Wilkinson are in daily danger in that hellish place."

Intrigued, Chris raised an eyebrow in question. Had something occurred between Stevens and the elusive Misses Wilkinson? They resided at the neighbouring estate with their unfortunate relations, but he had never seen them. Of course, he rarely stepped foot beyond his property lines and, he would grant, only on bright, pleasing days. He could not abide the pain in his knee otherwise.

"You plan to journey with both young ladies?" he asked Stevens.

"No." Bram quickly shook his head. "Just Miss Rose Wilkinson—under pseudonyms, naturally. Miss Violet Wilkinson has another mysterious plan to escape Hale and his vile machinations."

Curious, Christian notched his chin toward Stevens and linked his fingers over his belly once more. "Tell me."

Bram raised his hands in a gesture of helplessness. "The woman is"—his friend's lips twisted in a grimace as he thought—"*spirited.* She demanded that Rose and I fall in with her plans despite her outright refusal to reveal them to me."

Both of Christian's eyebrows shot upward this time. "*Rose?*"

The movement was subtle, but he could sense his comrade's attempt to resist an agitated shift in his seat.

Chris narrowed his eyes and growled. "Bloody hell, Stevens, you know the rules!" His brows drew downward in a fierce frown. "You cannot engage in an illicit *affaire* with your quarry's niece. It is a conf—"

"I know, damn it!" Bram burst out, his gaze irate as he stood and began to pace.

The man was as taut as a caged animal, striding back and forth across the tasteful burgundy-and-emerald brocade rug. He was falling for the woman; Christian could see it clearly in every rigid line of Stevens' body.

Christian's jaw tightened, and his stomach dipped with dread. "Tell me you do not fancy yourself *in love* with the chit."

Bram recoiled. "Of course not."

"Good," Christian muttered. "I cannot abide a man so foolish as to believe in that fanciful emotion."

Bram's golden eyes widened. "You do not believe in—"

With a warning glance, Christian cut in. "Having an intimate relationship with a woman is accepted and encouraged." He softened his tone in an attempt to tame his abrupt, riotous reaction. "Provided she does not interfere with your assignment and you do not place her in harm's way."

Bram spun to face him. "She was *already* in harm's way! Hale is a despicable blackguard! The things he has done to those sisters…" His golden eyes darkened with intense loathing, and the muscles jumped in his clenched jaw. "It disgusts me."

Christian inclined his head. "I've had minimal contact with the family, but I concur with your sentiment, Stevens. However—"

"No." The man cut him off with a shake of his head. "You shall not alter my course. The sisters require aid. I refuse to condemn them to such a…*non*existence."

Chris watched his friend and fellow spy with a gimlet eye. Bram's eyebrows furrowed in concern and frustration while his eyes burned with fury.

Christian had not realised that the sisters' circumstance was as dire as all that, although he ought to have guessed. If Bram rescued the distressed maidens at the risk of his position with the Home Office, then Christian would not point out the folly in such an action. Nor would he report it to Hydra. This was Bram's decision, and, morally, Christian supported his friend's choice.

"Go on with you, then, Stevens." Christian stood to face his comrade. "It would appear that we both have early departures."

He could not conceivably leave until he had completed his assignment for Hydra and had sent it to London. It was going to be a long night.

Bram's lips twisted in a wry grin. "Indeed.

"And do remain vigilant of pursuit." His golden eyes warmed with concern. "I know for certain that Hale and his cohorts are aware of your identity, and while their apparent superiors instructed *them* to deal with you, there is still a chance that whoever issued the order will look for you on their own."

"Noted, Stevens. I've been warned."

The man inclined his head. "Be safe, will you, Samuels? I would hate for another one of us to end up injured, killed…or worse."

Christian nodded sagely. He had heard that their fellow, Barrows, had not yet regained consciousness after being attacked some time ago. Many others of their group of spies had their identities compromised, but none had experienced such lasting injuries.

"Understood," Christian grunted. "Likewise, I'm sure. A betrayed man seeking retribution is capable of many an evil thing."

Chapter 2

The predawn air nipped at Miss Violet Wilkinson's cheeks as she tore across the land separating her uncle's estate from their neighbour's. The tall grass was a pale, milky green in the fading moonlight, but she scarcely gave credence to its beauty. She was on a mission.

Her pulse raced as she sprinted, beads of perspiration gathering between her breasts. This was their chance; they *must* succeed! The hatbox and reticule clutched in her hands bumped rhythmically against her legs, the sound muffled against the thundering of her heart in her ears.

A shrill whistle streaked along the air, and Vi glanced over her shoulder toward the noise without breaking stride. Lantern light flickered dimly in Lord Hale's stables, and her stomach twisted with nerves.

Blast. One of her uncle's grooms had likely been awakened by the noise. Her pulse tripped, but she continued on. Her sister, Rose, would be safe with her charming footman, Mr. Smithe, at her side. He had vowed to protect her, and Vi trusted that he would deliver Rose safely to London.

It was Violet who was entirely exposed in the open field. Should her uncle or one of his men spot her, she was finished. But she wouldn't give them the chance. Returning her gaze forward, she pumped her arms and legs faster.

The loud *crack* of a pistol echoed over the hills, and Violet gasped, halting to stare wide-eyed at her uncle's stables.

No! It couldn't be! "Rose!"

Her heart caught in her throat as she watched for any sign of Rose and Smithe. Time seemed to slow as she painfully waited for an indication that they were all right. Even at a run, she wouldn't make it to Rose in time to block an attack. Violet had claimed it as her duty to protect her sister, to take on any punishment that her relations deemed acceptable, but she was too far now. Vi had to trust that Smithe would take on that role, no matter how difficult it was for Violet to let go.

There! A carriage tore out of the stables. Vi squinted her eyes and counted. *One. Two. And a dog. They're safe!* Her shoulders slumped in relief while she caught her breath.

Then the shouting began. More lanterns were lit in the stables, as well as candles in the windows of Willow Hall. The house was awake. The Marquess of Hale would be furious once he realised what she and Rose had done.

Violet's fingers tightened around the ribbon of her hatbox as she spun, pumping her legs fast through the tall grass. She swung her arms at her side, the reassuring weights of her reticule in one hand and her hatbox in the other giving her the courage required for this outrageous venture. Despite her dire circumstances, the sharp pain of healing bruises on her person, and the simply mad scheme she and Rose were embarking upon, Violet could not restrain the powerful wave of anticipation that rushed through her.

She was going to be free!

Vi dashed across the boundary of her uncle's land and onto the next property, sweat beading at her temples and sliding down her spine. The cool night air felt blissful against the high heat in her cheeks and beneath her bodice.

Her stomach flip-flopped as the grand *maison* came into view. It was an enormous—if slightly daunting—black shape against the charcoal-grey sky. Violet briefly wondered if the man who owned it was equally intimidating. But just as quickly as the thought entered her mind, she dismissed it with a light—and entirely inelegant— snort. No man could be as intimidating as Lord Hale. If Violet had managed to survive her uncle's malevolent machinations for these two years, she could endure anything. She could face any man and perpetrate *any* scheme to escape.

She pushed herself, her legs propelling her rapidly across Viscount Leeds' land. Her ragged black skirts whipped and pulled over her knees and calves, and the *maison* drew ever closer as she ran.

Anticipation and relief swirled in her abdomen as she slowed to skirt shrubbery and weave through his lordship's garden. She avoided the gravel path, keeping her footsteps silent as she drew near. Her breath still came in rapid puffs, the staccato beat of her heart echoing like drums in her ears.

Moonlight lit her way, the creamy glow illuminating the large, dark building before her as it rose high into the sky. She rounded the side of the *maison* in search of an open or unlatched window.

Lord knew that it made more sense to ring at the front door, but for this particular plan, she needed to catch his lordship unaware and alone. While concocting her plan, she had naturally considered all of her options, including—God forbid—begging. But she was no longer willing to be indebted or subservient to a man. She would damned well *take* what she needed.

The viscount was an elderly man with a limp, and while Violet anticipated his compliance with her scheme, she was prepared to take on this journey alone if necessary. In her reticule was a map that she'd torn out of a book, notes on the mail coach route, and a small amount of money—things either collected on her own or gifted to her by Smithe.

She checked one window, then another…then another. Each one was barred from within and impossible to enter without breaking the glass. Violet crept along the dark stone façade, feeling with her hands to the next window. She pressed the tips of her fingers into the crack between the panes and pulled.

At last! The window swung outward to reveal a broken latch, much to her good fortune.

Vi darted her gaze into the darkness of the room beyond, watching for any sign of movement. *Nothing.*

Careful to remain silent, Violet looped the hatbox ribbon over her wrist and pressed her palms against the window's frame, lifting herself until her hips held her weight upon the sill. Vi dangled there for a moment before working her feet against the stone façade in an effort to tip the balance. With an unladylike grunt and a surprising amount of effort, she raised her knee to the sill.

The edge of the window bit into the tender skin at her knee, and she hissed but lifted herself forward regardless. Then, she tipped, fumbling gracelessly as her arms flailed for purchase, the movement pulling painfully at the bandages covering her back. It was to no avail. Her frock caught at her knee, swinging her awkwardly to the hard wood floor.

Violet grumbled under her breath. "Bloody rotten *hell!*"

* * *

Christian's spine straightened, his hands pausing in the action of placing another item in his saddlebag. The hair on the back of his neck stood on end as a scuttling, huffing sound reached his ears. Someone was attempting to enter his home. *Again.*

It had been several hours since Bram had made his exit, during which time Chris had decoded the intelligence and had it sent express to Hydra by one of his recently awakened footmen. He'd then doused himself in wash water and begun packing for his departure.

Had Lord Hale and his French spies come for him already? Their stolen correspondence had not been specific about when they would make their move, but, Chris supposed, he should be prepared for anything.

Christian slid his arms into his banyan once more, his still-damp skin sticking to the smooth material, and tied the sash about his waist. He pressed a hand to the comforting weight of his throwing daggers in his pocket and made his way through the dark corridors to the source of his unease.

Anticipation boiled in his gut. Gone were the days when his heart rate was affected by fear for his mortality or the heat of a waged battle. Even the impending row with Hale's men gave him little more than a slightly elevated pulse.

His training was his good fortune; it had kept him alive these many years. His instincts never failed him.

Faint grunts echoed through the parlour and into the hall, forcing him to pause briefly in the darkness. Someone was trying to come through the window. *Damn Bram for breaking that latch.*

Chris stepped into the doorway, his hand slipping into his banyan's pocket until his fingertips reached the thin handle of one of his throwing daggers.

A hunched figure was silhouetted against the moonlit sky. Christian frowned. Something was not right about the figure. It appeared…inept. Had Hale sent a new recruit to kill him as a first assignment? New recruits could be dangerous, so zealous and eager for their first bout, but also clumsy or not fully prepared for what was to come.

Chris pulled the dagger's handle into his palm, where he squeezed it reassuringly.

Suddenly the figure vaulted forward through the window to land hard on the parlour floor with a *thud*.

"Bloody rotten *hell!*" the intruder grumbled in a markedly feminine voice.

A woman! With a distinctly foul vocabulary, it would seem.

Christian's reaction was brief, and entirely unexpected. His hand opened, releasing the dagger among its fellows in his pocket. But almost instantly, he returned the weapon to his hand. He knew better than to let down his guard, even if the intruder was a woman. Lord knew he worked with enough female spies to recognise that they could be as deadly as any man—if not more so.

He withdrew the dagger, his spine stiff and breathing slow, as the woman rose to her feet.

A low gust of wind blew through the window, further mussing the woman's dishevelled locks and, *bloody hell*, he could smell her. *Cinnamon*. His stomach knotted unnervingly. How could a woman carry such a scent? And why did it...*affect* him so?

Damn it, he was supposed to be immune to these charms.

Christian stiffened his spine once more, pushing aside the off-putting stirring of *something* within him, and focused his attention on her stuttered movements.

The woman held what appeared to be a hatbox in one hand and an absurdly large reticule in the other. Was she unarmed? Perhaps she excelled in physical combat.

Christian watched, his senses attuned, as his clumsy intruder crept cautiously through the room.

Engrossed by her every awkward movement, Chris instinctively tightened his fingers around the dagger's handle. The woman would seek to distract him, to unarm him. But he would not allow that to happen.

She froze; her breath hitched. *She knows I'm here*, Christian's conscience whispered.

The woman fumbled with her reticule. Christian instinctively raised his arm in preparation to throw the dagger.

With a *click* and trembling movements, the woman pointed both hands in his direction, her reticule and hatbox swinging gently from her wrists.

"Wh-who is there?" Her voice wavered.

Christian narrowed his eyes and lowered his hand.

"Sh-show yourself."

That was not the voice of a threat, and she clearly hadn't the faintest idea how to hold a pistol. In fact, the nervousness seeping from her put guilt in Christian's chest for even considering the woman a danger.

"What are you doing in my home?" Christian put as much anger into the question as possible while he discreetly slipped the dagger back into his pocket.

Though the truth of it was...he was far from angry. He was downright curious.

Chapter 3

It took all of Violet's will to still her trembling hands as she aimed the pistol blindly into the darkness. She had pulled back the little lever at the top, but she hadn't the faintest idea whether or not it was loaded.

"I shan't repeat myself thrice, madam," the rough voice in the darkness rumbled. "What are you doing in my home?"

Violet bristled at his imperious tone. Annoyance. It was the perfect emotion to still her nerves and strengthen her resolve. The old man had a right to his displeasure, and he could scarcely know that she would never hurt him in truth. But while this method mightn't begin with them on the best of footing, it would result in her freedom and his knowledge that he'd saved a life. And she was determined to have her freedom.

She would not relinquish the upper hand. But she could not threaten him properly if she could not *see* him. "Lead me somewhere that I might see you, sir, and I shall answer your question."

There was a moment of silence before the sound of shifting silk reached her ears. Vi cautiously followed the sound, the pistol extended unwaveringly before her.

She was led into a long corridor and up a flight of stairs, following his tall form and the sound of his uneven gait. Disoriented or not, she would secure and maintain the upper hand, and dratted well save her own life.

Low light shone from a chamber down the corridor, which grew brighter as they neared it.

"I would allow you to enter my study first, madam"—Lord Leeds' gruff voice drifted back to her—"but I presume you wish to keep that pistol aimed at my back, etiquette be damned."

For the first time, Violet *looked* at him. *Oh sweet heaven!* He wore a cerulean banyan that scarcely reached his knees. His muscular calves were peppered with curling black hair, and his feet were bared.

Despite herself, her pulse gave a small leap. *Is he entirely nude beneath the banyan?*

The thought startled her, and she nearly lowered the weapon. *Keep a hold of yourself, Violet!* She could not afford any distractions from her purpose, no matter the curious nature of his lordship's *casual* attire.

They turned the corner into what Vi could only assume was his study, and her thoughts were torn back to their current circumstance.

"If you would be so good as to answer my question, madam, perhaps we might do away with the weapon." The Viscount Leeds turned slowly in the centre of the room, and Violet was struck speechless.

He was far younger than she had thought him to be. And far more handsome. She had observed from afar and heard rumours from her uncle's servants that Lord Leeds was grey-haired; Vi had simply assumed that he was elderly. The man before her, however, was a surprise.

Viscount Leeds did, indeed, have grey hair, but his youthfulness was entirely apparent. He could not be far above the age of thirty. He was tall, his body lean, with broad shoulders and narrow hips where he had loosely tied the cord for his banyan.

Violet's abdomen quivered before she snapped her gaze upward to meet his striking blue eyes, brought into full relief by a shaft of moonlight. Lord, but they were like the sky on a clear summer's day.

"Do I meet with your approval, Miss…?" He trailed off, clearly hoping for her to introduce herself.

Irritation at his knowing gaze and cocksure smile sprang forth in her breast.

Vi straightened her stance and tightened her grip on the pistol, the weights of her reticule and hatbox straining the muscles in her arms.

"Indeed not," she said tartly. "I had rather hoped that you would be elderly. You are quite the disappointment."

The brief frown of disgruntlement that crossed his ridiculously attractive features almost made Violet smile. *Almost.*

He crossed his arms over his chest and rested his bottom against the front of his large desk, one eyebrow arrogantly raised.

"I kindly request, your lordship, that you—"

"Kindly?" the viscount interrupted. "It is hardly *kind*, madam, when you hold a pistol to my chest after having invaded my home."

The man was right, damn him, but he needn't be so rude as to interrupt her! Vi clenched her jaw before releasing a slow, calming breath. *5...4...3...2...1.* "Please, your lordship, do refrain from boorish interrup—"

"Am I boorish?"

"*I* am in control!" Vi stepped toward him until she had all but closed the space between the barrel of the pistol and the scant curling hairs on Lord Leeds' chest. "*I* have the pistol."

Her arms began to quake with exhaustion, and she fought to control it. Drat, but her hatbox and reticule were rather heavy when held thusly.

The haughtiness in his blue gaze cooled until his eyes were veritably frosty. "Indeed you are, madam. And indeed you do." The muscles in his jaw jumped. "Pray tell me, what is it that you want with me?"

Violet's confidence returned, and she notched her chin higher to meet his gaze directly. She had practised this sentence in her head countless times after formulating her plan of escape. It felt satisfying to be able to say it at last. "Lord Leeds, I have need of a male escort for my journey north, and I've chosen you to be that man."

She thought she saw something flicker in his eyes, but just as quickly as it arrived, it was gone.

"What is your name?" he grunted.

That threw her off. "I would prefer not to reveal my identity until we are well enough away..."

His lordship pursed his lips in thought, and Vi squelched the urge to growl in frustration. The man was unaccountably irritating. He did not even have to speak, and yet his haughtiness radiated from him.

It was disconcertingly alluring.

It made her want to punch him in the nose.

* * *

The woman was angry with him. *Miss Violet Wilkinson* was angry with him.

She had the appearance of a woman brimming with tightly wound annoyance: fierce frown, thinned lips, clenched jaw. And her eyes... Those striking deep blues held fire. Determination. A fight for life.

This woman was in danger, and she was willing to do anything to free herself of it.

It was simple enough to deduce her identity from the black bombazine frock, her inexperience with a pistol, her relatively easy access to his estate without the use of a horse or carriage, and her burning desire to escape.

Christian quickly sifted through his options. He could refuse, disarm her, and have her returned to Hale. That, of course, was not an option; he would never condemn her to a life such as the one she'd fled.

He could reveal his own identity as a Crown spy in His Majesty's Secret Service and offer his protection. His identity was already compromised with Bonaparte's spies, but something compelled him to keep his lips sealed.

His third option was vastly more entertaining: he could satisfy his curiosity with the woman, meet her demands, allow her to believe she possessed the control, and enjoy a jaunt to the north while simultaneously taking leave of his estate—as he had already intended to do.

Christian uncrossed his arms and straightened. "As I have no wish to be shot, I suppose I must do as you demand."

Miss Wilkinson's heart-shaped face lit with satisfaction, and her sultry lips curved upward in one corner. Christian's cock twitched, and he frowned fiercely. The woman was, as Bramwell had said, *spirited.*

"Allow me to dress, pack a trunk, and have a phaeton prepared." He started to step past her toward the corridor when she lifted a hand to his arm to halt him.

Her reticule bounced against him, but that was not what had him gritting his teeth.

"I insist on accompanying you." Her soft, lilting voice washed over him while her cinnamon scent teased his senses. She lowered her arms to hang at her sides.

The woman could not accompany him; she would see his saddlebags already packed with his belongings and would know that he had already planned to take a journey.

Christian lowered his eyelids and leaned toward her, the space between them thick with intended meaning. "You would observe while I disrobe, madam? I assure you, I have no objection."

Chapter 4

Despite the shock that rippled through her and the telling flutter to her heart, Violet scowled at him. *Damn his hide.*

She inhaled deeply, prepared to loudly refute any interest in what was beneath his banyan—lie though it would be. But she halted, her lungs full of his dratted, alluring scent.

He smelled of soap and *man.*

She shook herself. "That, sir, is the *last* thing that I would wish to do." She stood her ground, outwardly uncaring that he was so near. "I shall remain here while you prepare for our departure."

His blue eyes glittered dangerously before he nodded and swept past her into the hall.

Violet held her breath as she listened to his nearly soundless, uneven steps retreat down the corridor. When he was out of hearing, she released her breath in a *whoosh.*

Lord Leeds was *not* what she had expected. Against her will, her thoughts drifted to the book that was hidden among the black bombazine in her hatbox. Her heart pumped faster, and she forced the thought away.

Vi returned the pistol to her reticule and strode toward his lordship's desk. It was distressingly neat. Only an inkpot and ancient quill sat in one corner; the rest was bare. So meticulous, so...*maddening.*

She turned her gaze upward to the walls of books. Firelight flickered over the many spines.

How long had it been since she had seen such a collection of books? Her father had been an avid collector. She wondered briefly what her uncle had done with them all. The thought sent a pang of pain and regret through her heart. It had been two years since the passing of her parents and her dear sister, Helen. Two years of living in a forced purgatory with the spawn of the devil.

She daren't tell Lord Leeds her name until they were well enough away, God forefend he alert her uncle…

A shiver wracked her shoulders, and Violet straightened them against it. She and Rose had finally left Lord Hale's estate, and she would ensure that their escape succeeded. Rose was under the protection of her Handsome Footman, Bramwell Smithe, and Vi… Well, her safety was in her own hands at the moment.

As of yet, her scheme was progressing *mostly* as intended. She would simply have to close her senses off from Lord Leeds. The man was a walking puzzle; how could he possess such a practical and arousing scent, be shockingly attractive and yet have the air of a haughty prig?

* * *

The trunk closed with a *whomp* before Christian secured it, the small gust of air ruffling his coat. He'd dressed and transferred his belongings from saddlebags to trunk quickly enough, but he found himself unnervingly distracted.

He was *never* distracted.

Chris' thoughts kept drifting to the woman belowstairs. He knew she was likely rifling through his desk or snooping through his bookshelves. She would not find anything, however. Christian had taken care to burn any and all documents in his possession after he had completed his last assignment.

But it wasn't what she wouldn't find that had him so focused on her. Despite his better judgement, he was *intrigued* by her. After what Bram had said about the twin sisters, he had thought them both fragile creatures. He supposed he should have listened to Bram when he'd called Violet Wilkinson *spirited.* Indeed, that was an apt description of her. Brave, brazen, and mad were also fitting.

Christian placed his trunk by his bedchamber door then turned to glance at himself in the mirror.

Could all of the stories he had heard about the Hale household be true? Bram certainly seemed to believe them. If they were, those sisters had been living in a nightmare.

What does she have planned for our journey? he wondered. She had said they were to travel "north," but how far? Did she have an ultimate destination in mind?

Chris briefly wondered if Miss Rose Wilkinson was just as confoundedly alluring as her sister. Did Miss Violet Wilkinson taste as spicy as she smelled?

He frowned at his reflection as he internally scolded himself for the inappropriate thought.

Christian ran his fingers carefully through his prematurely silver hair, adjusted the knot of his cravat, and tugged on his dark-grey coat. His weapons were adequately concealed. He most assuredly would not be required to use them on Miss Wilkinson, but one could never be over-prepared.

Clearing his throat, he spun from his reflection to tug on the bell pull near the hearth. He hated to awaken his staff at this hour, but they would have ample time to sleep once he had departed and they all had retreated to safety.

He felt the sleeve of his coat. *Blast.* He'd forgotten his last blade. He strode quickly to his chest of drawers, withdrew the thin, sharp blade, and slid it into the sheath strategically hidden in his coat sleeve.

"You rang, milord?"

Chris turned at the sound of his butler's voice. He marvelled at how quickly the man had managed to dress himself.

"Yes, Henry. I do apologise for disturbing your sleep."

The butler bowed. "Not at all, your lordship."

"Have my phaeton readied, will you? And gather any provisions that Cook has in the larder and package them for me." He strode toward the butler, speaking in low tones. "I am closing Maison Leeds until further notice."

Henry frowned. "I beg pardon, milord?"

Chris put as much meaning behind his gaze as he could manage. "This is a code-three evacuation."

Henry's shining shoes *clicked* together as he saluted. "Yes, your lordship."

"Get on with it, then." He notched his chin in dismissal.

The butler bent to retrieve Christian's trunk and hurried away. He knew the seriousness of a code-three evacuation. Soon the estate would be bustling with maids and footmen gathering their things and piling into carriages, hopefully vacating before the break of dawn.

Christian strode through the corridors and down a flight of stairs before nearing the light from his study. The gentle, spicy scent of cinnamon drifted through the air, and he had to shake himself of it. He'd nearly forgotten how intoxicating that scent was.

With an extra tug to his black striped waistcoat, Chris marched through the door.

* * *

Despite her determination to remain aloof, Violet's heart leapt when Lord Leeds re-entered his study. It seemed impossible for him to appear taller and more attractive with his clothes *on*. It was vexing, indeed.

His eyes glittered with arrogance, as though he knew what he did to her. She would not allow him the upper hand.

Violet fumbled with her reticule, and the smug countenance slipped from Lord Leeds' features. He stepped forward and stayed her hands with his.

A bolt of...*something* jolted up her arms and through her chest to settle somewhere in her stomach. She cursed soundly in her mind. *What was that?*

"You needn't display your lethal power by waving your pistol about." His blue eyes bored into hers. "I can assure you that I will do as you wish. I haven't a desire to be mortally wounded, and I must think of my staff."

She blinked the shock from her gaze and jutted her chin outward. "Nor have I a desire to mortally wound you." Her eyebrow quirked. "I require an escort to the North."

He retreated a step and clasped his hands behind his back, his expression frustratingly unreadable. She narrowed her eyes before sweeping past him into the hall. She hadn't any idea where it was she was going, but she certainly wasn't about to remain in that study with him and his fresh, manly scent any longer.

Her grip tightened on her hatbox and reticule as she navigated the suddenly bright halls. A maid scurried past with a mumbled apology. Had Lord Leeds awoken the household?

Terror squeezed her heart. *Did he alert my uncle?*

Vi spun abruptly on her heel. Her breath caught in her throat as he almost bumped into her front. She hadn't heard him walking behind her.

He raised a placating hand as though sensing her distress. "No one but you and I"—he gestured over her head—"and that maid know of your presence."

She nodded her thanks.

Lord Leeds cleared his throat. "The foyer is in *that* direction." He pointed down the hall the way they had come, and the corners of his eyes crinkled.

Her heart stopped. Was he laughing at her?

A footman dashed past them, a bundle of material in his arms.

Vi blinked, her questioning gaze intent on Lord Leeds. "Surely you do not mean to bring your staff along with us." She had not accounted for the fact that a lofty lord might wish to bring a bevy of servants on their journey.

The crinkling in the corners of his striking eyes deepened. Was that his way of smiling?

"Most assuredly not," he rumbled. "I have given my staff leave to spend time with their families." He stood aside and gestured for her to follow. "Shall I lead the way to the foyer?"

Chapter 5

Violet was amazed to see that dawn had not yet broken when they exited the grand *maison*. His lordship's stable hands had been busy, indeed, for a phaeton awaited them on the drive. A lantern hung to one side of the perch, prepared to light their way through the dimness.

Something did not feel right to Vi, however. The hair at the nape of her neck stood on end.

Lord Leeds preceded her down the front steps of his grand estate, limping but seemingly at his ease. Violet halted mid-step, clutching her reticule to her abdomen. She had the eerie sensation that someone watched them.

Her gaze darted about the drive, searching for a shadowed figure or any other indication that someone was observing them. Could her uncle have seen her leave the estate? Surely not. He and his staff had been so thoroughly distracted by Rose and Smithe's departure that it was not likely they had thought to watch the fields.

Violet breathed deeply of the cool country air and forced her feet forward. She abruptly wished that she'd had time to don a bonnet before she'd escaped; that would have offered a modicum of concealment.

Lord Leeds halted beside the phaeton, watching her with an air of impatience. Vi approached him quickly, not to appease him but to dispel the disconcerting tingle at the back of her neck.

He helped her onto the perch, where she settled on the seat, eager and ready to be well away from Eastbourne. Vi placed her hatbox at her feet as Lord Leeds rose to the perch beside her. Without warning, he clasped the reins in his gloved hands and flicked, urging the horses into a trot.

Fluttering erupted in her abdomen, and Violet confidently believed it was from the sense of urgency. Despite herself, she turned to look behind them as they departed.

* * *

Lord Americus Chaisty, Baron of Bristol, put his nose to the air, his chest burning with desire and vengeance. He could scent his cousin from here. *Cinnamon.*

He focused his gaze on the retreating phaeton. It would appear the filthy wench had run off with Lord Leeds. He snarled, his lip curling to reveal his perfectly straight teeth. He should have known.

A sense of predatory possessiveness swept through him. He *would* get her back. And when he did, he would teach her a lesson she would not soon forget.

* * *

The further from his estate that Christian drove the phaeton, the more he sensed Miss Wilkinson relaxing. Anxiousness still held her spine stiff, but the rest of her seemed to droop with relief.

His curiosity about her heightened.

Bright hues of red and orange streaked the sky, the clouds above them shadowed with purple, as the sun awoke the day. A rolling fog curled low upon the ground, stirred into whirling billows by the horses' hooves.

Chris flicked the reins, urging them faster.

"Might I inquire, now, as to your name?" He hedged a sideways glance at the termagant.

Miss Wilkinson chewed on her plump bottom lip as she considered his question. Tearing his gaze from her, he returned his attention to the dimly lit road. Would she tell him the truth?

She spun in her seat to look around the side of the phaeton, as though ensuring that no one would overhear her.

Christian's stomach knotted.

"I suppose there is no great harm in telling you," she muttered just above the din of the horses' hooves and the phaeton's wheels. "My name is Violet Wilkinson."

He inclined his head as…*pride?* swelled within him. He felt absurdly pleased.

"Ah yes," he returned. "Miss Wilkinson from the neighbouring estate."

A small amount of surprise registered on her features.

He wouldn't push for more information, for Lord knew the woman had been hesitant enough to reveal her name. But while she mightn't wish to divulge her past, Christian damned well required certain information.

"While you are understandably reticent to reveal your secrets," Chris clipped out impatiently, "I must at least know our destination."

"North." Her light voice hardened.

A frown tugged at his brow. He could not quite ascertain what it was about her that irritated him so thoroughly, and that alone bothered him. "You said as much when you waved a pistol about in my parlour, Miss Wilkinson. Shall I deliver you to London, then? The edge of a dirt road near Cambridge, perhaps? Or mayhap you wish for me to take you to my familial seat in Leeds?" His voice grew steely as he spoke. "All of which are *north* of our current location."

Despite having offered the suggestion in anger, the thought of having Miss Wilkinson stay in his home made his gut clench in damnable anticipation.

She huffed. "You, my lord, are infuriating."

He scowled. "Not as infuriating as you are, Miss Wilkinson, I assure you."

Her lips had gone red from chewing. "I would prefer to avoid London."

Christian took a deep breath in an attempt to slow his heartbeat. "So noted."

He guided the bays in a gentle turn, taking them toward the road that would lead them away from London. He supposed it was prudent of them to avoid town; it would be the first place that his enemies would look for him, and with Miss Wilkinson under his protection, he would prefer to avoid a confrontation.

They drove in silence for some time. The sky grew dense with clouds, the threat of rain intensifying the ache in his knee.

The bays had begun to snuff and snort some time ago. Guilt assailed him. He did not wish to mistreat the beasts, but they hadn't passed an inn for a long stretch of road. He flicked the reins with a low murmur to the animals. It had been mere months since he had driven this road, so he should have recalled the scarcity of inns.

Several minutes had passed before he saw a familiar curve leading to a wide innyard. Grateful for the possibility of a respite, Christian led the bays toward it.

Miss Wilkinson gasped. "What are you doing?"

"The inn," Chris grunted. "The horses require water, feed, and rest. We might well eat and take care of our own needs as well."

"No!"

He looked sharply at her. "I beg your pardon?"

"*No!*" She carefully enunciated the word, as though he did not comprehend its meaning.

Infuriating woman!

* * *

Violet's heart hammered ruthlessly in her chest as they neared the innyard. Her gaze scanned the patrons nervously. What if her uncle— or heaven forbid her *cousin*—had journeyed after them? If they tarried, they might well be caught... And then her very life would be in peril.

"I shan't allow you to—"

He pulled the horses to a stop and rounded on her. "While I wither under the supremacy of you and your mighty pistol, Miss Wilkinson, I will *not* allow my horses to run themselves to death."

Outrage and guilt warred within her. She gritted her teeth. "You haven't the faintest notion of what awaits me, should—"

"*You will not tell me!*" he shouted. He clenched his jaw and took a deep breath before he continued in a moderated tone. "At the very least, allow me to change horses and visit the privy."

Her gaze caught on his, intense and bright blue. He was angry, she knew. She could hardly blame the man. She had crept into his home in the wee hours of predawn, pointed a pistol at him, and demanded that he fall in with her plans. But, dash it all, she needed him!

She conceded that they could not very well condemn the horses to running themselves to death. Vi inclined her head. "A *short* interlude, if you please." Lord knew how close any pursuer might be...

The muscles in Lord Leeds' jaw jumped as he faced forward and flicked the reins, expertly leading the bays into the innyard. The building was commonplace for an inn, though smaller than any that she and her family had stayed at when they were still alive. A maid leaned out one of the second-story windows and waved some bedclothes in the air.

They rolled to a stop, and a groom dashed out of the stables to hold the horses' bridles, a dog barking at the quick movement.

A pit settled hard in her gut as she allowed another groom to aid in her descent. She clutched her reticule to her chest as she rounded the equipage, her gaze unable to settle on any particular thing as she anxiously searched for a potential attacker. Chickens clucked and flapped as they passed, drawing her nervous stare.

Dash it, Vi, stop this behaviour! she admonished herself. She had endured two years at Willow Hall, so she could certainly withstand escaping it! If one of her uncle's or cousin's men came upon her, she could scream, make a scene, and commandeer an equipage to get bloody well out of there.

She could, she supposed, use the respite to refresh the bandage covering her aching back. It stung with every movement of the phaeton, and she'd been forced to sit so stiffly—to keep her back from rubbing against the seat—that every muscle felt taut and creaky.

Lord Leeds appeared at her elbow. "I have provisions if you're so inclined, or if you wish to purchase a meal from the innkeeper to have packaged—"

"N-no." Violet shook her head. She couldn't spare even a ha'penny on an unnecessary meal. Instead, she would request a maid to help her with her bandages inside. "Your provisions will be fine, I'm sure. But I am not hungry," she lied.

Leeds nodded. "Very well, then. I will be a quarter of an hour at least to arrange a change of horses and address my own needs." He glanced up at the sky. "The collapsible roof will need to be raised, for rain is surely upon us. Await me inside."

With that imperious demand, his lordship spun on his booted heel and strode toward the inn's door. Violet resisted making a face at his back. Await him inside, indeed. Everything the man said begged a contradiction. It was in the way he spoke, as though he knew everything and intended to flaunt it. Even if she agreed with what he said, her instinct was to defy him.

It was for that reason that after Vi had changed her bandages inside, she returned to the innyard. The clouds had darkened throughout the morning. She wished they hadn't so Lord Leeds, the overbearing scoundrel, would be proven wrong about the weather.

A dog ambled by to sniff at her skirts before passing on his way to the trees. It looked something like her sister's running partner, Dog: tall and lanky with wavy, spotted fur. She wondered how Rose and Smithe fared. Had they come across any of their uncle's henchmen?

A single rider on a horse galloped into the innyard, and Violet's heart froze. Her gaze darted up to the man's face, and relief rushed through her.

She'd spent the past two years endeavouring to battle her own fear, to stand firm against the torrent of anguish and hopelessness that consistently threatened to take over her heart…her soul. And yet, while she'd managed to face down her uncle and cousin and succeeded in convincing her mind that she was somewhere else during their abuse. And yet, now she'd had a taste of freedom, it seemed that she could not outrun her terror.

Chapter 6

Christian kept his gaze on the innkeeper and head groom intent and imbued with meaning. His leg ached, and his patience for the circumstance had been worn parchment-thin.

The head groom adjusted his footing. "I don't understand ye, milord."

Remarkably, Chris felt little irritation for this man, for it was Miss Wilkinson that had fired his seldom-felt anger.

"I," he stated in low, calm tones, "am paying you handsomely to have one person driven to London in a four-wheeled equipage immediately."

The groom frowned. "I'll do as ye say…" He scratched the top of his balding head. "I just don't rightly know why."

Christian could not very well tell the man that he required a decoy to disguise their true path. He was certain that they were being pursued, but by men searching for either Miss Wilkinson or himself, he knew not. If good fortune were with him, this carriage would distract their pursuers long enough for them to find themselves well enough away.

He ignored the man's implied question. "I am much obliged." He handed the innkeeper and head groom several pound notes each. Their eyes widened with avarice at the outrageous sum, and Christian knew he'd bought their compliance.

"Right away, if you would," he reminded them.

"Of course, milord." The head groom bowed deeply before hurrying away.

"Is there anything else that I might help you with, your lordship? *Anything* at all?" The innkeeper eyed him with disquieting adoration.

Chris offered him a tight smile. "I thank you, no."

The innkeeper nodded. "The grooms will have had your horses changed—"

"Of course." He cut off the man. "I thank you again, sir."

With a short bob of his head, Christian turned and left the innkeeper's back office. The taproom was bustling with patrons, which was surprising for the time of year.

His boots clipped on the wood-planked floor, barely audible over the buzz of conversation around him.

The front door swung open, and Miss Wilkinson rushed in, her chest heaving. Christian frowned as his instincts came alert. Her expression was impassive, but her eyes gave her away. There was fear there. Deep, bone-chilling fear.

Despite his desire to detest the woman, a vexing protective instinct reared its head. The damned irksome thing. He strode forward with long, purposeful, uneven strides until he reached her side.

"There you are." Her voice was breathless and trembled around the edges. Christian's frown deepened.

"What is wrong?" he asked in an undertone.

Miss Wilkinson shook her head. "Nothing."

Chris' ire returned at her unwillingness to confide in him. *But why should she? And why the devil should I feel angry about it?*

"Have you a need of the facilities?" The question came out far rougher than he'd intended.

She blinked her striking cobalt eyes, her hands tightening on her absurdly large reticule. "I've already been," she stated defiantly, her chin notching higher and a stray lock of her wispy brown hair falling across her forehead.

He had the absurd desire to curl it behind her ear.

Chris' jaw tightened as he sidestepped the vexing woman. "Very well, then."

Closing off his senses from her cinnamon fragrance, he led the way through the inn's front door and into the courtyard. His phaeton awaited them, the collapsible roof erect and in place and a handsome pair of bays securely harnessed.

A groom stood by and aided Miss Wilkinson into her seat while Christian climbed onto the perch on his own. He nudged her large hatbox aside with the toe of his boot, earning a sniff from *The Woman*.

He reached in his pocket and withdrew a coin, flipping it to the groom. The man caught it in the air with a "Thank 'ee kindly" before turning on his heel and jogging toward the stable's double doors.

Miss Wilkinson settled herself in her seat, her too-alluring bottom bumping against his and her spine impossibly stiff. But Chris' gaze was on the carriage leaving the stables. One passenger sat within, and the coachman tapped his hat in greeting. Chris sent him an imperceptible nod then flicked the horses' reins and took off in the opposite direction.

Their route was by no means direct, but despite the winding and isolated country roads, they were still driving *north*, as Miss Wilkinson had demanded. Christian knew that while she wished for a speedy journey to wherever it was she had in mind for a destination, they must also lose their shadow. He had plenty of experience, of course, but he'd never had to lose a tail while in the company of a maddening woman. One could not simply disappear into the night with a loud and infuriatingly attractive woman in tow; people would remember her.

It was for that reason that Chris was prepared, should they not manage to lose their tail soon, to make use of the latticework of spies and safe houses scattered along the countryside. He couldn't put their contacts in danger, however, so Chris simply hoped that they could outmanoeuvre their pursuer.

Several hours passed while they drove in silence. A light rain started, sprinkling over them, lending a damp stickiness to the air. His knee ached something fierce, and a chill had settled into his skin. Why the devil hadn't he put on his hat before leaving his estate? Both he and his staff had been preoccupied, and it didn't even register in his thoughts as he left. It was ungentlemanly and foolhardy; he felt unaccountably lonely without it. Did Miss Wilkinson feel the same without her bonnet? Why had she not worn it?

He gnashed his teeth together, feeling perversely cross that his thoughts had turned once more to *The Woman*. There was most definitely something wrong with him. And he was damned near ready to settle down for the night.

* * *

Violet pressed a trembling hand to her stomach as a loud rumble filled the air between them. *Curses*. She had gone hungry for far longer than four and twenty hours before; she could survive this time as well. Vi much preferred to find herself far away from Eastbourne—and, more particularly, Willow Hall—than stop to satisfy her trifling hunger.

Without a word, Lord Leeds pulled back on the reins, slowing the bays to a stop in the middle of the muddy road.

"What are you doing?" Violet asked over the din of the falling rain.

He sent her a coldly superior glance before descending the side of the phaeton.

"Lord Leeds!" She half rose from her seat to scowl at him.

He arched a lofty brow at her and disappeared behind the equipage. Her scowl deepened as frustration rode her. Had he a need to relieve himself? This was hardly the location to stop if one had such a requirement.

Vi's stomach rumbled once more, and she pressed her reticule to her abdomen. She looked up at the dark sky, the rain finally out of her face due to their lack of motion. The clouds were opaque and dreary. To her, however, they looked like independence.

This was the farthest from Willow Hall she had been in two years; no matter how chilled she felt, she had her freedom. For now.

Lord Leeds reappeared with a satchel in his hands. He thrust it toward her as he resumed his seat at her side. His arousing scent of soap and damp, warm man wafted toward her, and she resolutely resisted the urge to lean close and sniff him.

"What is this?" She looked at the worn leather in her hands.

"Sustenance," Leeds grunted as he resumed his seat. "Eat."

Her curiosity overruled her desire to argue, and she opened the satchel. Her stomach howled in anticipation as the aroma of cured meats, buns, and cheese reached her nose. *Oh heavenly day!* She swallowed her pride and reached in for a slice of beef as Lord Leeds started them off at a trot.

Despite herself, she groaned in appreciation as the spicy, savoury flavours of the meat spread across her tongue. She chewed eagerly, then reached in the satchel for another.

Water soaked through her thick bombazine skirts as the rain grew heavier, but she paid it little heed as she ate to her heart's content. *Bloody hell*, she cursed soundly in her mind. She must look like a street urchin, lusting after food in such a vulgar manner. As quickly as the thought entered her mind, she pushed it away. She cared not what *Lofty* Leeds thought of her. No, indeed.

She abruptly realised that he was speaking.

"… just ahead." He notched his chin forward.

Violet swallowed her mouthful of bread and closed the satchel. "I beg your pardon?" Water sprayed from her lips as she spoke, the rain trickling down her face and obscuring her vision.

Lord Leeds' jaw jumped as he clenched it. "We will stop for the night at the inn just ahead."

Fear, and a desperate sense of self-preservation, leapt in her chest. "We must continue on!" she called over the tumultuous rain. They must stick to her plan!

Lord Leeds scowled at the muddy road ahead of them. "You are foolish, indeed, Miss Wilkinson, if you believe I will drive through this weather in the dead of night!"

"Foolish or not, your lordship, I intend to put as much distance between myself and Eastbourne as possible. I mapped out our journey, and while you've chosen an odd route, the inn at which we must spend the night is yet a few miles ahead. If we alter course now, it will impact the remainder of our journey!"

With a harsh growl, he pulled on the reins, guiding the horses into a swift stop for the fourth time since their journey had begun. He spun to face her, his prematurely grey hair wet and flattened to his scalp and his blue eyes blazing behind moist lashes.

"*Have you a death wish?*" he hissed.

Violet frowned in defiance, notching her chin higher. She opened her mouth to utter an acerbic remark, but Lofty Leeds cut over her.

"While you might be enjoying a jaunt '*north*,'" he spat, "I have been doing my damnedest to keep these horses from slipping their traces or breaking a leg in this mud. Our wheels could easily become stuck or our phaeton overturned and your pretty little neck broken." Vi ignored the leap to her pulse at his calling her pretty, and instead focused on the fire in his gaze. "So I will repeat once more, *have you a death wish*, Miss Wilkinson?"

For the briefest of moments, Vi's terror took hold; her breath stopped, her back twinged in anticipation, and her soul cried out. Instinct told her to hide, to curl into a ball, but two years of practice kept her still with forced bravado.

But Lord Leeds wasn't her uncle or her cousin, and it was she who was meant to be in charge. She had worked diligently to perpetrate her plan, and she knew this could work.

If they walked the horses slowly and carefully, they should reach the intended inn in just over an hour, perhaps two. It was worth the added effort to begin tomorrow as she'd planned.

Chapter 7

Miss Wilkinson's gaze grew firm as she matched Christian's stare. "We *will* continue, Lord Leeds," she stated boldly.

Chris resisted the urge to scoff at the woman. She *was* mad if she thought he would bend to her will so easily. It was reckless to continue in this rain.

His damned leg felt nigh unusable, and he had a need to use the facilities—but he'd take a bullet before he admitted it to *The Woman*. While he could understand her plight, he had no desire to die this night.

He blinked at her through the rain. "You are welcome to hire a hack from the inn, at which *I* intend to bed down for the night."

"I shall not waver from my resolve, your lordship." Miss Wilkinson's chest heaved with her deep breath, and Christian battled with his desire to drop his gaze to her bosom.

Cinnamon, his mind whispered. *I wager they taste like cinnamon.*

He shook his head to clear his wayward thoughts. *What the devil is the matter with me?*

Chris turned his gaze to the trees and shrubbery around them. Where were they, precisely? *Ah!* He kept his expression carefully impassive as he faced Miss Wilkinson once more, a devious plan formulating in his mind.

He sighed dramatically. "Very well; I concede."

The combination of shock and pride that stole over her features was almost enough to make him feel guilty for deceiving her. Almost.

Christian picked up the reins and guided the horses into a gentle trot. Miss Wilkinson sat primly beside him, seemingly unaffected by the rain soaking them both.

"Thank you." Her lilting voice rose above the rain.

Chris' jaw tightened. He wanted to despise her but, damn it all, she didn't gloat. Nonetheless, he had better turn his attention away from *her* and focus on creating a soothing ride. He had one mere hour in which to encourage Miss Wilkinson to succumb to the lure of sleep.

* * *

Three quarters of an hour later, the rain had strengthened into a steady roar on the phaeton's fold-up roof. It was a wonder that Miss Wilkinson could sleep with such a noise—and in sopping skirts—but there she bobbed in her seat beside him, appearing for all the world like a half-tossed chit unable to hold her drink.

He'd had to drive the bays in circles for a quarter of an hour while she gradually slipped into sleep. Lord forbid they arrive at their destination before she had fully surrendered, or he would be on the receiving end of another tongue-lashing, several threats, and would doubtless have to continue driving until he fell ill with the ague.

Taking pity on the maddening woman, Christian transferred the reins to one hand and reached an arm around her back. She gave in easily as he pulled her toward him, resting her head on his shoulder.

A disconcerting buzzing sensation wove through him, and he scowled. Her warm, spicy cinnamon scent drifted along the humid air to tease his senses as she settled her frame against him. He wanted to growl. He wanted to curse. Damn it, he'd *never* felt anything remotely akin to this with any woman before her. Why did he have to encounter it with *her*? He didn't even know what "it" was.

He cursed soundly under his breath as he led the bays down a sodden dirt road. The horses' hooves sucked at the mud, kicking up more filth as they trotted through the deep puddles. Only one dim light ahead told him that he was headed in the correct direction.

It had been many months since he had been to this particular cabin, but he knew that he would be welcome, even without an invitation.

Christian squinted through the darkness. The shadow of a large man briefly obscured the light. It would seem that Hades was aware of their arrival.

* * *

Lord Americus Chaisty, Baron of Bristol, slammed his fist on the wooden table of the devil-knows-what inn, his rage riding him, deep and intoxicating.

"*Where the devil are they?*" His voice boomed low and dangerous in the large room.

The taproom's occupants had long since grown silent as Americus interrogated a groom and a stableman, their curious, frightened gazes burning holes through his sopping riding coat.

"I-I don't rightly know, yer lordship." The groom's throat bobbed as he swallowed.

Americus took delight in frightening servants, but at that particular moment, he was too furious at having lost Violet's trail to enjoy the man's snivelling.

He clenched his jaw, long past the end of his patience, and grabbed a fist full of the man's coat, lifting him from his seat. The coarse wooden chair scraped along the floor, the high-pitched noise causing several of the room's patrons to groan.

"Tell me where they went," Americus spat.

"Th-the man paid us te drive 'ere. 'E gave us coin to buy a meal, sleep, an' return. We's jus doin' as 'e says! We don' know nothin' else, I swears it!" He put his hands up in a gesture of surrender and Americus dropped him to the floor.

He cursed soundly. The bitch had evaded him. Damn it, he would curst well find her again. It would be difficult to retrace his steps and find their path, but he would do it, if only to have a taste of what he'd been wanting for two bloody years.

His father's rules and the chit's arranged marriage be damned, Americus *would* have her.

* * *

Christian gritted his teeth as he mounted the first step to the second floor of the cabin, pain shooting up his knee and through his thigh. He shouldn't have led with his bad leg.

"Christ, Samuels, I offered to carry her up the stairs," Hades—Jacob McKinnon—uttered softly.

Hades had been so named by his three fellows: Sir Charles Bradley, Hydra; Andrew Smith, Ares; and Kieran Richards, Hermes. All were named for their areas of expertise in the world of spying. Hades was superior at being unseen; he was stealthy and quiet, and absurdly large—though gentle as a lamb. He was also a startlingly accurate shot.

Christian shook his head sharply. "I am well, I assure you."

"But your knee—"

"Just follow with the luggage, if you will. I shall manage."

Chris forced his legs to move one step at a time, the sweet burden of Miss Wilkinson warm in his arms.

"Though I do apologise for ruining your rug." Christian winced at the puddles he was leaving behind.

"Please do not worry yourself," his old friend murmured kindly. A low rumble came from low in his throat. "The young woman's reticule is unexpectedly heavy."

Christian grunted. "It contains a pistol."

There was a brief moment of silence before Hades muttered, "I beg your pardon?"

Christian explained their circumstance while they strode toward Hades' guest bedchamber, where Chris laid Miss Wilkinson upon the coverlet.

Hades stood beside Christian.

"You describe so much fire in her, Samuels," his friend whispered, "but all I see is sadness and suffering etched in her fine skin."

Chris sent Hades a withering glance. "You have not yet seen her conscious."

But despite his assertion, Hades' words rang distressingly in his ears.

His friend's quiet voice echoed in the diminutive bedchamber. "Perhaps we should remove her sodden frock and allow her to sleep comfortably."

Christian's heart abruptly hammered against his ribs. The intense desire to peel every bit of cloth from her person clutched him so powerfully that his very breath stilled.

He could feel Hades' gaze, but for the life of him he could not tear his own away from Miss Wilkinson's rosy cheeks or the gentle column of her neck…

Hades clapped Christian on the back. "I suppose, however, that if she awoke nearly nude, she would cut off your cods, what? Come"—he patted Chris' shoulder once more—"I have brandy waiting."

Chapter 8

Shouting drifted down the hall from the family room, and dread consumed Violet. Rose! As quickly as her skirts would allow, Vi dashed toward the commotion.

"God damn it, girl!" Her uncle's voice became clearer as she neared.

There was a shuffling noise that stopped as Violet dashed into the morning room.

"Will you not answer my bloody question?" Hale shouted at Vi's beloved sister, Rose, his face purple with the force of his temper.

Rose whimpered. "I-I'm sorry, my lord, but I don't—"

"She's thick in the head," their cousin Americus interjected, his expression smug as he watched from his position on the settee.

Incensed, Violet stepped forward. "There is nothing wrong with Rose! It is you who is thick."

Her uncle's eyes widened. "How dare you speak to us in such a manner? Insolent bitch!" He raised his hand and delivered a back-handed slap to her cheek.

Violet's eyes felt like they were going to pop as pain radiated through her skull. Rose stood, but Vi gestured for her to stay back.

"You think you can protect her from what she is due?" Americus rose and slowly prowled toward them. He spoke to Hale but kept his dark gaze on Violet. "What say you, Father? Ought we not to deliver them a lesson for their tart tongues?"

"A mighty fine suggestion, son." He eyed Vi's twin with malice. "Mighty fine, indeed."

Violet stepped between Rose and their uncle, effectively cutting off his stare. She could feel Rose's questioning pokes at her back, but she ignored them.

Vi met her uncle's malevolent gaze. "I will accept the 'lesson' for both of us."

* * *

Bright light shone beyond Violet's eyelids. She rolled to her back, a grimace on her lips and sweat beading her brow. She let her nightmare fade from her consciousness. It was in the past now, and she oughtn't continue to fear. They would reach her grandparents in Scotland, and life at Willow Hall would be all but forgotten. She stretched languidly, her arms reaching high above her head. The spicy-sweet scent of cinnamon swirled around her.

Just a moment…

Violet's eyes snapped open to stare at a deep-green canopy covering dark wood bedposts.

She sat up. The room matched the bed; rich greens and dark wood filled the small room. Only a narrow wardrobe, a minute round table with a washbasin, and a chair filled the space, each pressed tightly against the walls. Personal items sat upon a dressing table, and books were piled upon the floor next to the bed. This was very clearly someone's bedchamber, and decidedly *not* the inn at which she had anticipated a night's rest.

Vi pushed aside the voluminous counterpane that had kept her warm and edged toward the foot of the bed. *A bath!* Someone had drawn her a steaming, cinnamon-scented bath.

Frustration at having been deceived warred with the desire to bathe. While it was thoughtful of Lord Leeds to draw her a bath, she knew it was merely his way of attempting to calm her temper. Well, it would not work.

Violet slid from the bed, her booted feet muffled on the emerald-green brocade rug. She dashed to the window above the table and looked outside.

Bright light shone in, the tall trees surrounding them notwithstanding. Her gaze scanned the land. It did not appear to be overrun by her uncle's men. In fact, it would seem that they were quite isolated.

Relief swept through her, but she remained alert. They might not have been discovered yet, but that did not mean that Lord Hale's men weren't on their way. She would have to keep her ablutions brief, for as much as she would like to find Leeds and give him a verbal lashing, she was intolerably matted, chilled, and musty-smelling.

As quickly as she could, Vi divested herself of her damp, rumpled clothing and stepped into the tub. Grateful for the easily accessible soap and cloth, she made short work of washing. Gradually, the chill seeped from her bones, and she felt her muscles relax.

With a sob of regret, she stood from the water and reached for a towel. She found her hatbox near the door and withdrew her last spare bandages, a fresh set of undergarments, and her only other black bombazine frock—a dreadful, wrinkled mess—for the day's travels.

The hatbox was dismally empty but for one item: the book. The *naughty* book. The book that she had bought for her sister in preparation for her twin's nuptials. That day had never come, however, Rose's fiancé, Peter Jones, having died in battle before the wedding could ever take place. The book had since remained with Violet.

Unable to separate from the book, Vi had purchased a second copy for her sister, which she'd kept hidden until she'd gifted it to Rose a few weeks ago. She missed Rose. Missed their written conversations as they fell asleep at night, and the way they brushed each other's hair...

With a small shake of her head, Violet pushed the maudlin thoughts aside. Rose was well: she was with her Handsome Footman and her own naughty book. Vi couldn't worry about Rose. Smithe had said that he would protect her, and Vi trusted him.

With awkward movements, she hastily bandaged her back, wrapping the cloth around her body to hold it in place, and donned her painfully old undergarments. She stepped into her dark frock and fastened the front buttons and bows, allowing her anger to return. She could not allow Lord Leeds to take control of their journey. Violet must make a *proper* escape, must follow her plan, not take a leisurely journey. She simply was not willing to risk her life for the sake of restful nights of sleep and full meals. Concessions could be made for changing horses and taking care of their most basic needs, but from now on they would stick to her plan.

With her determination renewed, Vi knotted her dark locks loosely at her crown and picked up her reticule.

Her heart stalled as the weight of the bag registered in her mind. *This is far too light.* The organ in her chest resumed its beating but took to fluttering wildly.

She opened the drawstring and looked within. *The pistol is missing!*

Dread and ire clashed in her chest. *That devious, loathsome, rotten blackguard!*

She clenched her fists to match her jaw and stormed from the room. Vi hadn't the faintest notion of where she was going, but she continued her determined march nonetheless. She spotted a staircase and stomped down the steps, entering a small foyer.

There, she stopped. Where was he? There were no servants...no footmen, no maids, no housekeeper. All was silent. Could Lord Leeds be asleep? Had he abandoned her here?

Violet's heart hammered, but her mind rebelled. *Civility be damned.*

"*Lord Leeds?*" she called. "Lord Leeds, where are you, you dratted nuisance of a man?"

* * *

Christian grimaced at the shouting coming from the foyer.

"I believe the young Miss Wilkinson is awake, Samuels." Hades grinned, and Chris shot him a dark look.

He swallowed his sip of tea. "In the kitchens, Miss Wilkinson!"

A low growl came from Hades. "You could have gone to fetch her."

"Kindly shut up." Christian frowned, waving a hand in his direction. "Mind your own matters. I will handle *The Woman.*"

Hades arched a brow and turned his gaze back to the blackened cloth in his hands.

Chris shifted his seat on the smooth wooden bench at the long kitchen table. Hades did not have a formal dining room, nor a room in which to break one's fast, but took his meals in the kitchens. He employed no servants, but that hardly signified, for the man certainly knew how to keep a home and cook some bloody fine food.

"You...you...*blackguard!*" Miss Wilkinson stormed into the small room, her spine stiff and her gaze venomous.

She was striking. *Damnation*, her cinnamon scent teased his senses. He should never have drawn her a bath, and he certainly shouldn't have added cinnamon. What the devil had he been thinking?

His gaze slid down her rumpled black bombazine frock, past the limp reticule clutched in her fist, to her stocking-clad feet. He almost laughed.

"Of all the insufferable things for you to do—"

Christian put up a hand to halt the disgorging of insults from her lips. Her gaze locked on his arms and he abruptly realised that he was still in his shirtsleeves. *Oh hell.* He'd forgotten to slip his coat on, and the damned thing was in the parlour. Though he had to admit that her interested gaze warmed him something fierce.

"Good morning, Miss Wilkinson." He smiled at her. The skin of his cheek pulled. Hades' razor was remarkably sharp; he'd very nearly skinned himself shaving.

She blustered. "Do not 'good morning' me, Lord Leeds!"

Putting her fists on her hips, she glared fiercely at him. She embodied vengeful beauty. Sultry, arousing, and furious.

He groaned, frustration riding him. Why did he think such things?

"What were you thinking, stopping here for the night?" she shouted. "I have a map! I have a *plan*!"

Chris could feel Hades' laughing gaze boring into him. Damn the man!

He returned Miss Wilkinson's glare. "That road was perilous! The horses could have broken a leg, or we could have had a carriage accident. We would have been stranded in the rain and mud all night!"

"I shan't engage in this pitiful argument again, your lordship." She pointed a finger at him. "*I* am in charge of this journey. It is *my* life at risk if we tarry, and I will not let you—"

Christian scoffed, interrupting her. "I sent out a decoy carriage at the last inn. Rest assured, Miss Wilkinson, you are safe."

The fire in her eyes began to bank. "While I appreciate the forethought, that does not guarantee that anyone in pursuit might not simply continue following our tracks."

"Whomever it is that you are afraid of will lose our tracks, particularly after this rain." Chris raised one eyebrow at her impassive expression. "As a peer of the realm, I am trained from a very early age in how to use a pistol. I can defend us if need be."

The fiery anger returned to her azure eyes as she held her reticule out in front of her. "With the weapon you pilfered from my reticule?" Her voice rose in both pitch and octave.

"My apologies, Miss." Hades' deep, soft rumble rolled through the air as he gestured to the pistol resting with a cloth on his lap. "Your pistol was wet; I thought I would give it a cleaning."

Miss Wilkinson's eyes widened alarmingly before she released an ear-splitting scream.

* * *

Violet couldn't stop it, could not keep the shriek from escaping. It was as though the man had appeared from nothing, suddenly there, before her eyes.

Both men stood, their hands held out in pacifying gestures.

"Where did… He… Who are you?" Violet sputtered.

"Miss Wilkinson, this is my friend, Mr. Jacob McKinnon. This is his home. Jacob, this is Miss Violet Wilkinson."

She turned her gaze on Mr. McKinnon as he bowed.

"A pleasure to make your acquaintance, Miss Wilkinson."

Mr. McKinnon straightened, and Vi's breath all but left her. He was large in both height and build. He wore the clothes of a gentleman farmer: a well-tailored brown cutaway coat and grey waistcoat and trousers. He had short, wavy black hair; a closely cropped beard over a strong jaw; and eyes the colour of brandy.

"God blind me," she whispered. "You're beautiful."

The heat of embarrassment flushed over her chest.

Lord Leeds cleared his throat, frowning.

"P-pardon me, Mr. McKinnon." She curtseyed haltingly. "I meant to say that it is a pleasure to meet you."

Lord Leeds' friend graced her with a charming smile, his teeth white and even and his arresting eyes crinkling in the corners. He was beautiful. It made her wonder why she didn't feel that excited flutter in her stomach at the sight of him.

"I apologise for relieving you of your pistol." He handed it to her, his palm open.

"Thank you." She accepted the weapon from him and placed it carefully in her reticule.

"The shot was damp, so I took the liberty of reloading it," he added. "Do be careful."

She nodded her thanks, a smile on her lips.

"Tell me, wherever did you acquire such a piece? That particular double-barrel flintlock pistol is quite rare…and was very obviously made for a man."

Vi's heart hiccoughed, and she cleared her throat. "It is mine, I assure you." *It is mine* now.

Mr. McKinnon twisted his perfect lips. "It might be yours, Miss Wilkinson, but I am quite certain it was designed for a man. You see"—he gestured toward the weight in her reticule—"the barrel is roughly twelve inches in length. Women's pistols range anywhere from six to eight inches in length." He was silent for a moment, the air around them heavy. "Did you purchase it second-hand?"

She swallowed, grateful for the easy lie. "It is second-hand, yes."

He nodded, a grin pulling at one side of his mouth. "Ah, yes. I'm afraid to say that whomever it was that sold it to you should have known better than to supply you with an ill-suited weapon. If you would like, I have a pistol that might suit—"

"While I thank you for the gracious offer, Mr. McKinnon, I am rather anxious for Lord Leeds and I to resume our journey." She smiled openly at him before turning to frown at Lofty Leeds. "I will return to the foyer in one quarter of an hour. Please be sure to have yourself decent, packed, and with the phaeton readied."

Decent, indeed. When first she'd noticed Lord Leeds in his rolled-up shirtsleeves, she'd nearly swallowed her tongue. The man had the most alarming effect upon her. She despised it.

Chapter 9

"The devil you will!" Christian growled. He'd told himself that what he felt was anger, but he was terrified that it might be something *else* flaring in his chest. Something decidedly more discomfiting.

The Woman's eyes first widened, then narrowed on him. "I beg your pardon?"

He took a breath to calm himself. "While I appreciate your sense of urgency, Miss Wilkinson, I'll not have you fainting from hunger. Jacob has prepared a fine morning meal, of which I urge you to partake." He gestured to the bench opposite the one he'd previously occupied.

She chewed on her bottom lip, and Chris had to refrain from groaning. That tore it. It had been far too long since he'd bedded a woman; it had gotten to his head, for certain. It could also be a matter of too few hours of sleep; he'd had a fitful night on Hades' lumpy chaise longue in the parlour. Whatever the reason, he needed to either find a willing woman or take care of these curst needs on his own.

"First, I expect something from you." *The Woman* imbued her gaze with meaning—a meaning that was lost on Christian.

Did she wish for him to fetch her food? To retrieve her boots from the guest bedchamber? Did she—

Hades cleared his throat. "An apology," he murmured.

Chris' scowl caught him off guard, but he quickly schooled his features. The blasted woman demanded an apology? For what— potentially saving her life? He clenched his jaw and took a deep breath. If it would get her to eat and find them on the road quickly, he would relent.

"My sincerest apologies, Miss Wilkinson."

Her smile of satisfaction both irritated and aroused him. *Maddening woman.*

He waited until she was seated before he resumed his place across from her. Hades strode to the warming pots above the fireplace and began to heap food upon a plate.

"How are the two of you acquainted?" Miss Wilkinson placed her reticule upon the bench beside her pert *derrière*.

Hades' back stiffened at the fireplace. The man hated telling falsehoods. It was why he excelled at being invisible; no one noticed him enough to ask questions.

Christian answered. "Jacob and I were introduced by a mutual acquaintance."

It was mostly true. Hades had met Christian's superior, Hydra, while on assignment on the continent, working directly under Lord Wellington. Upon their return from war, they'd been introduced to Chris as fellows working for the Home Office.

Miss Wilkinson nodded, her blue gaze locked on his. He silently dared her to inquire further. While he preferred not to, he was skilled in the art of telling falsehoods.

* * *

"I admire her tenacity," Hades rumbled.

Christian shot his friend a sharp glance. The damned thing was...he admired Miss Wilkinson, as well.

"Come now, Samuels, you must admit that she has—"

"Yes, yes, I know," Chris growled irritably.

They were silent for several moments as Christian slipped on his coat and ensured his trunk was closed properly. Miss Wilkinson had returned to the guest bedchamber to gather her own belongings.

Hades' soft voice sounded behind him. "You suspect that she is being pursued."

Chris nodded his head. "I do. In fact, I'd been warned by Stevens that my identity has been compromised and that someone is coming for *me*. I cannot be certain if our pursuers are mine or Miss Wilkinson's. I expect, however, that they are not far behind us, even with the poor weather and the diversion."

"Would you care for an escort? I could follow discreetly behind you."

"I thank you, no; that is not necessary." Christian lifted an eyebrow at his friend. "I am armed."

Hades crossed his arms over his chest. "If you should defend yourself, you must know that Miss Wilkinson might discover your true identity."

Christian tilted his head with a grimace. "An unfortunate circumstance, to be sure, but one that cannot be helped."

He gripped the handle on his trunk and lifted, hiding a grimace at the pain jolting through his knee. The skies were clear for the moment, but rain would be upon them again soon enough. His knee was never wrong.

"You care for her," Hades observed, his expression pensive.

Christian's brows drew together in a frown as something altogether bewildering knotted in his gut. "Don't be daft."

He started for the parlour's door, but Hades stopped him.

"Deny it if you will." The man strode forward, his hulking frame towering over Chris. "You mightn't see it now, Samuels, but—"

Christian sliced his hand through the air, frustration pumping his blood rapidly through his veins. "*No.* I admit to being curious at first, but now, if I feel anything for the woman, it is irritation and a desire to be well away from her. I have no wish to see her harmed," he conceded, "and I shall do what I can to deliver her to her destination, but damn it, the woman drives me mad with annoyance!"

A throat cleared in the hallway, and both men swung their gaze toward the sound.

Christian cursed inwardly. Miss Wilkinson stood in the doorway, her hatbox and reticule in her hands, and, if he wasn't mistaken, a glimmer of hurt in her gaze.

"Miss Wilkinson, I—"

She put a hand up to stay him. "Save your words, Lord Leeds. I am well aware of your feelings." She arched an eyebrow at him. "After all, what man takes delight in having his masculinity and control stripped away by a mere woman?"

* * *

Wind nipped at Violet's cheeks and tugged at her half-fallen chignon. The sky was dark with the threat of rain. The horses' hooves splashed through puddles from the previous evening's torrent. Their snorts of exertion and the wheels rolling through sucking mud were the only sounds surrounding them.

Lord Leeds had been stiff and silent beside her since they had embarked several hours before. Despite what she'd said, his words had hurt...and continued to hurt. She had suspected that he didn't think kindly of her, but hearing it from his lips stung her pride. What was worse, the realisation struck that she'd begun to *hope* he would like her. At the very least, it would lessen the awkward silence and simmering animosity between them.

She clutched her reticule tighter as they rounded a curve in the road. She'd added *The Book* to her burden, for fear that her sodden dress would ruin it once placed in her hatbox. It wasn't particularly valuable, but it was one of her only possessions, and therefore valuable to *her*.

"Will you tell me, now, where it is that we are headed?" Lord Leeds' low voice broke through their long silence.

She opened her mouth to speak, but he spoke first. "And pray, do not say *north*."

Vi supposed there was no harm in telling him. While he might not be fond of her, he'd expressed a desire to see her unharmed and safely to her destination; she could trust him not to abandon her.

"To my grandmamma and grandpapa in Glasgow."

She watched him from the corner of her eye as his eyebrows rose. "You're part Scottish?"

"No." Part of her wanted to leave it at that, but while she would likely never see the man again, and he very possibly cared nothing for her family history, Vi felt compelled to continue. "My grandparents merely *wish* they were Scottish. As soon as my mother left home, they purchased a house in Glasgow and have been enjoying the Scottish life ever since."

Lofty Leeds nodded as she spoke.

Her bladder gave a twang, and Vi reached into her reticule for the torn book pages. Ignoring her irksome escort's curious glances, she examined the map and read the notes she'd added along the edges.

She cleared her throat. "There is an inn just up the way where we can change horses and refresh ourselves before resuming our journey."

"It is nearing the luncheon hour; we will have a repast and a rest as well."

Violet was hungry and desirous to stretch her legs, but he spoke with such imperiousness that she had the overwhelming need to contradict him. "We haven't the time for a meal. A change of horses and taking care of our immediate needs should suffice."

His scowl was instant. "I shall not engage in this same argument with you, Miss Wilkinson—"

"I do not trust you to not trick me into staying the night," she lied.

He scoffed. "Of course you should bemoan your night of sleep and warmth when the far more appealing option of perishing in a carriage accident presented itself." He put a hand to his chest. "My most sincere apologies, Miss Wilkinson, for sparing your pitiful life when I should very clearly have left you to die."

Her jaw dropped despite herself.

"Is that not what you wished to hear?" Sarcasm veritably oozed from him. "You came to me for a reason, Miss Wilkinson. I am your escort. Your *protection*. Your lofty ideas of superiority and control notwithstanding, you *rely* on me." He cut her a scathing sidelong glance. "I know the land, I know how to drive, I provide funding for your little escape. You might wave your pistol about, but you would—"

"That is quite sufficient, Lord Leeds. Your point has been made." Vi clenched her jaw and counted backwards from five in her mind in an effort to quell the spike of anger that swelled within her. "And while I thank you for your compliance and your generous aid, I will not stand for cruelty."

The truth of his words grated. She would admit that she hadn't shown him any kindness; her tone was sharp and her words sardonic. Despite his not being kind, either, it did not excuse her rude behaviour. Indeed, Vi was the aggressor, and he was allowing her control while also taking on the brunt of the burden for their journey.

Despite the powerful need to challenge his every word, Violet relented. "Very well, your lordship. A meal would be acceptable."

With a terse nod, Lord Leeds guided the horses down the inn's drive.

Chapter 10

His stomach sufficiently filled and his needs satisfied, Christian led the quiet Miss Wilkinson to their equipage. The air was heavy with moisture and unspoken words. The mist clung to his skin, and his knee throbbed.

A stable hand aided *The Woman* onto the perch before Chris took his own seat. He murmured his thanks to the young man and flipped him a coin before accepting the reins.

With a gentle flick, the horses and their burden jolted into motion.

Luncheon had been fraught with tense silence. He should have apologised for his harsh words; it was certainly not his finest moment, but he'd be damned if he bent wholly to the woman's demands. She knew precisely how to aggravate and arouse him simultaneously, which only turned his mood increasingly foul.

He regretted that Miss Wilkinson had overheard his discussion with Hades, for he'd had no intention of hurting her—her obvious distaste of him notwithstanding. Frankly, he did not know why he'd said those things. For years he had been growing accustomed to a careful neutrality toward daily life, not feeling any particular anger, irritation, or intense desire. Suddenly having these feelings was far more unsettling than he would have imagined.

In agitation, Christian urged the horses faster.

Lord knew how long their unconventional route to Scotland would take, particularly while evading pursuers, and while he, himself, required a means to escape, he hadn't envisioned his journey alongside a puzzling, Machiavellian Amazon.

"Perhaps we ought to reduce our speed…" Miss Wilkinson called above the squelch of horses' hooves and rattling wheels.

Damn.

The phaeton abruptly jolted, and the loud *crack* of splintering wood rent the air.

Christian's heart stalled; he clutched the horses' reins before the phaeton shook and lurched, expelling Chris from his seat.

Miss Wilkinson's shriek echoed in his ears as he landed upon the dirt road, the very breath knocked from him. Pain radiated across his hip and ribs, his hands tightening instinctively on the reins.

The horses whinnied, their cries terrified, before they started at a wild gallop. Chris cursed soundly before the reins grew taut and the horses dragged him along the road. The muscles in his arms screamed in pain, and agony tore through his ribs, back, and arse as stones and twigs minced his coat.

His mind worked in a frenzy. They required the horses in order to outrun potential pursuers, but regaining control was nigh impossible, and riding a carriage horse even more so. With a hiss of pain and regret between bared teeth, Christian let go.

* * *

Spots danced before Violet's eyes, and she blinked rapidly in an attempt to dispel them. Her head swam and her body ached, and a groan rattled in her chest.

"What…" she croaked. *What happened?* She lay flat on her back, her mind whirling. With another blink, her memory rushed back. *The carriage! Lord Leeds!* Vi flexed her muscles one at a time, testing the amount of pain. Nothing seemed to be broken, but no doubt she would soon be covered in bruises. Her view of the rolling grey sky blurred, and she closed her eyes against the sight.

Her ears rang, the distant thudding of horses' hooves slowing to a light patter. There was a shout. Then another. Vi frowned. *What did it say?* There it came again, but much closer.

"Miss Wilkinson!" Lord Leeds crouched over her as the first drops of rain began to fall, his clothing torn and covered in streaks of dirt and blood. His brows were drawn together in concern, his lips white with tension. "Miss Wilkinson, can you speak to me?"

She licked her lips. "Yes." Vi moved to sit up, and her head spun briefly before she blinked away the dizziness.

Her assurance notwithstanding, his frown deepened. "Breathe slowly," he murmured soothingly.

Lord Leeds leaned forward to gaze searchingly into her eyes. "We might be required to keep you awake into the evening to ensure that you are not concussed. Does your head or neck pain you?"

"Not terribly."

In a not-altogether-unwelcome movement, Leeds put his hands to her bared skin. His thumb and fingers roamed the column of her neck, and his other hand cupped her jaw. "How does this feel?" His breath teased the fallen hair at her temple, sending a tremor through her.

It felt far too good.

Her eyelids suddenly felt weighty, her heavy blink leading her eyes to roll.

"Miss Wilkinson?" Lord Leeds' frown intensified as he caught her gaze once more.

He repeated the motions with his hands, and Vi's stomach quivered and her pulse fluttered erratically. She scowled. Her dratted body was betraying her. Lord Leeds was a supercilious, *annoying* man. But he also showed compassion and kindness. In her current hazy state, she almost thought she *liked* the man. Perish the thought.

He narrowed the distance between them, gazing intently at her. "How does it feel, Miss Wilkinson?"

Her breath stalled. One thing was for certain: she was attracted to the blasted man.

Vi took a quavering breath. "Pleasing," she whispered.

Surely he must hear her heart beating, could feel her pulse against his hands. Surely he realised that there, in that moment, she wanted him to kiss her. To press his lips languidly against hers, to tighten his hold on her and then plunder her mouth...

His gaze dropped to her lips. Lord, but her bosom swelled and a quivering began low in her belly. Violet had extensive knowledge but, unlike her sister, very little experience in the physical intimacies between the sexes.

What would he taste like?

Lord Leeds' chest expanded and contracted with each breath, his features tense—but no longer with concern. His gaze fixated on her lips as he slowly drew near.

Violet paid little heed to anything else. The heavily falling rain that drenched them slipped from her conscious thought as his arousing scent of soap and man surrounded her.

Then, with a bright flash of light and a quickly following *clap* of thunder, the moment was gone. Lord Leeds sprang back, his gaze darting around them. Vi felt abruptly chilled, the rainwater seeping through her gown and settling into her bones.

Lord Leeds stood, offering her his hand. "Are you able to rise?"

"I believe so, yes." She accepted his proffered hand, though her muscles protested the movement. Her head swam, and her eyesight blurred briefly before it cleared.

The phaeton lay on its side, the wood of its wheels and frame twisted and broken. The horses were far up the road, their reins caught on a tree's branch.

"What happened?" she asked his lordship dazedly.

He shook his head with a wince. His silver hair was caked with mud, blood, and rainwater, his coat torn up his side and back... *Lord*, but he was in a state!

"I intend to find out," he muttered.

He strode past her, his limp weighing heavily in his step.

Vi watched as he passed, and a gasp rose unbidden from her throat. She could not close her eyes; her gaze was transfixed on Lord Leeds' partially exposed bottom.

He spun to face her, and Violet's stomach swooped at having been caught staring.

"What has happened?" He watched her intensely.

Her mouth went dry, and her tongue refused to cooperate. *Damnation*. She ought to be far beyond such prudish discomfiture. "Your..." She gestured toward him. "Your...er...bottom is showing."

He cursed, twisting to see the state of himself.

"My apologies, Miss Wilkinson. Perhaps you had best avert your eyes while I examine the phaeton."

"Certainly not!"

His eyebrow rose, and something decidedly wicked shone in his eyes. "I beg your pardon?"

She clucked her tongue, though she could not deny that watching his *derrière* as he focused on his task was certainly tempting. "I aim to *help* you, presumptuous man."

With a swish of her skirts, Violet swept past him, her stomach fluttering unremittingly.

She wiped at the rain dripping down her face as she bent to examine the wreckage despite the protest of every muscle in her body.

The phaeton was awfully damaged. One wheel was all but entirely splintered, the seat was cracked down its centre, and the rails were crushed. It was a sad sight.

Lord Leeds uttered a dark curse as he crouched beside her.

"What is it?" she asked, worry knotting her stomach.

He turned his gaze up at her, his eyes clouded with fury. "Our equipage was sabotaged."

Chapter 11

"*What?*" Miss Wilkinson's eyes grew alarmingly large in her sopping, slender face.

Christian battled with the anger surging through him. The blackguard that did this would meet his fist, by God!

He rose from his crouched position and scanned the muddy road and tree line.

"Sabotaged, Miss Wilkinson," he confirmed. "We must leave. *Quickly*. Whoever did this cannot be far behind us."

"*Bloody hell.*" She somehow managed to whisper the unladylike curse with venom in her voice. Chris' lips twitched.

Naked fear shone in her eyes, which only urged Chris to move faster. He bent to detach his trunk from the rear of the phaeton, then searched for *The Woman*'s hatbox. He spotted a bit of ribbon poking out from beneath the wreckage and crouched to examine it.

"Blast. I fear this might prove difficult." He glanced at her over his shoulder.

"Please, do not trouble yourself." She watched the road behind them with worry. "All that was within was my ruined frock. What I care for is in *here*." She hugged her mud-spattered reticule to her chest. "We have tarried too long…"

Something tugged within him. He would have brushed the feeling aside, but the same odd emotion had struck him several times since she had broken into his home. It must mean something. He'd certainly felt attraction to her just moments before, but this wasn't the same.

Christian shook himself.

One thing she'd said replayed through his mind, and he suppressed a scowl. She had only two frocks? He hadn't much knowledge about women's fashion, but he knew for certain that women typically had numerous gowns—some that they would only wear once. Hell, even his maids had more uniforms than Miss Wilkinson had dresses. And why only the bombazine? What happened to the dresses that she'd possessed before moving in with her aunt and uncle?

Despite his many questions, and the outrage burning through him on Miss Wilkinson's behalf, he was very aware of their dwindling time.

He stood and cupped Miss Wilkinson's elbow. "Come," he muttered, directing her toward the horses.

"How will we hide?" she asked. "The copse of trees does not seem dense enough for—"

"We will ride," he interrupted.

She was clearly taken aback, but continued along with him unfalteringly. "They are carriage horses, Lord Leeds, and are not meant for riding."

"They are horses, Miss Wilkinson, and we require a means for escape." Though he'd been thinking much the same only minutes ago.

She pulled her elbow from his touch, indignation spread across her features. "Those horses are not accustomed to running with weight upon their backs; we will be thrown for certain."

He spun to face her, anger burning in his gut. "If we remain here or attempt to escape on foot, we will undoubtedly be set upon." The skies opened further, the heavy droplets of rain creating a nigh-deafening din. "Whoever has been following you has become a common enemy. We are *both* running now, and I will not risk remaining and waiting for certain death." It could also be someone in pursuit of him, *but* he daren't mention that. He raised his voice above the rain, pointing a finger at her. "You forced yourself into my charge the moment you waved your pistol at me, Miss Wilkinson. Your wellbeing has become my responsibility, and I will *not* fail in keeping you safe."

Her jaw worked as she thought, her pretty brow furrowed.

He extended his hand to her. "Come."

She relented with a sigh.

They approached the horses cautiously. The beasts were frightened from the accident, their eyes wild and their coats slick with sweat and rain. It was a foolish course of action, Christian knew, but what other choice did they have?

He put a hand to the mare's flank, uttering low, soothing murmurs in an attempt to calm her. He'd ridden an unbroken gelding in training, but that horse hadn't been spooked by a carriage accident…and it had taken several tries and a broken foot to ride it successfully.

* * *

"I will not fail in keeping you safe…" Violet recognised his truth in the line of his lips, the stern arch of his brows, and the softness in his eyes. She'd not revealed much about her life in her aunt and uncle's home in an effort to shield herself from reliving the emotional torment and pain, and she would *never* tell him all that had happened to her. The man thought his words were comforting, but they only re-established her growing awareness that she wouldn't have been able to succeed on this venture on her own. She owed this man her life.

"That's a good girl," Lord Leeds uttered softly, rubbing his hands along the mare's body and neck. "You're a sweet beauty, aren't you?"

Violet watched, mesmerised, as Lord Leeds effortlessly soothed the nervous bays. He ran his palms over their muscled shoulders, up the columns of their necks, through their manes, and to their jaws.

"There we are," he murmured.

The rumbling timbre of his crooning had an unnerving effect on Violet as well. She'd thought herself under his spell when he'd come to her aid moments before, but *this*… This made her long to hear him whisper such things in *her* ear, to have him put his hands on *her* body, comb his fingers through *her* hair.

It made her want to read the book that weighed heavily in her reticule.

A distant trundling and a squelch from behind them echoed along the thin tree line, cutting over the roar of the rain, and Vi's heart froze. She turned wide eyes on Lord Leeds, but he had already sprung into action.

"We've no more time for pleasantries, I'm afraid." He put his hands to her waist and lifted her high into the air.

Violet would have enjoyed the tingle up her spine and the gooseflesh upon her skin at his familiar touch, if impending doom had not been galloping down the road behind them.

"Put your legs astride," Lord Leeds directed her.

Now was not the moment for modesty. She did as he bade, tucking her frock around her thighs. The mare danced to one side, but Lord Leeds soothed her directly. He led the horses from around the tree, untangling their joined reins, then mounted the other mare, settling his small trunk in front of him.

Cutting Vi a sideways glance, he shouted, "Hold on!" He flicked his mare's reins and she jolted into motion, leading Vi's mare to do the same.

Her stomach leapt in alarm as they jostled forward. The horses protested the unfamiliar weights on their backs by throwing their manes and kicking their hind legs. She held on tightly, her arms wrapped around the beast's neck as they ran through the rain.

Her muscles protested each movement. Her bones ached and her teeth clattered, the rattling echoing in her ears.

"We must get off the road!" Lord Leeds called over the thunder of hooves and the rattle of her shaken bones.

The forest gave way to a rolling hillside, and Leeds led them at a gallop over the grassy hills, the horses' hooves squelching in every patch of muddy grass. Wind and rain whipped at Vi's sodden clothes and hair and bit at every inch of her exposed skin.

They crested a hill, and as providence would have it, a cottage appeared just beyond the next hill. Lord Leeds led them toward it at a punishing pace.

It felt like an hour had passed, but it could not have been longer than one quarter of an hour before they reached the small home.

A wiry stable hand dashed out to aid in Vi's dismount and to hold the tired horses. Vi stood on unsteady legs, her gaze darting about the small building.

"Whose home is this?"

Lord Leeds shook his head. "I haven't the faintest, but we shall beg their aid regardless. Whomever damaged our phaeton, whether they were on the horses we heard or not, will soon be after us," he whispered in her ear, suddenly beside her. "I assure you, it will not take them long to examine the wreckage before they realise where we've gone." He stepped back and gave a nod toward the front door. "I shall inquire with the homeowner."

With that, he limped away, his back stiff and his bottom all but entirely exposed. Vi's chest tightened, but she followed to stand nearby, rainwater sluicing down her head and sodden shoulders.

The door swung inward before he could knock, and a fair, elderly gentleman stood in the doorway. He gazed impassively at the two of them, his warm brown eyes curious.

"May I help you?"

Lord Leeds gestured vaguely with his hands before clasping them in front of his sternum. The older man followed the movement with his sharp gaze before offering Lord Leeds a nod and an encouraging half smile. Could *Lofty* Leeds be nervous?

"Yes. My name is Christian Samuels. My companion and I were in an accident, and I must humbly ask if you have any mounts that we might be able to trade for our bays?"

The older man glanced past them at the winded horses standing with his groom, and he nodded thoughtfully. "Very well. I accept the trade. My man will ready a gelding and a mare for you directly."

Lord Leeds bowed. "We are in your debt, sir."

"Think nothing of it." The man smiled. "The name's Briggs."

The two shook hands, then Leeds scratched at his chin. "We are in want of a pair of saddlebags; do you know where we might acquire some?"

Mr. Briggs blinked, then a slow smile grew on his lips. "You've come to the right place. I make them myself with the pelts of rabbits and the like."

Lord Leeds returned the man's smile. "Splendid! I shall take two." He handed the man several pound notes, and the man's eyes widened.

Violet admired how his lordship worked, always managing to endear himself to others But most assuredly not Violet.

Leeds glanced at Vi before turning back to the man. "Would you happen to know where we might find a shop at which we could replace our ruined attire?"

Fear at the possibility of Hale catching up to her and excitement at the possibility of a new frock warred within her.

"Of course!" Briggs grinned at them. "Mrs. Cora West has the best used frocks and suits around these parts. Her shop is just on Firth in the centre of town."

The kind man gave them the direction as Lord Leeds handed him another few coins with gratitude.

It was only minutes later that their horses were saddled and awaiting them in front of the cottage. Violet's body protested, but she mounted the mare quickly. The longer they tarried, the more anxious she became.

His lordship removed a few select items from his trunk and placed them discreetly in the newly purchased saddlebag strapped to his gelding. He handed the half-full trunk to the awaiting groom, and mounted.

"Here!" Mr. Briggs called out to them as he hurried out his front door, his shoulders hunched against the rain and a wrapped parcel in his hands. "For your journey."

Lord Leeds accepted the parcel with an appreciative, "Thank you," before placing the item in his new saddlebags.

"That's so thoughtful," Vi said over the rain. "We are very grateful."

Mr. Briggs tugged on his forelock and stepped back. "It was my pleasure, madam."

Leeds glanced at her over his shoulder. "Are you ready?"

Violet dipped her head in a nod.

He returned the gesture and nudged his gelding forward with a *click* of his tongue.

* * *

Christian slowed his mount to a trot as they neared the centre of town. The streets were markedly busy for the time of year and the size of the town, though the activity paled in comparison to the bustle of London.

The rain had stopped long enough for the sun to shine through the clouds, lending warmth to the once-dreary day.

Miss Wilkinson hadn't uttered a word since they'd left the safe house—thank Christ. She'd stood so damned near to him when he'd given David Briggs their safe house hand signal that he'd been certain she'd noticed. The signal, of course, had alerted Briggs to Chris' connection with the Home Office and communicated their need of aid before he'd even spoken.

Like many urchins and pickpockets pulled from the streets of London, Briggs had been saved, given a home, and educated. He'd then been offered the choice of becoming a spy—like Chris and his fellows—or of turning his future home into a safe house. Not many turned down the life of a spy, but those who did were scattered across England. And now Christian needed their help.

He eyed the lively groups of tittering ladies and stodgy gentlemen, an unsettling sense of discomfiture quivering in his stomach. He had been in many compromising and dangerous circumstances in his life, but never had he felt so *exposed.*

"There! What a clever name."

Miss Wilkinson pointed to a hanging wooden sign that read "Mrs. West's Twice-Loved Attire."

They rode toward the shop and halted. Christian dismounted, grinding his teeth at the sting to his back, and tied the horses' reins to a nearby post. He should have taken them to the stables, but he'd be damned if they wasted any more time, and he was optimistic that no one would commandeer their mounts.

Chris turned and clasped Miss Wilkinson about her waist, but stilled. Her ribs lifted with her swift intake of breath, and her fingers dug into the material at his shoulders… His stomach flipped over and his cods tightened.

Her gaze met his, keen desire and some alluring, unfathomable emotion shining in her eyes. His mind swam with heated images, just as it had after their accident. He'd been about to kiss her then, and he was damned tempted to kiss her now. He clenched his jaw against the sensation.

Time. He needed time to think this through, damn it.

With regret, he lowered her to her feet and released her. "I must request something unconventional and potentially upsetting from you." His lips twisted in a grimace of remorse as she watched him expectantly. "As you have likely surmised, I intend to purchase two new frocks for you, in replacement of those you have lost on our journey. But although we have very little time in which to shop—as our pursuer is very probably moments away from coming upon us— I must also ask you to purchase a men's suit of clothes, that you will don at our next stop."

She blinked. "I beg your pardon?" she breathed.

"Men's clothing," he repeated. "Those that follow us are searching for a man and a woman. If we can fool those we pass, even enough for them to be uncertain, we might be able to lose our pursuers' trail." He waited a moment before shaking his head at her silence. "I hate to request it of you, Miss Wilkinson, but I require at least one decent night of sleep, a bath, and a modicum of peace if we are to continue on this mad journey. If we change our appearance, we should be—"

"Very well. I will do it." She jutted her jaw at a stubborn angle. "To be truthful, it has been well over two years since I have worn anything other than those two bombazine frocks. I am rather eager to wear something different. And quite frankly, after that accident, I am reticent to ride through this night."

Something in Christian's chest tightened as his lips pulled into a smile. "Thank you."

Chapter 12

"I think ye've made a right fine choice, Mrs. Platts." Mrs. West smiled as she accepted the bundle of cloth from Violet's arms.

They had been in the shop for no more than one quarter of an hour—the swiftest shopping of her life—by the time they were ready to pay.

Mrs. West had four attendants employed in her busy shop, and had devoted all of them to Lord Leeds and Violet. His lordship had purchased three suits of clothing for himself—for the ones he'd brought were ruined—two frocks and sets of undergarments for Vi, and one suit of clothing for "Mr. Platts' nephew," who just happened to be very near to Violet's size.

They hadn't the time to try on their purchases, but one patron of the shop happened to share Violet's measurements and had donated several gowns; all Violet was required to do was choose which colours she preferred. She'd hastily donned the fetching Pomona green paisley walking dress and overlong black cape. They hadn't any riding habits, but she thought the cape would disguise that nicely.

"How kind of you to say, Mrs. West." Violet smiled at her, the motion strained with anxiousness. It was miraculous that they were able to find attire *and* hurriedly change in one quarter of an hour, but Vi still felt that they had taken too long. For surely their pursuer was already in town searching for them…

Vi's stomach twisted with nerves.

Lord Leeds stepped forward in his black woollen trousers, crisp white shirt and cravat, deep green waistcoat, and brown cutaway. The sight of him nigh stalled her breath in her lungs. The clothing appeared to have been made for a gentleman farmer, for they were made of sturdy wool and cotton, with no silks or other luxurious fabrics. Violet thought him rather dashing.

He smiled at Mrs. West. Impatience lined his face, though he attempted to hide it. "I am much obliged for your wonderful service, madam. Never have I visited a finer shop than yours."

The young woman wrapping their clothing in paper blushed fetchingly as Mrs. West beamed. "You flatter me, Mr. Platts."

Violet eyed the front window, anxious to be on their way. The pleasantries were taking far longer than she had anticipated. They were nearing twenty minutes since entering the shop; surely they would be soon discovered!

As though sensing her nervousness, Lord Leeds handed several pound notes to the matron and accepted the wrapped parcels. With a salute to Mrs. West and her employees, his lordship ushered Violet from the shop.

The jingling of the shop's bell rang above them as they stepped onto the walk. It had been a whirlwind inside, and she'd donned her frock so quickly that she was likely missing a button or hook somewhere, but they'd done it.

"Thank you," she said softly to Lord Leeds' back. "This purchase was entirely unnecessary, and not within the terms of our agreement, and I am grateful."

"You're welcome," he replied, his voice floating back to her.

Lord Leeds added the parcels to their saddlebags, but stilled as he was fastening the last buckle. Despite the bright, warm sun heating her through her new clothes, Violet felt a sudden chill race down her spine.

Then she heard it. Above the low chatter of voices, laughter, horses' hooves, and rattling carriage wheels, there was a shout. "*Violet!*"

Her heart sank heavily to her stomach. She knew that voice. It filled her with dread. Time seemed to slow, her abruptly pounding heart echoing loudly in her ears. Then she was lifted into the air until the solid weight of her mare rose beneath her. Almost mechanically, she curled her leg around the lower pommel.

"*Go!*" Lord Leeds was shouting at her. "Miss Wilkinson! *Ride!*"

Time flooded back in a blink, and she flicked the reins. They navigated their way quickly through the crowded street, an apology on her lips murmured to passers-by. The moment they reached a clear stretch of road, Vi urged her mount into a gallop.

She could feel their pursuer's vindictive gaze boring into her back as she rode, and both fear and regret threatened to overwhelm her.

They had lingered too long. They ought to have ridden through to the next town.

Countless minutes passed as they ran their horses side by side, the feeling of being watched slowly dissipating the further they rode. The mounts snorted and huffed, their manes flying wildly in the wind and their coats slickening with sweat.

"We need to change horses," Lord Leeds called over the din of pounding hooves and rushing wind. "These are tiring."

Violet hated to stop, but if their horses required respite, then so would their pursuer's mounts.

* * *

Christian slowed his horse to a walk, allowing the beast to catch its breath. They'd been running hard for far too long. He pushed through the sting to his abraded skin, moving with the horse as though he felt nary a thing. But, Christ, it hurt.

Miss Wilkinson matched his pace beside him, her back stiff and eyes wide with fear as she gasped for breath.

He hated to cause her distress, but the matter had to be discussed. He cleared his throat. "I believe I know the answer to this question, Miss Wilkinson, but I must ask it—"

"Lord Americus Chaisty, Baron of Bristol."

Chris' jaw clenched at the confirmation. "Why is he pursuing you?"

She pursed her lips but remained silent. He had come to his own conclusions after his discussion with Sir Bramwell Stevens, but if he were to protect Miss Wilkinson properly, he had to know the truth. He waited for several moments before she finally spoke.

"Lord Bristol is my cousin. My sister Rose and I lived with him and his sister, Uriana, under my aunt and uncle's care in the two years since my parents' death." Her gaze turned tormented as she watched the road ahead of them. "They were...unkind to us."

Bram's words floated through Christian's mind. *"The Misses Wilkinson are in daily danger in that hellish place... Hale is a despicable blackguard! The things he has done to those sisters... It disgusts me."*

Chris had agreed with Bram's sentiments, but could there be more of which he was unaware? How far had Hale and Bristol gone in their abuse of the sisters? Had it been verbal attacks, or something decidedly more nefarious?

His gelding sidestepped, agitated from its rider's distress. Chris forced his fists to unclench from around the reins.

"Lord Bristol, in particular, took an interest in tormenting me," she continued, her voice barely audible.

Christian's gut churned.

"Rose and I decided that we would be better suited living elsewhere, and perpetrated our escape. I believe that my cousin and uncle are displeased with our actions and wish to pull us to heel."

Miss Wilkinson pressed her lips together, and Chris knew that was all he would glean from her. She was undoubtedly leaving much out of the discussion. Anger burned inside him. There was no mistaking the dread in her eyes or the alarming blanching of her complexion when she'd heard her cousin's voice. The man must be a monster, indeed, to frighten a strong, spirited, and courageous woman like Miss Violet Wilkinson.

He wanted to say something encouraging, but he hadn't much experience in doing so. "I give you my word that you will arrive at your grandparents' home safely. Lord Hale and Lord Bristol will soon become a distant memory."

Her lips quirked up in one corner. "You have my gratitude, your lordship."

Chris eyed her carefully as their horses walked down the muddy road. She did not believe him capable of protecting her. It should not have irritated him—he had given her nary a reason to believe otherwise—but damn it, it did.

What bothered him more, however, was the very real possibility that their entire journey was futile. Miss Wilkinson's cousin was so determined to reach her that he would likely cause trouble for both her and her grandparents once she reached them in Scotland. And he couldn't bear the thought of it.

Indeed, seeing her safely to her grandparents was only a part of how he would help. He must teach her ways in which to defend herself, and how to hide her identity in order to throw her cousin off her trail.

"While I do not doubt your ability to fend for yourself, Miss Wilkinson, I feel obliged to offer my counsel," he said. "At our stop this evening, I intend to teach you some methods with which to protect yourself. For now, however, I have a few pieces of advice for how to get away, should you need it."

She glanced over her shoulder, her spine stiff. "I thank you, Lord Leeds, but...do you believe that I will require such knowledge?"

Not every stop they made could be a safe house, nor could he guarantee her safety, but he would damned well do his best. "Yes," he said honestly.

* * *

Violet's mind whirled with information as they awaited their fresh mounts at their next stop.

"Have you any questions?" Lord Leeds asked.

Vi blinked into the slowly setting sun as she stood on unsteady legs. "I have many."

The man nodded. "I shall do my utmost to clarify things for you once we begin a true lesson this evening."

A gust of warm wind blew past, ruffling her already-mussed hair, and she glanced about. The inn was much like the others, though this one employed cats—most likely to catch mice. The drive opened into a cobblestoned courtyard that was in great need of repair; the building had three floors and cracking mortar; and the stables, though small, were well stocked and bustling with stable hands.

They stood just inside the stable's doors, watching as the grooms worked.

"How do you know so much about fighting?" Violet asked in an undertone, her nerves buzzing with the desire to be on their way yet aware that the wounds on her back needed dressing.

Lord Leeds stiffened beside her but replied casually. "Gentleman Jackson's. Most men who frequent the academy for pugilists learn such things, or have simply experienced them themselves."

After seeing his reaction to her inquiry, she'd prepared herself to accuse him of a falsehood, but it was certainly a believable reply, and he'd answered quickly enough. Perhaps he was merely as sore as she from both the accident and the hard ride.

"Our horses are nearly saddled," he said, interrupting her thoughts. "I must advise you to make use of the facilities before we depart."

His bright-blue gaze caught hers and, all at once, something entirely foreign to Violet rushed through her veins.

He cleared his throat. "I will see to getting a simple helping of provisions packaged."

With the spell broken, Violet did as his lordship suggested. She did, indeed, need to use the facilities, and fresh bandages would be just the thing.

She located a maid willing to help her, and together they cleaned and redressed her wounds in a private dining room before Vi gave the young woman a coin and sought out the facilities. She found them swiftly toward the rear of the inn and took care of her needs. Pouring water from the pitcher into the washbasin, she worked the soap into a lather and washed her face and neck.

She wished that she could have a hot bath, but with Americus so close behind them, they hadn't the time. Perhaps once she'd changed into her men's clothing, they would—

Her mind halted mid-thought as the door to the facilities opened with a bang. And Lord Americus Chaisty, Baron of Bristol, entered.

Vi's heart all but stopped beating, her throat closing and her palms and neck going clammy.

His eyes narrowed menacingly as he locked the door behind him. His dark gaze swept her as he combed his fingers through his closely cropped dark hair. If not for his vile personality, one might call him handsome. "You filthy *bitch*," he spat. "You've led me on a merry chase, but now I've got you."

Violet sucked in a desperate breath before she released it in an ear-splitting scream.

Chapter 13

"I am much obliged." Christian smiled as he accepted the small parcel of food from the innkeeper's wife.

She sent him a suggestive wink. "It's me pleasure, it is, Mr. Platts."

His smile sagged. "I'd best find my wife."

Turning, he limped from the taproom, his leg afire and throbbing with every beat of his heart, and ventured back into the stables. With just a glance, he knew that Miss Wilkinson had not yet returned from performing her ablutions, and while he didn't wish for her to rush, he couldn't be certain how close their pursuer might be.

Whose pursuer? The question filtered through his mind once more. And indeed, it was a pertinent one. Was it someone in Hale's household in search of his charge, or, worse, was it someone come in search of *him*?

And what could—what *would*—he do once he encountered their pursuer? His days of combat were over, and he hadn't a wish to kill, even should his life be threatened. Was he even the right man to protect Miss Wilkinson? Could he—

A chilling scream rent the air, sending gooseflesh across his skin. Instinct kicked in. Christian dropped the provisions and dashed out of the stables toward the taproom.

Onlookers watched his every move, some rising from their seats in the taproom to sate their curiosity. His mind driven, Chris paid them no heed as he ran toward the retiring room.

He tried the latch, but the damned door was locked. He pounded his fist on the wood. "Miss—Mrs. Platts?" *Damn it.* "Violet?" he called. "Violet, is everything all right?"

Silence greeted his inquiry, and the pit in his gut sank further.

He rammed his shoulder into the door. "Violet? *Violet!*"

* * *

Americus swooped in to clutch Violet's throat in his thick hands. Her heart fluttered wildly as she gasped for breath. *Not again, not again, not again,* her mind and heart screamed simultaneously, the litany of words racing through her as she fought to maintain her composure.

This is the same as before, Vi, and you've survived. But no, it's not! She'd had a taste of freedom, even while knowing that Americus was in pursuit, and that hope… That hope being torn away could very well kill her.

She didn't *want* to hide in her mind, to disappear into the vast reaches of her imagined paradise where she'd sought solace for the past two years.

"You'll pay for what you've done," he breathed in her ear. "But I shan't let you off so easily as to kill you now." He licked her cheek, the hot slime from his tongue sending a shiver of revulsion down her spine. "I intend to have some enjoyment from you first."

Her throat squeaked a breath, and she clawed at his hands. No, she wouldn't allow him to win this time. Dizzying recollections of Lord Leeds' words buzzed through her mind, but none stuck.

Distant pounding filled the room, and someone frantically called her name, but she steadfastly ignored them, focusing instead on remembering Leeds' words.

"If you are facing a male attacker, always remember one thing. One swift kick to the ballocks will fell any man."

Violet grimaced. "Come now, your lordship…"

"It might sound distasteful to you, Miss Wilkinson, but I can assure you, it will work." He raised one silver eyebrow at her. "But…do not give him any clues as to your actions before you strike, else he will guard his loins."

Spots swam before her vision, but her course of action was clear. She would fight.

Without hesitation, Violet lifted her knee with as much force as she could muster, aiming it at the sensitive area between her cousin's thighs.

His reaction was instantaneous. His hands dropped to cup his injured area, his eyes widened, and a vein on his forehead bulged. Clutching her hands to her neck, Vi stumbled backward, putting as much distance between them as the room would allow as she gasped for breath. The bastard dropped to his knees on the rough, wood-planked floor, his face red with strain and fury.

"*Bitch*," he sputtered.

The door crashed open, and Lord Leeds entered, blazing fury mixed with dread etched on his features.

"Violet!" His glinting blue gaze caught hers before it zeroed in on Americus.

His face turned thunderous, and he stormed past Vi to grip Americus by the cravat, lifting the man half off the floor.

"Miss Wilkinson left your father's home and shan't return," Leeds hissed. "You'd best abandon your pursuit of her if—"

"Fuck you!" Americus spat, his face reddening further.

Lord Leeds' other hand fisted so tightly at his side that Vi was certain he would punch Americus—and rightly so. But he didn't.

"*Leave* her," Leeds gritted out before dropping the man back to the wood floor.

Leeds spun to face her, his eyes full of fury and concern. "Are you well? Did he hurt you?"

Her hand still clutching at her raw throat, Vi croaked, "I am fine."

Leeds' gaze dropped to her neck, and his expression darkened.

"I will…find you, Violet," Americus wheezed, rising slowly to his knees.

With that threat hanging in the air, Lord Leeds spun around and punched Americus square in the cheek. With a great *thwump*, her cousin flopped unconscious to the floor.

He turned back to Vi. "I apologise for that, Miss Wilkinson." His concerned gaze lowered to her neck once more. "Would you care for a refreshment?"

"No." She shook her head. "I am well enough."

His lips thinned, but he nodded, his fingers nimbly undoing the knot of his cravat. "Very well. I must bind Lord Bristol's wrists while he is unconscious. I will see him to the local magistrate before we continue on our way."

Her gaze was wholly riveted on the corded column of his neck that was slowly being exposed. Lord above, it was lean and appeared soft to the touch. The scent of soap and salty skin reached her nose, and the desire to press her nose to his throat came over her in a haze of want.

Crash!

Vi squeaked, shaken from her reverie as a dark figure flung itself out the window.

"Damnation!" Lord Leeds cursed, rushing forward. "*Damn*!" He slapped his hand against the window's frame. "He's gone."

* * *

Christian ground his teeth together as he attempted to garner control over his body. A deep, red rage had woven itself seductively through his veins when he became aware of what the bastard Baron of Bristol had done to Miss Wilkinson, and no matter how much distance he put between them and the man, his muscles would not unclench. He wanted to turn his mount around, ride back to the inn, and thrash the blackguard.

But Chris wasn't a murderer. He'd never killed unless he'd had no other choice. Most spies in their band—with the exception of the assassins—found alternate means to handle their opponents besides killing. There was Newgate, extradition and, most commonly, a trial and potential hanging. The only time Christian had killed had been in self-defence. Some villains would not quit until someone was dead.

If he'd but been able to rely on his title and money and seek help from the innkeeper and his staff... But no. Chris must maintain anonymity as a precaution, in the event that someone came looking for *him* as well. A man with money would be noticed, and the word of a gentleman farmer against that of the baron he had just assaulted was poor, indeed.

His only recourse had been to apprehend the man himself. He'd told Miss Wilkinson that he would bring the baron to the magistrate, but he'd *intended* to take him to a local safe house to await retrieval by Hydra. If the cur hadn't slipped away...

He pushed his horse faster along the grassy field, forcing Violet to keep up with him. The setting sun had broken through the clouds, though a chill still clung to the air.

Chris wanted to run fast and hard until his anger abated, until he no longer felt the effects of his fear. *Hell*, that had been like nothing he'd ever felt. He'd been frightened before, to be sure, but never had he experienced such a visceral reaction so deep in his core—a *need* to keep someone safe from harm.

"Your lordship!" A shout caught his attention, and he slowed his mount.

Miss Wilkinson drew up next to him, her chest heaving with each breath. He realised that he, too, was breathing heavily. *Damn.* He hadn't meant to run them so hard. The horses were likely exhausted.

"We ought to consult my map," she gasped, shaking her head. "There must be something more we can do than run."

Christian walked his horse alongside hers. "There is a home just up ahead." He nodded toward a billow of chimney smoke from a safe house beyond the next copse of trees. "We will seek help."

A swift frown clouded her features. "But Americus—"

"We will not tarry," he hurried to assure her. He couldn't put the safe house's location at greater risk than necessary. And in the meantime, he would think on a way to apprehend the Baron of Bristol.

* * *

"Samuels!" Erasmus Russell, safe house owner and Chris's old classmate, clapped him on the shoulder in greeting. "To what do I owe this honour?"

Christian glanced back over his shoulder toward *The Woman* and their mounts, a gust of wind mussing her skirts and half-fallen coiffure. Her skin was pale in the early moonlight, and something at the sight tugged at him. He frowned. Whatever this strange feeling was, it irked him. Distraction, heart lurches—

He cleared his throat and spoke in an undertone. "It's great to see you, Erasmus. But I'm afraid that I'm in need of aid this evening."

Erasmus' brown gaze sharpened with awareness. "Of course. Whatever you require. I've space in the servants' quarters, or if you're able and willing to make the short ride, the hunting cabin is vacant. Just refreshed its supplies two nights past."

Chris nodded. "The hunting cabin is perfect. You have my thanks." He started to turn away, but paused and added softly, "We have a tail. I cannot be certain that they'll not find this place, so please, be careful."

"So noted."

With another nod, Christian returned to Miss Wilkinson's side. "He says that there is a newly vacated hunting cabin just beyond that copse of trees." Chris gestured to the small forest beyond Erasmus' modest home.

The woman frowned and winced as he helped her onto her mount. "But surely we're to continue on?"

Frustration stiffened Chris' shoulders, and he gritted his teeth against the emotion as he mounted his gelding. "I've no desire to engage in this argument with you again, Miss Wilkinson. We *cannot* ride through the night on tired horses. Both we and the mounts require respite—"

"Enough. I relent—for now. I need you to finish the lesson you'd promised, and I intend to study my map. I believe that I can arrange our route with adequate horse changes…"

Throughout the ride to the hunting cabin, the woman sat stiffly and ineffectively stifled her groans. Chris imagined that her muscles ached much like his, and for that reason, he would not push her during her lesson.

They reached the two-storey hunting cabin, and Chris strode with the horses to the crude, open-sided shelter that was used as a stable while Miss Wilkinson went indoors with their saddlebags. The shelter had old gates to keep in the horses, a roof to keep them dry should it rain, and the necessary supplies to care for them.

He worked quickly, seeing to their mounts' comfort before venturing indoors. The cabin featured an open, rectangular room with two closed doors against the back wall and a wooden staircase on the left-hand side. To the right was a stone fireplace, which was surrounded by the dark wood panelling that encompassed the room. There was a large, faded rug of indiscernible colour in the middle of the floor, a sitting area near the fireplace, and a desk, table, and chairs by the stairs.

Candles had been lit around the room, lending the surfaces a faint golden hue.

Miss Wilkinson sat at the table, peering closely at a map that sat upon its surface. She looked up at his entrance.

"Where are we, precisely?" she asked.

"Just north of Banbury."

She nodded, and bent back to her map.

"I had difficulty with the fireplace, so I left it cold," she muttered while she worked.

She clicked her tongue. "We could reach Birmingham tomorrow. I'd thought about going to a magistrate as you'd mentioned, but would they not see me as my uncle's property and thus side with

Americus?" Her troubled blue gaze lifted to meet Chris'. "No matter how violent my family, the law will side with them."

Chris merely stood there, his heart nigh beating out of his chest for God knew what reason. The woman was frustrating and maddening, and yet...she was clearly also trying to find a way for them to travel safely.

"Do they not know of your grandparents in Scotland? *Will* you be safer there?"

Her chest heaved in a sigh. "I imagine not. My uncle would undoubtedly already suspect my destination, but I do not think that Americus would yet think of it. I suppose the lessons that you're to give me will prove invaluable after all."

Chris' stomach dipped. "Are you ready, then?"

"Just one more moment, please." She gestured over her shoulder toward the closed door. "There's a washbasin in the kitchen. I've already taken the liberty of washing up, though the water was frigid."

"Thank you."

Chris strode past her and into the dimly lit kitchens, his muscles stiff. Damn, but he ached all over. He found the soap and cold water, and set to giving himself a cursory wash.

It had been a damned hard day, but he had certainly learned a valuable lesson. Miss Wilkinson's pursuer, Lord Americus Chaisty, the Baron of Bristol, was possessed of a devilish determination and would stop at nothing to reach her.

Despite the change in attire and countless hours of rain, Miss Wilkinson's cinnamon scent somehow surrounded him. He frowned. *Damned woman.*

* * *

"You hold it just so," Lord Leeds instructed, tapping Violet's elbow and urging her to straighten her arm. "Imagine that the pistol's barrel is your index finger and you're pointing at your target. Hold it straight, sight down the barrel, and pull the trigger."

A tremor ran up Vi's spine at his continued touch and his nearness, but she did as he instructed. *Click.* The unloaded pistol discharged.

"Very good." His smile was encouraging. "Now, if you've used your shot, but your opponent is still able to fight and is coming after you, what do you do?"

"Run?"

His lips quirked. "A sensible option. You might also use the handle of your pistol to subdue your opponent by connecting it to their temple, here. Just like so." He tapped the side of his head, then swung his fist in an arc. "The nose and eyes are also suitable targets."

Violet nodded her understanding as she watched Lord Leeds. Pale firelight flickered over his features, the space warm and close. A heavy summer rain splattering against the windows created a dim hum in the cabin's main room.

"Before we depart in the morning," Leeds continued, "you ought to practise loading the pistol and shooting at targets out of doors."

"I shall. Thank you for the instruction." She placed the pistol on the table near her neatly folded map.

His eyebrows lifted. "We've only just begun, Miss Wilkinson. Take this."

He withdrew a large kitchen knife from within his coat, and Vi gasped. *Bloody hell, where had he been hiding that?*

He held it out to her, handle first. "Stab me."

"*What?*"

He sighed. "I shall block you, but I want you to *try* to stab me."

Knots formed in her stomach. "I have no wish to hurt you."

One of his eyebrows lifted sardonically, and she accepted the knife with a huff. The blade glinted in the candlelight, and she gave a half-hearted lunge. Leeds easily swiped her hand aside and changed positions, stepping back to give her some space. She swung the blade in an arc, and he moved effortlessly out of the way.

A grin stole over his features, and frustration gnawed at her. She swiped and lunged again, but he sidestepped and swatted at her hand. Again and again, she moved to attack, and the man danced around her.

At last, she growled, "What is this teaching me?"

All at once, he gripped her wrist and pulled, spinning her around until her back hit his chest with a dull *thud* and her breath left her in a *whoosh*. The healing wounds on her back burned at the contact, and yet she didn't struggle.

Pressing his lips to her ear, he whispered, "Do not let your guard down. Remain on the attack, or you shall be put on the defence. And be prepared for a dirty fight."

Her breathing turned ragged and her pulse sped ever faster, curse the man. With a grunt she pulled out of his grip and spun to face him. "Have we concluded with the knife, then?"

He examined the hand that clutched the knife. "Your grip is good. Here." He rounded behind her and extended his arm alongside hers, holding the knife with her. "When you swipe, do it like so."

Moving their arms together, Leeds attempted to instruct her, but her thoughts were centred entirely on the contact of their bodies. Her arse sat cradled against the most intimate part of him, her aching legs against his, and his head pressed against the side of hers, his breath ruffling the hair at her temples...

"Does that make sense?" he asked, his voice slightly husky.

Vi cleared her throat. "Yes. Thank you."

She felt him nod against the side of her head, and then he was gone, cool air rushing in to replace the heat of his body against hers. He took the knife from her slackened fingers and placed it on the table next to her pistol.

His tongue darted out to moisten his bottom lip, and she watched, transfixed by the movement.

"Now we must focus on holds and hand-to-hand combat," he said. "If someone were to come in for a slap or a punch and you hadn't a weapon to hand, what would you do?"

"Run."

He quirked an eyebrow. "And if you're cornered, captured, or they've grabbed you?"

"Scream?" She scrunched her nose. "Oh! Kick him in the ballocks!"

"Aye, that could work. If someone is coming in for a hit to your face, however, you ought first to block, then knock them back or attack. Like so." He put his hands to the sides of his head and thrust his right elbow forward. "An elbow to the chest or neck will incapacitate your attacker for time enough to attack or flee. You try."

Violet lifted her hands to her temples to block a slow attack from Lord Leeds.

"Good," he urged. "Now thrust your elbow into my chest."

She hit him with a muted *thunk*.

"Very good. Faster, now."

They rehearsed the move several times, until Violet felt that she was comfortable with the movement.

"Excellent." His lips tugged in one corner. "Now, if someone were to grip your neck with both hands in an attempt to strangle you, there are several moves that would work to throw them off, but you must move quickly. When someone is squeezing your neck, you don't have much time before the lack of breath causes your limbs to weaken. So, when their arms are extended, you must thrust both of your arms up and between theirs, pushing them wide apart. Try it with me."

He put his hands lightly to her neck, and she flinched, recalling with painful clarity what her cousin's hands had felt like choking her.

Leeds stopped, his eyes dark and serious as he said softly, "I need you to know that I will not hurt you. If, however, this is Lord Bristol's preferred method of attack, you will need to know how to release yourself from his grip."

She nodded, perhaps too vigorously, for it jostled her hair. "I understand."

With his gaze steady on hers, he lightly gripped her neck once more. "Now, slide your arms up between mine, and push out."

She followed his direction and, to her astonishment, it had been rather easy to remove his grip. "Again."

They tried twice more, before Leeds clasped her wrist. "Once you've freed yourself, you have several choices for attack. Your best options are the eyes and nose. If you can jab your attacker's eyes with stiff, extended fingers, like this"—he positioned her hand for her—"then do so. Or, break their nose using the heel of your palm and an upward motion; this will not only cause pain, but it will also blur their vision and thus incapacitate them. Try the motions with me."

Her heart fluttered, but she ignored it, instead focusing on the movements he'd taught her.

"Very good." His eyes crinkled in a not-smile, and her stomach swooped. "I've only one more for tonight, as this is a great deal to process." He rounded behind her and wrapped his arms around her body, pressing her arms to her sides and her back to his chest.

Vi's breath caught once more, her pulse skipping.

"If someone grabs at you from behind," he murmured in her ear, "you must strike their nose with the back of your head, stomp as hard as you can onto one of their feet, elbow their ribs, and, once your attacker has let you go, turn and break their nose."

Not able to trust her voice, she nodded. They practised slowly, though even while she committed the movements to memory, her body wouldn't cease its reaction to his close proximity. Mayhap she was too tired to regain control. Her body, the dratted thing, veritably hummed with his nearness.

"Again," Leeds grunted, wrapping his arms around her from behind once more.

Vi's eyes slid closed, and she breathed in his scent of soap and man. Her belly quivered, and instead of simulating breaking his nose, she tilted her neck back to rest her head on his shoulder. Almost instantly, he bent to press his nose to her neck, and inhaled. A delicious shiver travelled down her spine, before they both stilled.

With a muttered curse, Lord Leeds released her and stepped away. "My apologies, Miss Wilkinson."

"Y-yes, of course." She curled a tendril of hair behind one ear, nervousness and the sting of rejection warring in her stomach. "I must bid you good night. Thank you for the instruction."

The air was heavy with unrequited desire, unspoken words, and utter humiliation, and Violet was grateful to retreat abovestairs while Lord Leeds secured the cabin.

Chapter 14

Violet huffed an exasperated breath. She was very nearly losing grip of her sanity.

"It has been *four* days since we've had a full night of sleep, Miss Wilkinson!" Lord *Lofty* Leeds held his fingers up with the number. A gust of wind ruffled his silver hair, and his pale blue eyes glinted, distressingly brightened by his grey waistcoat and charcoal cutaway coat.

Putting her hands to her hips, she scowled at the blasted man. Four days, indeed. Travel with his lordship had been a trial on her nerves. One moment fluttering would erupt in her stomach and her pulse would race, but then in another moment, he would make so imperious a statement that it set her teeth on edge.

The sun at her back, she strode toward him, the tall grass to the side of the dirt road brushing her skirts. "Think you that this has been a pleasing jaunt for me, your lordship? I experience exhaustion, hunger, and frustration just as you do."

His shoulders stiffened. "All I ask is for a decent night of sleep. I know of an estate in Brampton. A school, of sorts. They have—"

"*Of sorts?*" She squinted against the brightness of the sun.

Lofty Leeds' lips thinned in annoyance. "The school is secluded and well protected. I have friends in residence. We will have the opportunity to sleep, eat, and bathe, and I will be able to shave this damned beard." He scratched irritably at the coarse silver hair on his chin.

The prospect of a bath was exceedingly tempting, but the man's overbearing manner was not to be borne. "We've looked at my map, and I believe that my plan is sound—"

"We have been travelling for a sennight, Miss Wilkinson," he cut over her. "No matter what you might think or feel about me at the moment, we both deserve a respite."

Blast the man. She pursed her lips as she considered her options. While she despised giving in to the man, he was correct. They'd been fortunate enough to encounter several crofters and gentlemen farmers who had permitted them time for respite, though they hadn't spent a full night anywhere since... *Four days*, her inner voice reminded her. It had been four days since Leeds had instructed her, and since she'd felt the sting of rejection.

Perhaps *that* was why she'd been determined to maintain her distance? She internally shook herself. It did not bear thinking on at the moment.

Another gust of warm, mid-June air blew past them, pulling with it a loose lock of Vi's dark hair and the skirts of her Pomona-green paisley walking dress. The sun shone down on them, giving the grass around them an unearthly green glow. A bird flew past to land on the short fence marking the border of a nearby estate, and called out a fetching tune.

"I believe the mounts have caught their breath," she said into the silence between them. "And you are correct, of course. I apologise for being so demanding these past days. I believe it was a combination of fear and..." She cleared her throat, refusing to admit to the tension that she felt around him. "Well, the temptation to sleep in a bed, bathe, and eat a proper meal is simply too great to resist. Surely Americus is far enough behind us now."

Lord Leeds' eyes crinkled in the corner at her response. A thrill jolted through her at the sight, and she hid a frown. His not-smile had become rare in the past four days...and it was curst attractive. She hated it.

* * *

Christian slowed his mount to a trot as they crested the hill. Rising above them, the grand expanse of Grimsbury Manor came into view. He hadn't seen the building since he'd taught cryptology the previous semester, and damn, but it felt good to be back!

It had taken some time, but Chris had come up with a plan for Lord Bristol. He couldn't take down the man on his own, not without putting Miss Wilkinson in harm's way, potentially endangering innocent bystanders, and alerting anyone following *him* to his location. This school was his best hope.

Chris' comrade, Kieran Richards—better known to those in the Secret Service as Hermes—owned the estate. The man had inherited the ostentatious piece of land from one deceased family member or another. There were several outbuildings and crofters' cottages on the land, all faced with red brick. The windows of the main building varied in size, some small and situated high along the many roof peaks, and others, great in number and aligned side by side, taking up entire walls. The sun glinted off them, giving the glass a sparkling quality while simultaneously obscuring the rooms' interiors.

"Blimey," Miss Wilkinson breathed, her eyes wide as they neared the front entry.

Christian swallowed his mirth. The woman had a mouth on her.

They reached the edge of the drive and pulled their mounts to a halt, the beasts' hooves kicking up dust from the gravel.

From the front, the building appeared to be in the shape of a squared horseshoe, with two long wings of classrooms flanking the circular drive. From this vantage, one couldn't see that the building webbed outward at the back.

Two young recruits dashed out to grab the horses' reins, allowing Christian to dismount. He nodded to the lads.

While changing horses at the inn in Carlisle, Chris had taken it upon himself to send a letter ahead of them, warning his fellow spies that an outsider would be visiting. He had given them sufficient time to hide anything damning. Furthermore, it was beneficial to the recruits' training for them to rehearse normalcy.

It's a pleasure to see you, milord," one of the young men said.

"You as well, Milford."

Before the other recruit could aid Miss Wilkinson to the ground, Christian stepped forward and placed his hands on her waist. A *frisson* of awareness sizzled up his arms and he ground his teeth against it. The woman, even while rousing his curiosity, could be a damned nuisance, and the fact that his body had such foreign reactions to her grated. But he couldn't seem to help himself.

He settled her on her feet and stepped back, nonsensically tempted to wipe his palms on his trousers to dispel their tingling sensation.

"We'll 'ave these 'orses watered and fed, your lordship," Milford said, a congenial smile on his lips. He handed Christian the horses' saddlebags, which he draped over one arm.

Hermes had had the stables custom-built to suit the needs of a school for spies. A piece of the land was dedicated to the horses; they had a ring in which to train, a plot on which to run, and another field solely for the use of those that were unbroken. The stables had space in which to hold well over 200 horses, though less than half of the stalls were ever used.

With another nod to the lads, Christian put a hand to Miss Wilkinson's elbow and led her to the front door. The entry was directly off the front drive, the double oak panels tall and wide.

As they approached, the door swung inward to allow them admittance, and one of the headmasters, Lachlan MacLean, strode forward to take Christian's hand.

"Welcome to Grimsbury! We're so pleased to see you again, Lord Leeds." The man nodded, shaking loose a lock of his bright copper hair.

Chris inclined his head. "A pleasure as always, Mr. MacLean." He turned, gesturing to his confoundedly alluring burden. "Might I introduce Miss Violet Wilkinson?"

MacLean bowed and *The Woman* curtseyed as they uttered pleasantries.

"You both appear to be wearied." MacLean clasped his hands together behind his back. "We have prepared rooms and have hot water on the boil. Why do you not freshen up while your meal is prepared?"

A recruit acting as a footman accepted a saddlebag from Chris and ushered Miss Wilkinson up the grand, curving staircase. The interior, while ostentatious, was elegant and sophisticated. Creams and dark browns appointed the space, the walls adorned in wood panelling and the floors a marbled cream.

Lachlan leaned toward Chris and murmured, "Samuels, we must speak privately."

Christian rubbed a hand over his face. "Yes, we must."

MacLean put a hand to Chris' arm, his green eyes imbued with concern. "While our discussion is of great import, your mental presence is paramount. What we must say will not change in one hour. Go. Take care of your needs." He notched his chin toward the stairs.

Relieved, Christian strode across the foyer, but halted. "MacLean," he said over his shoulder.

"Samuels?" his fellow replied gruffly.

"Miss Wilkinson requires cinnamon for her bath."

Apparently, Christian enjoyed torture.

* * *

A deep, satisfying sigh escaped Violet as she sank deeper into the brass bathing tub. Every muscle cried out in pain, the ache somehow worse now that her body was not in motion. Lord Leeds had been right: they needed this respite.

Cinnamon swirled through the steam to tease her senses; she was grateful for the modicum of comfort the familiar scent provided.

Though she had already concluded her wash, Vi was reluctant to leave the water. Despite the midday hour and the sun shining brightly through the expansive windows in her guest bedchamber, she felt the seductive pull of sleep. The room she had been given was light and cheerful, the walls painted a vibrant pale yellow and the furniture painted white.

The past four days of rough riding and snatching only moments of sleep while their horses rested had taken its toll on her, in both body and mind. While she'd had good cause in pushing them, she felt obliged to admit that perhaps she had been a mite harsh.

They had not seen her cousin since the incident at the inn several days past; however, Vi had nary a doubt that he was still in pursuit. Lord Leeds had accepted her proposed route of lanes and side roads, but she was unsure if any of their stratagems to delay Americus had worked, or how many days behind them her cousin was.

If they could but press on come dawn, she would feel more secure in her circumstance. Surely by the time they reached Grandmamma and Grandpapa in Glasgow, Americus would have either lost interest or given up his search. If not, then the defence techniques Lord Leeds had taught her might prove useful.

Suddenly, his last words rang in her ears. *"I will find you, Violet."*

Her chest squeezed. What if he *did* follow her to Glasgow? To what extremes would he go to have her in his clutches? A shiver ran through her, despite the warmth of the bath.

Unable to sit still a moment longer, Violet left the comforting bubble in which she had briefly surrounded herself and rose from the tub.

She wrung out her hair, the raining droplets returning to the cooling water. Swiftly drying herself with a towel, Vi retrieved her saddlebags and peered inside. And frowned.

Brown and grey wool, sachet of buns and apples, white lawn shirt…a cravat! She marked the items off in her mind. *Bloody hell, this is* Lofty *Leeds' saddlebags.* That would mean that he—

She gasped, her eyes widening and her heart all but stopping in her chest. *No, no, no!* Lord Leeds had her book!

Chapter 15

"What the devil—?" Christian stood, stark naked, in the middle of the crimson guest bedchamber, a well-worn leather-bound book in his hand. This wasn't his saddlebag. That would mean that Miss Wilkinson had his. Chris cringed. He hoped she didn't find his throwing daggers. They would certainly be difficult to explain.

He turned his attention to the saddlebags clutched in his fist. A suit of clothes, a set of undergarments, and one of the frocks that he had purchased for Miss Wilkinson were within, along with her absurdly large reticule. He scrutinised the small tome he'd withdrawn. Now, he supposed, he knew why the damned reticule was so heavy.

Turning the book over in his hand, Chris examined the cover. It was devoid of any engravings but for the initials "M. M." on the weathered spine. He set the saddlebags aside and opened the curiously blank cover.

A startled choke escaped him, his eyes widening and his neck growing red enough to match the room's wallpaper. *Bloody hell!* The title page sported an image of four women examining a table covered in cocks, and scrolling script that read *The Schoole of Venus*.

Christian's heart pumped erratically. Miss Wilkinson was in possession of *pornographia*! Suddenly his perception of her skewed sideways, his thoughts going in several directions at once. Had she actually *read* the book? Why did she have it? Clearly it was the only belonging—with the exception of her pistol and ruined frocks—with which she'd escaped Willow Hall; did the book mean that much to her? If so, *why*? Was she...? God help him for wondering, but, was she still an innocent? Or was she, perhaps...more *experienced*?

Despite himself, his cock swelled. Miss Wilkinson was under his protection, damn it; he shouldn't feel lust for her.

A knock sounded at the door and Chris cursed. Spinning, he hid the book beneath his discarded clothes and wrapped a towel around his waist before returning to the door. He pressed the latch and peered into the hall.

MacLean grinned at him. "I'm sorry for disturbing your bath, Samuels." He held up Chris' saddlebags. "Miss Wilkinson informed us of our mistake. Might we make an exchange?"

Christian gave a cursory nod, his mind still whirling. He accepted his things and gave MacLean Miss Wilkinson's in exchange—her erotic book excluded.

* * *

"If you would, MacLean, get to the crux of your point." Christian rubbed at his freshly-shaven jaw thirty minutes later.

The man's shoulders tensed. "Hermes is missing."

Chris stilled. "Good God, man!" He rose from his seat in the sparsely furnished headmaster's office. "*Missing*? How many men do you have out searching?"

MacLean held out his hands, urging Chris to resume his seat. "Rest assured, Samuels, we have sufficient men looking for him. Word has been sent to Hydra and Ares. Hermes' absence is not the only event of import in England at the moment. With the war on and Bonaparte's spies abound, we must remain vigilant. It is what Hermes would wish."

Christian's lips thinned. "How many men and women remain at the school?"

"Roughly thirty men and ten women. Most are our newest recruits. And, of course, we have some children, but they are keeping to their studies." His green eyes watched Christian closely. "With your identity compromised, I'm afraid our school is not as safe for you as it would have been with Hermes and our other men and women in residence. We are at a diminished capacity."

"I am not afraid to face the danger presented to us by Miss Wilkinson's pursuer, but I confess, having her to protect…" Chris sighed, shaking his head.

"It adds to the challenge," MacLean offered.

"Indeed, it does." Chris nodded. "Bramwell Stevens was on assignment at Willow Hall, observing Lord Hale and his heir, Lord Bristol. When he came to me prior to his departure, I believe he had evidence against Hale, but I am unsure about Bristol. Undoubtedly, there is incriminating evidence against Hale and Bristol. But while I would prefer to seek justice by finding a way to incriminate the men and seeing him through a trial, part of me wishes to have it out and done with by *any* means possible."

"Your disquiet with violence does you credit. Lord knows you've seen enough of it to send any man to Bedlam." MacLean tapped his narrow oak desk. "But while you've trained for longer than the rest of us, and are entirely capable of taking the man out, prudence is key."

"Naturally," Christian drawled.

MacLean pursed his lips, curiosity written on his expressive features. "About Miss Wilkinson…"

Chris' body buzzed at the mention of *The Woman*, her decidedly lascivious reading material burning a metaphorical hole in his breast pocket. "She beseeched me to bring her to Scotland, and that is precisely what I will do. The Baron of Bristol is a dangerous man, desirous to see Miss Wilkinson harmed. As I have sworn an oath to England and her people, I will do whatever I must to keep the woman safe."

"You've come here for a reason, I take it? There aren't many left, but those students who remain in residence are young and eager— albeit inexperienced—and would certainly be up for any task."

Chris nodded. "I thank you, Lachlan. And yes, I need help. I've a plan to lure and capture Lord Bristol. I need him questioned and prepared for a journey to London. Miss Wilkinson and I will spend the night and return to Carlisle on the morrow. There, we shall dine in the taproom, talk to the innkeeper, walk about town, and be *seen*."

"Very good; a classic bait. I will have some men stationed about town. Once word reaches them of Lord Bristol's arrival, they shall strike."

* * *

A warm gust of June air ruffled Violet's skirts as she descended the front steps of Grimsbury Manor the next morning. She'd had a pleasant enough sleep, though her mind had been reeling.

She'd searched her saddlebags upon their return to her chambers, and yet her book was not within. Had Lord Leeds seen it? Or—perish the thought—did he have it with him? Hell, she hoped not. Perhaps it had somehow been lost along the ride.

Her stomach clenched. The possibility that her book was lost hurt more than the thought of Lord Leeds being in possession of it. That book had shown her a world outside of pain for the past two years; being without it felt akin to being without hope.

"Good morning, Miss Wilkinson," Leeds said, trotting down the front steps and striding onto the gravel drive. "The mounts are ready; are you?"

"Yes." Ignoring how dashing the blasted man looked with his hair coiffed and his jaw freshly shaven, she withdrew her map and opened it. "I've taken into account the need for longer rests, proper meals, and sleep, and have come up with what I believe to be a suitable plan for the remainder of our journey to Glasgow. If you'll look—"

He turned to face her. "I appreciate the effort that you've put in, but we'll not follow your plan."

Her spine snapped straight, and a frown tightened her forehead. "And whyever not?"

"I've a plan, myself."

She scoffed. "And you imagine yours is superior to mine?"

"I do."

Her frown turned into a scowl. "Why are you so...blasted...*annoying*? I detest feeling as though I'm being moved about as a pawn on a chessboard. You set me aside when you haven't a need of me, you engage in secret discussions, make plans without consulting me, and...and... And why in damnation did you purchase a men's suit of clothing for me if I'm never to wear it?"

His icy blue gaze locked onto hers, but he said nothing, jaw clenching and unclenching as he considered her.

"What is it?" she asked. "And what is your plan? I vow I shall not be stirred from this spot until we've discussed this properly."

Shoulders heaving in a heavy sigh, he said softly, "I aim to trap Lord Bristol. Today, you and I will return to Carlisle and go about town. If we are seen enough, then there will be plenty of accounts of our being in town, and your cousin will take time to track our movements. I've arranged to then have him apprehended."

Fear spiked in Vi's belly, and a slight tremble shook her fingers. "But what if the magistrate sides with my cousin? I am considered theirs to contr—"

"I'll not allow that to happen. I'm a lord of the realm as well, and I shall give my account. The magistrate will surely see your grandparents as adequate guardians."

Vi released a slow, shaky breath. "Thank you."

He nodded. "Now, if we're to be seen in Carlisle, I believe that you require practice."

"Practice in what?"

He strode forward until he stood within arm's distance. "Hit me."

Chapter 16

A swift frown caught Violet by surprise. "I beg your pardon?"

"*Hit* me," *Lofty* Leeds urged. The sunlight brightened the silver of his hair, drawing Violet's gaze.

"You wish for me to strike you? Come, now, Leeds, we've been over this."

"*Tsk,*" the man chided, clasping her arm and using her hand to bat him on the chest. "Not with your hands. Now, hit me," he repeated. "Strike, punch, jab, pummel. Come, now! *Hit me!*"

Violet's desire to slap the cocksure man quarrelled with her sense of decorum.

"Oh dear, Miss Wilkinson," the blackguard taunted. "You are unafraid to wave a pistol about, but striking me with your fist has you trembling?"

The poke to her pride shook her from her spell. She extended her arm, intent on making contact with his chest. She hit air, instead, Lord Leeds having avoided her blow.

He waggled his eyebrows in a taunt, and Vi frowned. She balled her hand into a fist and made to strike again, but he sidestepped out of the way. *Curses!* She tried again, and again, each of her attempts foiled by Lord Leeds' quick movements.

The scoundrel tapped her on the shoulder. As she moved to bat at his hand, he tapped her stomach. Her frown of frustration quickly turned to a scowl. Their movements increased in speed, Violet attempting to make contact anywhere on *Lofty* Leeds' person, and the infuriating man tapping her wherever he pleased.

She growled, her irritation growing.

Leeds laughed, and Vi's heart nigh stopped in her chest. In the sennight that they had been travelling, she hadn't even seen him smile, let alone laugh. The sound was low and gruff, almost like a gravelly bark. It seeped under her skin, warm and sweet like honey.

The bright front drive of the grand manor faded away. Violet stopped her onslaught, her breath coming quickly as she stared into his sky-blue eyes. The mirth slowly fled from his features, the tense air between them heavy with something she couldn't quite name.

He was close. *So close.* His scent of soap and man enveloped her in its tempting embrace, pulling her inexorably closer.

Why, when she detested the man so thoroughly, did her body betray her in its curst attraction? And, as much as it irked her, she *was* attracted to him.

Violet's heart raced as Leeds' gaze dropped to her lips. *Sweet mercy!* Was he going to kiss her? *Oh, please let him!*

They remained thus for countless heartbeats, the air veritably crackling with their static attraction.

With a softly uttered curse, Leeds broke the silence and swooped, catching her lips with his.

A jolt of arousal and relief filled her at the heated contact. His mouth melded to hers as he closed the narrow distance between their bodies.

An influx of anxiety flooded her mind. Where did she put her hands? How did she align her feet? *Oh, Lord,* what if she did it wrong?

Lord Leeds cupped her jaw, caressing her bruised throat with the pad of his thumb. Her jaw fell open on a gasp, and then he plundered. Violet's thoughts fled, her anxieties dissolving, as the tip of his tongue flicked hers. It was as erotic and as thrilling as any of the descriptions in her naughty book—the book now missing from her belongings.

Vi followed his lead, mimicking his movements with equal fervour. With a twist to his hand, Leeds guided her head back so he might plunge deeper with his searching tongue.

Her insides heated further, and a decidedly wanton—and delightful—liquid sensation flooded low in her abdomen as her feminine core throbbed in anticipation. Leeds fisted his hand in the material at the small of her back, moulding her body flush against his. *Oh Lord!* She could feel the hardness of his arousal pressing against her.

Vi wanted him closer, as impossible as it was. She stretched her arms over his shoulders and surged upward on her toes, throwing herself wholly and completely into his kisses.

His breath puffed against her cheek as he groaned, the sound vibrating over her skin.

She was gasping, unable to take full breaths as they clung to each other, locked in a passionate merging of lips and tongue. Her baser instincts urged her to take more, to *feel* more.

Then the sound of voices around the side of the manor forced them to spring apart. Violet's chest heaved. For a moment they remained as they were, their wide-eyed gazes locked.

Another shout came from around the corner, and Lord Leeds broke the spell by striding toward his horse.

Did that truly just happen? Vi's fingers drifted up to touch her lips, where the heady taste of him still lingered. Leeds had plundered her mouth as a pirate would treasure, and despite her distaste for the man's *lofty* nature…she wanted more.

Leeds glanced at her over his shoulder. "There is a group of travelling performers in town that I think we ought to see."

* * *

Christian had itched with the desire to pull Miss Wilkinson back into his arms since the moment they'd left Grimsbury Manor and reached their rooms at the inn in Carlisle.

He glanced at her from his spot near the window, where she sat re-pinning her hair after their ride. Her slightly rumpled appearance, pinkened lips and cheeks, and the dazed arousal in her deep, blue gaze were nigh irresistible. The woman's sweet kisses had him very nearly losing power over his urges.

Since the moment he'd met her, he'd known that she was different from any other of his acquaintance. Around her, his reason was constantly at war with his instinct. He *felt* things when Miss Wilkinson was around that he'd never felt before.

When it came to women, Chris relied on his logic. He took care of his needs when the desire arose and left when his needs had been satisfied. And he'd *always* been in control. Chris knew not what to make of *this* circumstance. The woman drove him mad, but, for some unknown reason, he seemed to respond favourably to her Machiavellian personality. She presented a challenge that he was curious to face.

An awkward beat passed between them before Christian cleared his throat. "The performance will begin soon." He walked over to retrieve his saddlebag and, with it, one of his throwing daggers. "I intend to arm you with something other than your pistol. Surely, if Lord Bristol has continued in his pursuit of you, he is aware of your arsenal. If you don your men's suit of clothes, I will hide this within your sleeve. It will be easily accessible; if at any time you feel threatened, you can retrieve it and use it to defend yourself."

Her brow furrowed as she eyed the small, sharp blade in his hand. "If we're to lure my cousin, why must I don my men's suit of clothes?"

"If he has followed us this far, he will be aware of our presence here, but I haven't a wish for him to get too close to you."

"Very well. Your precaution is appreciated."

"Of course. I promise not to leave your side," he vowed.

Miss Wilkinson pursed her reddened lips as she thought, and Chris' thirsty gaze drank in the movement. What he wouldn't give to take her against him once more, to taste the cinnamon on her skin, to peel that frock from her delectable body and have her in ways that even the book in his breast pocket hadn't thought to describe—

Christian halted his dangerous thoughts and turned to lift *The Woman*'s saddlebags in his hands. He cleared his throat once more. "What say you, Miss Wilkinson?"

"I accept your reasoning; I'm merely disappointed that I spent the time to re-do my hair." She stood and rifled through her saddlebags. "I shall change."

With a hooded glance, she withdrew behind the privacy screen. The swish of fabric sent lewd images thundering through Chris' mind, and he cursed inwardly. He couldn't let himself get a cockstand at such a moment, for Christ's sake!

Think of something neutral... He cleared his throat. "Tell me, Miss Wilkinson, do you have a favourite—" *Hell, don't say "book"! Think of something else.* "—dessert?"

She hummed, and his cods tightened. "I'm partial to cinnamon pound cake."

Of course. Damn it.

"Although I do enjoy fruit."

"Just fruit on its own? Not in a cake or trifle?" *Curious.*

"Yes, just on its own. And you? Have you a favourite dessert?"

"I've always been partial to baked custard and jam tartlets."

Her light, lilting laugh filtered through the privacy screen. "Really? I didn't picture you as the sort of man to enjoy those."

"And what sort of dessert man do I seem to be?"

She hummed and grunted. "I'm not certain; something sour, perhaps."

"Sour! Bah."

She grunted again. "How the devil do you men dress in these? It's so…scratchy."

"Do you require help?"

"I'm afraid I do, yes. I haven't a clue how to tie my cravat."

"Come out, then."

She rounded the corner, and Chris very nearly swallowed his tongue. The trousers hugged her hips and thighs, and even with the cover of the waistcoat, her generous curves were obvious. The collar of her shirt hung open to reveal the column of her throat and her collar bone. Damn, but he wanted to trail his lips along every inch of that exposed skin.

He cleared his throat and accepted the neck cloth from her. "Here now. We wrap like this, and knot…just so." The cloth conveniently covered the still-yellow bruises caused by her blackguard of a cousin, but neither thing diminished her beauty in the least.

With a breathy "thank you" and a short smile, she donned her boots. She then moved to fix her hair while Chris inserted her dagger discreetly into the right sleeve of her coat before she put it on.

"There." He cuffed her playfully on the shoulder. "You won't be able to fool anyone who looks well enough, but at a glance, this will suffice."

She beamed and strode toward the door, the gentle sway of her hips entirely giving her away.

Chris snorted. "No, no. We cannot leave yet. Not until you've learned how to walk."

She turned with a frown, affront written all over her features. "I do beg your pardon, but I know how to walk."

"Like a woman, yes, but not like a man. Come." He gestured her forward.

They walked together, side by side, while she practised. Chris attempted to minimise his uneven gait so as to better teach Miss Wilkinson, but the damned limp wouldn't relent. To his relief, she didn't mimic it, nor did she comment. Her walk, however, did improve slightly.

* * *

Awe filled Violet as she and Leeds entered Bitts Park. The open green space between the extravagant gardens had been transformed into an open theatre. Lanterns were lit and hanging high in the air, suspended from wire to appear as if they were stars in the darkening sky. A stage was set with deep red curtains, no doubt concealing the performers as they prepared, and chairs were arranged in curved rows for the audience.

The residents of Carlisle gathered in great number, many milling about while others had already taken their seats.

Despite her unnatural fixation on the way she walked, excitement bubbled within her and a grin stole over her lips. Though she had read about the experience, she had never before seen a travelling theatre troupe. She and Rose had attended only their come-out ball and other matchmaking events in the years before her family had taken ill.

"Shall we sit?" Lord Leeds' deep voice murmured in her ear.

Vi nodded, tugging nervously at the chocolate brown cutaway coat that she wore. She was entirely unused to the chafing of material between her legs, the cravat secured tightly around her neck, and the moving fabric around her bandage-bound breasts, but she also felt confident in her disguise and exhilarated about the diversion.

It took a great amount of focus to resist the urge to fidget with her hair. She wore it tied with a leather strap at the nape of her neck, her long dark locks flowing down her back. It was an out-of-fashion style for men's hair, but it was gratefully still acceptable.

They found seats in the middle of the audience, the hum of many voices surrounding them. The sun set fully, the lanterns brightening against the night sky. A bell jingled, and the seats around them quickly filled. Many men and women were forced to stand about the perimeter of the chairs, though Violet fancied that they had the best view.

Lord Leeds' thigh brushed hers, and a jolt of awareness quaked through her. Vi's stomach fluttered as memories of their kisses flooded her mind.

Leeds had not mentioned their kisses. Could he regret kissing her? Could she have done something wrong? Or...perhaps she was simply a terrible kisser. There had been tense moments between them, so surely it wasn't a lack of attraction? Oh, Lord, what if it was only *she* who felt it?

She slid a sideways glance at the stoic man.

He leaned sideways and whispered, "I saw some of the men I'd arranged for take their place among the crowd. We are in a good position to enjoy the show."

A man in a brightly coloured suit of clothes appeared on the stage, his hands held aloft as the hum of voices hushed. "Good evening…"

Violet twitched as Lord Leeds shifted in his seat. He spread his hands and slid them up his thighs, brushing her leg with the backs of his fingers. The performer on stage continued to speak, but Violet's attention was decidedly engrossed in the contact. Had he meant to touch her?

"…Prepare to be amazed!"

A low rumble came from behind the stage, followed by gasps of awe from the audience. From around the platform, a man emerged, riding a grand gelding. He wasn't in the saddle, however, but standing on the beast's back.

Violet laughed at the sight. She wondered if this was what it was like to attend Astley's Amphitheatre; she'd heard that men and women performed tricks while riding on a horse's back, but never would she have imagined that it would be so enjoyable to watch!

Man and rider rode around the audience, drawing everyone's gaze as more performers took the stage. A man wearing a bright mauve suit of clothes with absurdly long coattails stood beside an enormous dog that was made to look like a lion. The audience laughed as the man comically attempted to get the "lion" to sit on a pedestal and fit his head in the beast's mouth.

Leeds' hand brushed her thigh once more, her skin heating beneath the thin material of her trousers. He couldn't have touched her unintentionally *twice*, could he?

Violet hedged a glance in Leeds' direction and caught his intense gaze, his sky-blue irises darkening in the lantern light. *Perhaps it* was *deliberate.*

She wanted to kiss him again, and if the desire shining in his eyes was any indication, he did, too.

Laughter and applause erupted around them, forcing Vi's attention back to the stage.

A woman with three flaming torches in her hands strode to the centre of the platform, a large, pleasing smile on her round face. Rapid violin music came from behind the stage as the performer began to juggle the torches. All the while, Violet was exceedingly aware of Lord Leeds' fingers touching her thigh.

The performance went on, flaming torches flying through the air, higher and higher, the audience rapt with delight. Not Violet. Her heart tripped along, her lungs tightening.

Ought she to be outraged that he would presume to behave so improperly with her? Probably. But the little jolts of anticipation travelling up her spine, the quivering in her abdomen, and the speeding of her pulse told her that she was rather thrilled by it.

The audience's applause cut through her reverie once more as the flame-juggler left the stage and a sharply dressed man took her place. He bowed with a flourish, producing a bouquet of flowers as if from nowhere. *A magician!*

Violet was all too aware of Leeds shifting in his seat. As silly as it was, disappointment lanced through her as he moved his hand, her thigh suddenly chilled without his touch. Just as the feeling registered, however, another wholly unexpected one took its place. Aroused anticipation flooded her as Lord Leeds boldly clasped her hand in his; his palm placed flat against hers, their fingers seductively intertwined.

Her head spun so quickly to catch his gaze that she nearly became dizzy from it. His heated gaze was knowing, watching her with the lust that she felt for him. But, *dash it all*, she could not muster indignation, for *this* she wanted. What her grandparents would think was simply…not a concern. All Vi desired for her future was the freedom to make her own choices, and whether that came in the form of her growing into an elderly maiden or a soiled spinster, she cared not.

Gasps rose about them as doves flew through the sky. Violet laughed, watching the small flock of white birds skim the tops of women's bonnets and men's hats.

Then she saw it. A face. *His* face. Her smile aborted and her breath nigh froze in her throat. The man was handsome, with a square jaw, close-cropped black hair, high cheekbones, and full lips. His malevolent black eyes bore into hers, a glint of wicked victory in their depths.

She could feel the blood drain from her features, her mind spinning.

"Miss Wilkinson?" Leeds whispered in her ear. "What do you see?"

He followed her gaze, then let out a low curse. He gripped her elbow and stood. "Come," he muttered. "Quickly!"

With mumbled apologies to those around them, Leeds hurriedly led Violet to the centre aisle.

"*Run!*" he hissed, pushing her toward the standing audience.

Vi glanced over her shoulder, but Americus was gone. Abruptly awoken from the spell of shock and fear, Violet ran.

Weaving between men and women, she was desperate to be free and begin a sprint. Lord Leeds' smooth but quick breathing sounded behind her, urging her faster.

A shot rang out and Violet screamed, her voice overpowered by the cheer of the audience. Someone called her name, but she didn't turn to look. She just kept moving.

Someone shrieked, and another shouted, "He has a gun!"

Vi's heart nigh stopped at the shouts and scrambling people. This wasn't how it was meant to go! Lord Leeds had promised her that his *men* had secured positions around the performance, that her cousin would be caught!

Crack! Another shot sounded, and people screamed behind her, but she kept running. Finally, she broke through the milling crowd, her feet carrying her swiftly over the grass.

Heavy footfalls came up behind her and she nearly sighed in relief. Deep panting followed, and Violet glanced over her shoulder toward the noise.

A dark gaze met hers and a gasp rose in her throat. Americus' arm swung, and Violet shrieked, the sound cut off abruptly as her vision went dark.

Chapter 17

Christian pushed past the searing pain and damned ringing in his ear and ran through the park, a trail of blood flowing down his cheek and along his jaw.

The bastard, Lord Bristol, had sighted him charging after Violet and damned well shot him! And *bloody hell*, did it hurt!

He dashed across the grass, terror gripping him. He'd lost sight of Violet among the crush, but he was certain she was still running.

A broken scream rent the air, and Chris' gut churned. He followed the sound. *There*. He caught sight of a man carrying a lad over his shoulder, but Chris knew the truth. It was Violet, and Lord Bristol had her.

Chris pumped his legs faster. Shooting would do him little good, as he could very well injure Violet unintentionally.

He was too far away! Where were the spies-in-training? Bristol hailed a hack at the edge of the park and tossed Violet inside. *Damn, damn, damn!* Christian pushed himself faster, nearing the hack just as it pulled away. He followed the equipage down the narrow road, watching for their direction before he finally stopped.

"We'll follow, your lordship!" a tall student of the spy school said as two of them darted past. "We'll return with his location."

"Thank you."

Chris' chest heaved with each laboured breath, his body aching with exhaustion and his sodding damaged knee burning with every movement. Sharp instinct from a lifetime of training and conditioning took over. He raised a hand to the driver of another hack and tossed him a coin. "The Blue Bird Inn. There's a pound note in it for you if we can be there within five minutes."

* * *

Miss Violet Wilkinson smelled of fear. The odour radiated from her in waves. Her ankles and wrists chafed against their bindings, but the more she tugged against them, the tighter they became. Her fingers began to tingle as the blood flow struggled up her arms, which stretched above her head.

Her world was black beneath the blindfold, but she could sense the warmth of a fireplace and the gentle breeze of an opened window.

The bed beneath her was intolerably uncomfortable, lumpy and dishevelled with odd mounds pressing upward against her person. But it was the terror of what was expected of her, tied to the bed such as she was, that thundered mercilessly within her.

Where were Lord Leeds and his men? What had happened to their plan? Well, she certainly wouldn't wait to be rescued. This was up to her alone. It was her fault for trusting the dratted man from the start.

Retreating footsteps echoed down a corridor, and Vi strained to listen as they slowly faded away. Her cousin had promised his direct return as he went to fetch his meal in the taproom belowstairs; this was her only opportunity… If she could but manage to cut her ties, perhaps there was a chance for her after all.

Vi flicked her arms in an effort to shimmy the small blade hidden in her sleeve toward her hand. It was a trifling little dagger, similar in size to her little finger. It would not inflict much damage to her captor, but if jabbed in the correct locations, it could very well kill him, or at the least incapacitate him long enough for her to make good her escape.

The panicked organ in her chest fluttered faster than a butterfly's wings as she wiggled about upon the bed.

Further…further. Blast! The blade was stuck against her bindings. She must flip it at *just* the correct angle, else the dagger would drop to the bed above her head and entirely out of her reach.

Flick…flick…

Aha! The dagger jabbed into her palm, the sharp blade digging painfully into her soft flesh. The prospect of being free was worth the small sacrifice of drawn blood, however, for far worse would befall her should her captor return before she found freedom.

She bent her nimble fingers, bringing the blade to the tie linking her wrists, and began to saw. Violet was thankful for the little dagger's sharp edges, for the bindings slackened almost immediately.

Frantically, she continued to cut. How had it come to *this*? Never would she have imagined that she would find herself in such a circumstance. She wished her plan had played out differently.

A swift surge of victory pumped through her veins as the ties snapped open and she pulled the blindfold from her eyes. She gave a cursory glance around the room as she bent to tug at the ties on her ankles.

Her cousin had brought her to a hovel of an inn. The plaster crumbled from the walls and the paltry furnishings were dented and gouged. She hated to think of what bugs infested the soiled bedclothes that she had been tied upon.

A shiver wracked her frame.

One of her ankles slid free and she hastily moved to unknot the other. Within moments she had herself released from her bindings. She gripped her small dagger in her bloodied hand and strode purposefully toward the window.

The cooling evening breeze blew over her, tugging with it her dark hair pulled chaotically from the leather tie at the nape of her neck. The scent of manure, hay, urine, and soil assailed her nostrils.

Her eyes widened at the distance of the drop. Four floors separated her from the innyard below.

Ballocks!

Heavy footsteps echoed down the corridor outside the small, unkempt room. Terror snaked its way up Violet's spine, threatening her with its poisonous bite. Each ominous footfall added a weight of anguish to her troubled heart.

There is no escape.

"Knock, knock…" Americus' deep voice rumbled forebodingly through the door. "I have come to claim my prize."

A key slid in the lock and slowly turned, the scraping of metal on metal feeling like the final nail in her proverbial coffin.

Hide! Instinct screamed inside her head.

Before the latch could be pressed, Vi dropped to the floor and shimmied herself beneath the bed.

Something squeaked and skittered alongside her, and she bit her lip to keep from screaming. *Dear Lord!* She was going to die with her front pressed to a filth-covered, rat-infested, flea-ridden floor of a vile inn!

* * *

Christian pressed his signet seal into the melted wax before stuffing the ring back into his saddlebags. As tempting as it was to bring both bags with him, he hadn't the time to pack. If it was required, he'd damned well pay for new attire instead of wasting precious moments.

He hastily wrote the coded direction on the letter, then waved it about as he strode to the washbasin, his hidden inner pockets heavy with throwing daggers and his holster fastened about his shoulders and concealed beneath his coat. Putting the missive down, Chris dipped a washcloth into the water and swiped at the drying blood trail from his ear.

A hiss escaped him as he washed his sensitive lobe. The blackguard had put a hole through his damned ear! A swift cleaning would have to suffice until he could properly bandage it.

Missive in hand, Christian trotted down the flights of stairs to reach the taproom. He found the messenger used by his comrades—the very same lad whom he'd sent to Grimsbury Manor when first they'd arrived in Carlisle—and pulled him aside.

"Have this brought to MacLean. *Urgently.*" Chris handed the lad the missive with a meaningful glance. They had need of more men.

The messenger saluted before leaving the nearly empty taproom and dashing toward the stables. Christian followed him out, his rented horse awaiting him in the innyard. The cool air brushed past him as he mounted, but it wasn't the chill evening that put a shiver in his bones. Nearly a quarter of an hour had passed since he'd seen Lord Bristol ride away with Violet. Every minute that went by could mean a great many terrible things for the woman, even with the fighting techniques he'd taught her.

"Your lordship!" a student called, winded as he entered the inn's stable yard. "Lord Bristol has Miss Wilkinson at the King's Horse on the outskirts of town. Fourth floor."

Chris' gut twisted. "Very good. Thank you. Have the others assemble to pick him up; he won't be leaving Carlisle." With a nod, he nudged the gelding into a gallop.

* * *

Violet watched from beneath the bed, her heart fluttering wildly, as the door slowly opened. Americus' boots stopped on the threshold, the door swinging wide.

Instinctively, Vi ducked her head, resisting the urge to shimmy backward. She knew what he saw; the rumpled bedclothes, spots of her blood from her fumbled attempts to free herself with Leeds' dagger, and undoubtedly a flea or two. She suppressed another shiver. This inn was beyond vile.

Americus cursed, then slammed the door behind him, his tray of food dropping to the floor. "You *filthy whore*! How *dare* you presume to escape me?"

The lump on Vi's head throbbed with every beat of her heart.

Americus stepped toward the bed. "Think you that I wouldn't find you? That I wouldn't *smell* you?" He inhaled audibly, then groaned, sending another shiver of revulsion through Violet.

Suddenly, his arm appeared beneath the bed with her. Her heart all but stopping, Vi scrambled backward. The attempt at escape was futile. Americus gripped the long length of her hair, and pulled.

Pain screamed through her head as Americus dragged her from her insufficient hiding spot, lifting her to her feet in front of him. Violet grit her teeth, not giving the scurrilous bastard the satisfaction of hearing her cry out in fear.

He hauled her back against his chest, wrapping an arm about her midriff. "*You…*" Americus sniffed her neck and ground his hips against her bottom simultaneously.

Violet swallowed the bile that rose in her throat.

"I'm going to enjoy breaking you." His lips moved against the side of her neck, drifting down to where her shirt collar came open, her cravat having been used as her blindfold. "Father forbade me from having you, but I cannot resist. And I'm owed money for your retrieval, naughty wench. You were meant to be married by now."

Vi surreptitiously flipped the small dagger over in her hand, careful not to alert her cousin.

He squeezed her tighter, licking the column of her neck and leaving an abhorrent trail of cold slime behind. Violet shivered in disgust. "You'll never have me," she asserted, her jaw clenched.

"Ah, but there you are wrong, Violet. I *already* have you. And by God, I shall relish every moment." Without warning, Americus bared his teeth and sank them into her.

Her cry of pain reverberated loudly in her ears as agony burned through her neck. Sans hesitation, Violet swung her arm backward, stabbing Americus in the thigh with as much strength as she could muster, then withdrew, the bloodied dagger still held in her hand.

Americus roared, releasing her to grip his leg. Without looking back, Violet dashed to the opened door.

"You *bitch*!" he spat.

A string of foul curses followed her down the hall as she ran. The inn's patrons eyed her with a mix of curiosity and outrage as she passed; she must have looked a fright with her hair almost entirely pulled from the leather strap, a ruined men's suit of clothes, a dripping dagger clutched in her fist, and blood coating her head, neck, and hands. But she cared not what they assumed.

The taproom door swung inward as an intoxicated couple entered. Violet slid past them, the overwhelming scent of rum and ale assailing her senses. As soon as the aroma of horse, leather, manure, urine, and, beneath it all, fresh air engulfed her, Violet broke into a run once more.

Her booted heels crunched on the dirt and gravel innyard. Wind swept past her, a faint whistling rushing over her ears. The distant call of her name urged her faster. Americus would soon recover himself and resume his chase, but she would damned well put as much distance between them as she could before he followed.

Violet's arms pumped at her sides, her heart beating a wild tattoo in her chest. With the amount of running she'd had to do in the past sennight, she had a newfound respect for her sister's proclivity for it. No matter how much it burned her lungs, however, Vi would power through, because she would be damned if she let Americus catch her again!

* * *

Anxiousness clutched Christian as he rode. He nudged his gelding faster, the chilled wind ruffling his silver hair and whipping at his coat.

The dim lights of a decrepit inn glowed through the darkness just off the road, and Christian steered his mount toward it. The closer he got to the inn, the more ghastly it appeared. "The King's Horse," the sign read.

He spotted the other students loitering in the shadows, and he stopped in front of them.

"The moment I have Miss Wilkinson away from Lord Bristol, take him down."

The dimness notwithstanding, a light eagerness brightened the students' eyes, and they nodded their understanding.

Chris turned and stopped in the innyard, an intoxicated man and a blowsy woman stumbling past him as he dismounted. A slovenly groom lumbered out of the stables and accepted the horse's reins.

"Give him water and feed." Christian tossed the man a coin. "I will be but a moment."

The groom nodded and led the horse toward the stable doors.

Drunken laughter wafted on the night air toward Chris, a shaft of light coming through the opened door of the inn. As the inebriated couple entered, a slight figure dashed out. *Violet!*

Christian's heart tripped over itself at the sight of her. His glimpse was brief as she ran, but the sight of blood on her opened shirtfront twisted his gut.

"Violet!" he called.

She ducked her head as she entered a sprint, and Chris cursed. Spinning on his heel, he summoned the groom. "Oi! My man!" He dashed into the stables and handed the man another coin. "I've need of my mount." He glanced over his shoulder to see the students entering the inn, and a modicum of relief hit him.

"But 'e ain't been fed yet!" the groom yelled belligerently.

Christian grabbed the beast's reins and mounted him there in the stables. With a nudge to the gelding's ribs and a cluck of Chris' tongue, they were off.

* * *

Violet's body ached. The constant running and riding for her life was as tiring on her physically as it was emotionally. She wanted nothing more than to reach her destination, have a long, hot bath, a cup of tea, and a good night of sleep. And then to write a lengthy letter to her sister.

Past the rushing wind, her heavy breathing, the crunching of her boots on the dirt road, and her heart pounding in her ears, the distinct timbre of galloping hooves alerted her to a rider's approach. Instinct and a sharp spike of terror drove her to swerve into the nearby copse of trees.

Twigs and eagerly stretching roots littered the forest floor, and reaching branches tugged at her clothes and fallen hair. Without the aid of the early moonlight, Vi could scarcely see a thing. She held her hands out before her, the small dagger still grasped in her fist as she carefully guided herself between the trees.

A man cursed behind her, followed by heavy footfalls and the *snap* of breaking twigs.

Americus! Violet's pulse tripled its speed as she darted haphazardly between the trees. The rapid beat of her heart overpowered every other sound. *Thump-thump. Thump-thump.*

Her hands knocked into trees and her feet fumbled awkwardly over fallen branches as she ran.

"Damn it. *Violet!*" A pair of thick arms wrapped around her from behind, pulling her to a stop.

Violet screamed, the sound echoing in the vastness around them, when Lord Leeds' lesson ran through her mind. She quickly slammed her head back, the movement causing her a brief moment of dizziness, and stomped on her attacker's foot. The man howled in pain.

"Bloody hell!" the deep voice cursed as the man leapt backward. "Violet, it's Christian, for God's sake. Stop!"

Christian? Lord Leeds? She blinked into the darkness, trying to make out his shape.

"It's me," he restated, his voice slow and soothing. "I saw you leaving the inn and I called out, but you wouldn't stop."

A sob rose in her throat as profound relief flowed through her. Her face scrunched, and a hot tear spilled over her lashes, the sudden burst of emotion entirely overwhelming her.

Leeds cursed and stepped forward to grip her upper arms. "There, there," he muttered softly.

Absurdly amused at his ineptitude at comforting a weeping woman, Violet snorted, then covered the sound with the back of her blood-crusted hand. She could hear him smile, and she followed suit.

"Come." He urged her back the way they'd come. "We must return to my horse and be away from this place."

She stumbled forward with him, stepping awkwardly upon the roots of the trees they passed. "Americus will be in pursuit."

"The men I'd arranged for will have him in hand. How badly did he hurt you? What happened?"

Violet's stomach clenched at the thought of reliving the terrifying moments at the inn. "I can't... Not yet." Her fist tightened around the small, sticky dagger, her mind rushing with unwanted images of blood and Americus' rage-filled visage.

Leeds cleared his throat. "As a precaution, we will take rooms at each of the inns along the north road on our way back into Carlisle, though we shall stay in none," he began, swiftly changing the subject. "My acquaintances from Brampton ought to have apprehended him by now. We will be afforded a night of sleep before we resume our journey on the morrow."

Chapter 18

"I realise the hour is late, but we would be much obliged if you would prepare a meal of foodstuffs for us—anything you have in the larder will suffice." Christian smiled at the young maid as she stood just outside their bedchamber door.

She returned his smile, her sweetly rounded cheeks dimpling. "O' course, sirrah. An' I'll 'ave those bandages to ye right quick." She curtseyed and strode swiftly down the dim corridor.

Chris closed the door and turned toward Violet. "Let us have a look at your wounds."

She stood gazing at herself in the mirror, a grimace of pain on her fine features.

Christian went to the washbasin and dipped a cloth into the chilled water. His stomach was in knots. That amount of blood on a shirtfront wasn't an unfamiliar sight in his field, but damn it, on *Violet* it was beyond disconcerting.

"Allow me?" He gestured toward her wounds then toward the room's only chair.

She twitched her head in a halting nod and sat stiffly.

"This might sting," Chris warned as he gently pressed the cloth to her blood-soaked skin.

Violet hissed a breath between her teeth and Chris cursed, his stomach knotted sickeningly. He was startled by the feelings she evoked in him, and by the bewildering, vehement hatred of Lord Bristol that burned deep within him. She was confounding him with her remarkable—albeit foolhardy—bravery, her determined will, her frustrating—and alluring—tart tongue, and her damned annoying sexual appeal.

She gasped again, and Christian murmured an apology. He hated seeing her beautiful skin so damaged.

Violet tilted her head back, revealing the slender column of her neck, the movement pulling at the horrifying bite mark there. Christian pressed the cloth against it, cleaning away the freshly seeping blood.

When her neck was cleaned, he moved quickly on to the puncture wound on her right hand and dabbed the cool cloth to the rope burns on her wrists. The maid returned, bringing with her a tray of clothes, a poultice, and bandages beside an arrangement of foodstuffs. Christian blocked Violet from the maid's curious stares.

"Will that be all, Mister and Missus Platts?" The softly rounded woman clasped her hands before her, a polite smile on her lips.

Chris nodded. "It is, thank you."

The maid curtseyed and closed the door as she left.

Violet lifted her nose to the air and hummed low in her throat, the sound hitting Chris somewhere in his abdomen.

"That smells delightful," she noted, "and I'm famished!"

His lips tightened. "That will have to wait, I'm afraid. First, we must bandage your wounds—and my damned ear—and leave the inn."

A quick frown marred her brow. "But I thought—"

He held up a hand to stay her words. "I assured you that there would be no further travel this evening, and I intend to uphold that promise. Trust me."

* * *

Violet held her breath as a footman strode past them down the hall. Her back pressed firmly to the darkly panelled alcove wall, she hoped that she and Leeds blended into the darkness. His hand was hot in hers, the contact sending tingles and gooseflesh up her arm despite the tension of their situation.

The footman's treads faded down the corridor, and Leeds gently tugged her hand. They left their hiding spot, slinking through the dim hall toward a rear door of the inn. Leeds hadn't explained where they were headed, or why they must do so in secret, but she trusted him. No matter how much it grated.

The rapid beat of her heart pulsed in her ears as they sped quietly from shadow to shadow. Why she was so anxious about a maid or footman seeing them, she knew not.

Leeds adjusted the bundles over his shoulder, and they pressed onward. Voices echoed down the corridor from the kitchens, and Violet's heart hiccoughed. Leeds' hand tightened on hers. The door was just ahead!

"...Upon my word, 'tis true!" Two maids strode through the doors from the kitchens and into the hall.

Violet and Leeds froze in the darkness. Vi willed her heart to beat softer lest the maids hear it.

"Augusta got right bosky an' told Martin tha' she thought 'e was top o' the trees. Sarah says she saw them tossin' about in one o' the guest bedchambers, like."

"Thunder an' turf!"

The maids' voices trailed away, the sound replaced by their footfalls on a set of stairs.

Leeds released her hand to press the door's latch. He pulled, and a gust of cool night air rushed inward. He glanced into the darkness without before they crossed the threshold, carefully closing the door behind them.

"Come," he whispered, clasping her hand once more.

Then they ran, dashing through obscurity on quick feet. A burst of excitement rippled through Vi, followed by a peculiar urge to laugh. She'd escaped a dangerous situation and a dire fate this night. If Christian had so chosen, he could have considered himself free of her and made the return journey to Eastbourne. But he'd searched for her—he'd *saved* her—of his own accord, and he had helped her further by arranging to have her cousin apprehended.

He was still *lofty*, still in possession of his superiority and arrogance, but now there was another facet to him that she hadn't seen before. There was compassion, bravery, daring, and a part of him swathed in the base needs of man. Needs that she had the reckless desire to explore.

They came to a halt and pressed themselves against the exterior of the stables. A light gust of wind blew past, tugging gently at Vi's dark coat and partially fallen hair. The soft *whicker* of horses and the muffled shifting of hooves came from within. Christian nodded, apparently satisfied.

They crept toward the side door and silently entered. She was immediately greeted by the scent of horseflesh, manure, hay, and leather. It was a strangely comforting odour.

Christian gently squeezed her hand and led her down an aisle. But for windows at the end of the long corridor and high up in the hayloft, lending shafts of moonlight, they were engulfed in darkness. There were approximately twenty stalls, and only half were occupied. A closed door on the wall to the left of the entrance presumably led to the stable hands' quarters.

Several horses sniffed at them as they passed, their noses curiously poking over the stall doors.

They came upon the ladder to the loft, and Christian gestured toward it. "Up." He released her hand.

"The hayloft?" Violet questioned.

He nodded, the gentle moonlight giving his silver hair a faint blue glow.

Vi's bandaged palm throbbed as she climbed the ladder. She had never before slept on hay, but she imagined that it wouldn't be terribly comfortable: itchy, hard, and possibly lumpy. She couldn't bring herself to complain, however, for her living conditions in Willow Hall had been no better, and sleeping in a carriage was dreadfully difficult.

She was merely curious as to *why*, for Christian had not revealed the details of his plan.

The hayloft spread across the rear quarter of the stables. Hay covered the entirety of the space. Along the back wall and down the sides, more hay was piled, giving the appearance of a large, lumpy settee made of hay.

Violet smiled at the thought.

Climbing atop the bottom layer of hay, she stood. The instability of it caught her off guard and she stumbled. Behind her, Christian cursed, dumping their saddlebags and the bed sheet filled with their foodstuffs at his feet, and put a hand to her back.

"Steady, now. Are you all right, Violet?" he murmured softly as Vi caught herself. A shudder went through her at the sound of her name on his lips. When had Christian begun calling her by her given name?

Her eyes widened. When had *she* begun thinking of Lord Leeds as *Christian*?

* * *

Chris swallowed his last bite of cheese and dusted his hands together. It had been an adequate repast: cured meat, apples, biscuits as hard as stones, and warm, fragrant cheese. He had not brought plates or utensils, but the inn's bed sheet had served as a satisfactory picnic blanket for their extemporised midnight meal.

"Thank you," Violet whispered. "For everything."

Chris' gaze flicked upward. The genuine appreciation on her features had the oddest effect on him. He wasn't sure what she was thanking him for; perhaps it was nothing in particular, or their journey as a whole. It mattered not. She was welcome to it all.

His gaze travelled over her. Even in a bloodstained men's suit of clothes, Violet was ethereal in the moonlight. Chris had avoided looking at her while he ate, for he feared that once he did, he would not be able to tear his gaze away. Her dark, loosely knotted hair lightly framed her pale, narrow face. Her eyebrows arched elegantly over intelligent blue eyes, and her pert nose accentuated the permanently stubborn set to her intoxicating, plump lips.

There were so many overwhelming odours in the stables, but damn it, he could still detect *The Woman*'s cinnamon scent.

When it came to the maddening Miss Wilkinson, Chris was in danger of losing control of himself. He could feel his resolve crumbling ever further the more time he spent in her company.

He cleared his throat. "You're welcome."

"He anticipated it this time." Violet chewed on her bottom lip in an unconsciously alluring way, her gaze downcast.

A frown brushed Christian's brow. "Who anticipated what?"

Her troubled gaze rose to meet his once more. "Americus—Lord Bristol. He knew I would try to kick him in the ballocks. He deflected my attempt."

The sudden change of topic twisted his heart before he could guard himself against it.

Violet's fingers worried the edge of the bed sheet. "I-I tried the other methods you'd taught me, but he was stronger than I. He hit me from behind, and I don't..." She shook her head. "I don't remember anything until I awoke, just after he had tied me to that awful bed."

Christian closed his eyes. He didn't want to know more. Hell, he didn't think he could *stomach* knowing more, but he couldn't bring himself to stop her flow of words.

She looked at the bandages on her hand and wrists. "I managed to free myself, but he prevented me from fleeing. He..." She swallowed, the motion of her neck drawing Chris' gaze. The fading bruises from her encounter with Bristol several days before were still visible beneath the bandages. "Americus said he wanted to break me."

Chris cursed, the sudden roiling fury, abhorrence, and another disturbing emotion churning within him.

Violet nodded and shrugged simultaneously, an oddly endearing gesture. "So I stabbed the blackguard in the leg with the dagger you gave me."

A barked laugh escaped him before he could suppress it, and a horse whinnied in the stall below them. He admired Violet her tenacity to be free from her scurrilous bastard of a cousin. And as strange as it was for Chris to admit, even to himself, he was honoured that she'd chosen *him* to bully into escorting her.

Chapter 19

Vi didn't know it until that moment, but she'd been waiting to hear Christian laugh again. Despite the maudlin topic, she grinned at the rough sound.

"Tell me of your childhood," Christian said, interrupting her chaotic thoughts.

Violet smiled at him. "I had a wonderful childhood." She turned her gaze toward the haystacks beyond Christian, visions of her youth passing through her mind's eye as she spoke. "Our family estate was modest, but it was dear to all of us. Papa was the third son of the Earl of Huntley, and he had inherited the property from a distant uncle. Well," she amended, "it was more of a gift than an inheritance.

"We had a cook, several maids, a butler, and some footmen, nothing overly costly for Papa. The estate sits vacant now, under our uncle's control."

She worried the edge of her coat between her fingers, the thick, rough material somehow calming the riot of emotions that suddenly burst through her.

Vi cleared her throat. "Rose, Helen, and I used to run about the gardens, chasing butterflies, feeding birds, or making a mess of ourselves in the mud. Mama and Papa said that so long as no one outside our family witnessed it and we were polite young ladies in society, we could run as we pleased." She rubbed the fabric of her coat harder. "My parents were wonderful people; we felt their love for each other and us in everything they did. Before the illness that took them away, I desired a union such as theirs, built on affection and mutual respect. I daresay they would roll fitfully in their graves if they knew what life was like for Rose and me after they passed…"

Things were going so pleasantly. Why did I have to ruin it by getting maudlin? Vi breathed deeply, past the sudden lump in her throat. She was not one to fall apart easily, no matter how acceptable the reason. Why was she now being so weepy? *Ballocks*.

"Tell me about *your* childhood, Christian," she urged, taking a deep breath and retrieving an apple from atop the inn's bed sheet.

Christian stiffened. Was it her use of his given name or the abrupt change of topic? Or mayhap he had a troubled relationship with his family? Whatever it was, her question was left in the air between them and couldn't be withdrawn. Her curiosity about him had been growing since that fateful night she'd broken into his home and aimed a pistol at his chest. It was about damned time that she attempted to appease it.

She rubbed the apple upon her coat's sleeve before taking a bite. The sweet fruit crunched satisfyingly, juice dribbling inelegantly down her chin before she caught it.

"My father's name was Theophilus Samuels, and I never knew my mother," Christian stated abruptly. His jaw jumped before he cleared his throat again.

"How did she go?" Violet asked softly.

"Childbirth," he grunted.

"I'm so sorry," she whispered.

He nodded and began placing the remains of their alfresco luncheon on the haystacks beside the bed sheet. "I never wanted for family, however. My father was always desirous for more children and had the habit of picking them off the street." He grunted. "Not abducting them, mind. He would scour St. Giles for those who were homeless or in need, and he would give them a home, food, and an education. He couldn't abide an excellent mind without the means to achieve its potential. Father thought it a great tragedy."

"How noble! He sounds like a kind man."

Christian tilted his head thoughtfully, a faint smile on his lips and a teasing glint in his eyes. "Kind to his wards, yes, but a harsh taskmaster, indeed."

"Oh dear. Was he harsh to you, Christian?" Her lips curled upward of their own accord, matching his smile.

She could not imagine the man before her as a child. Had he brown hair then? Or was it a sandy colour, tousled and unruly in the exuberance of youth?

He caught her eye, and his own crinkled appealingly in the corners. "I had an extensive education."

"Clever evasion, your lordship."

With a small smile, he bowed his head. "I thank you, Miss Wilkinson."

Her smile grew. "Were you a trying lad?"

Christian's chuckle sent a delightful quiver through her. "Most assuredly," he said, his voice low.

Violet took another bite of her apple and chewed. How long had it been since she'd felt such a sense of peace? As harrowing as her day had been, and as sore as her body still was, she felt calm sitting there in the hayloft with Viscount Leeds. It could very well have been exhaustion, for Lord knew she was nigh ready to drop, but she knew it wasn't. Americus was, at the very least, sufficiently detained for the moment. She trusted that once they awoke come morning, Christian would be there to escort her on her—no. That didn't feel right anymore. It was *their* journey. He had proven himself to be as involved in this escape as she. The thought was heartening.

* * *

The hard fist of a riotous emotion knocked Christian in the gut. He resisted the urge to rub his abdomen.

Violet took another bite of her apple, the juices sluicing down her chin and making her lips glisten.

The bandaged gunshot wound on his ear throbbed in time with his speeding heart rate. He wanted to kiss her, to taste the apple on her lips, to hear her groan of delight. He wanted to make her feel happy, even if it was but a fleeting experience. At least she would have something pleasurable to look back on after this dangerous journey was concluded.

Hell, the truth of it was that his decision was not entirely selfless, for even the *thought* of having a small taste of her set his pulse to racing. He could never allow himself to be *completely* free, for he would never endanger a woman's life by getting her with child. Of course, he needn't take her innocence—*if* she in fact happened to be innocent, for Lord knew the book that sat heavily in his pocket suggested otherwise. There were other ways to enjoy themselves without soiling her entirely.

* * *

Christian's air changed, stirring something deep within Violet. It was a subtle change: the glitter to his eye, the set to his lips. But she saw it nonetheless. And, *oh*, how she longed for another of his kisses!

He leaned toward her, watching as she nervously licked her lips. A faint groan emanated from his throat, the sound sending Violet's heart to beating a staccato rhythm.

Chris' gaze flicked up in question, his nose a mere breath from hers. "I desire more than a kiss from you, Violet." His voice was low, rough.

Vi nodded, utterly incapable of speech. Her stomach buzzed with anticipation.

His piercing blue gaze bore into hers, searching. "I shan't take your innocence." His throat bobbed as he swallowed, a slight frown marring his brow. "I wouldn't deign to presume. B-but even if you weren't, I—"

With a nervous laugh, Violet pressed her lips to his. It was just as she remembered. Soft, heated, and utterly delicious. Their mouths melded, his tongue flirting scandalously with hers.

She would never have thought that *Lofty* Leeds could become so awkward in his speech. It was impossible to deny the slight sting of his words, however. Did he not *wish* to make love to her? While she was still in possession of her maidenhead, Violet was far from a maiden of the *haute ton*, confined to the whims and rules of society. She doubted there was a single man or woman—with the exception of her relations—who remembered her or even knew of her existence. Surely it would not affect her reputation if he possessed her fully. Oh, how she wanted him to!

Christian deepened their kiss, drawing Violet's thoughts back to him. His hand cupped her jaw, spreading gooseflesh across her skin. Careful to avoid her injury, he trailed his fingers down the column of her neck before settling on the edges of her coat.

The space between them was thick and charged with desire. Violet wanted to tear their clothes away and allow the passion to consume them. Fast, rough, and messy. The slow simmer that heated below her skin, the agonising need, was spectacularly tempting to appease.

Her heart hadn't slowed a beat since the moment they'd connected, but it nigh stalled when Christian drew the coat from her shoulders and began working on the buttons of her waistcoat. Their kisses grew ever more passionate, their breaths coming quickly as they worked at undressing.

It was precisely what Violet wanted: to see him, to *feel* him. To the devil with societal restrictions and unnatural expectations. Now that she was free, she wanted to experience everything that life could offer.

She drew off Christian's coat, opened his waistcoat, then spread her hands over the expanse of his broad chest and tight abdomen, his skin hot beneath the thin lawn fabric of his shirt. A smattering of dark hair poked out above the vee of his opened collar, and she caressed it with the tips of her fingers.

With a growl, Christian tugged at the hem of her shirt, untucking it from the waist of her trousers, and slid his hands beneath.

Vi broke their kiss; her head dropped back on a sigh as he explored. She was abuzz with nervous energy, but the needy, wanton excitement was too heady to ignore.

Then, his hands were gone; Vi nearly moaned at the loss. Christian folded his coat and placed it upon the sheet, creating an improvised pillow upon the bed of hay.

With a quirk to his lips, Christian advanced once more. This time his hands didn't stop. He pulled the shirt up and over her head, entirely exposing the binding over her upper body to the cool night air. She felt a moment of self-doubt at the reminder of her hidden wounds. What would he think of them? Would he be repulsed? Skipping nary a beat, he unravelled the bandages—Vi arching her back to give him space—and set them aside.

There he paused, gazing at her in the faint moonlight provided by the small window just above the hayloft. His chest heaved with each breath as he reverently glided his palms over her heated skin.

Her momentary nerves forgotten, Violet marvelled at her own daring. Another woman might shy away from a man's bold touch, but Vi not only accepted it, she desired it.

Christian's hands skimmed up her waist toward her ribcage, the gentle abrasion of his lightly calloused fingers sending gooseflesh spreading across her skin. He cupped her breasts, and Violet's breath caught in her throat. She'd always wondered what it would feel like to have a man's hands on her breasts. It was decidedly more exciting than she'd anticipated!

Her heart beat wildly beneath his hands; she was certain that he felt it.

"Lie down," Christian urged.

Violet didn't hesitate. She settled her back against the thin sheet and rested her head atop Christian's coat. She frowned. It was rather hard.

Christian leaned forward, but Vi stopped him. She propped herself on one elbow and reached for his coat. She eyed him curiously as she violated his privacy and searched his pockets.

"Er...Violet..." His eyes widened.

She turned her gaze down to what she held in her hand. *The naughty book!* She nearly laughed. Strangely, the discovery did not bother her as much as she'd thought it would. Not even embarrassment penetrated the happy ease that currently consumed her.

"Did you pilfer this from my bag, Lord Leeds?" She sent him a glance of mock reproach as she clucked her tongue. "For shame! Might you require punishment?"

The remorseful glint in his eye vanished, replaced with keen anticipation. He slid the book from her hand and placed it on the hay beside them. With a predatory grin, he leaned over her, forcing Vi to resume her supine position.

"Have you ever attempted any of the acts described within?" Christian asked, leaning forward to press kisses to the tops of her breasts.

Violet's eyes slid closed at the sensation. "No," she admitted.

"But you're curious?" He licked the area around her nipple, eliciting a gasp from her.

Vi's mind raced with lines from within the book. *"It is the most sovereign pleasure we poor Mortals injoy..."* Of course she was curious! This was likely her only opportunity to try some of the delectable acts written about in her book; she would not squander it.

"More than curious," she said. "Eager." She put her hands on Christian's shoulders, where his muscles bunched in an effort to keep himself hovering above her as he lavished attention on her breasts.

"Violet," he pressed, flicking the tip of his tongue over her taut nipple.

She gasped, a shiver running through her. A short, rough laugh escaped him, before he pulled her nipple into his mouth and lightly bit down.

A moan escaped her, and she arched her back, urging him to take more.

She could feel him smile against her breast before he pulled away. His hand quickly replaced his mouth, kneading and caressing, and keeping her desire burning.

"What would you have me show you?" he asked.

He watched her with heavy-lidded eyes as his hands worked on her breasts. Vi couldn't think; her thoughts were muddled by need.

"You," she stated. "I want to see *you*."

Violet had never seen a man move so quickly. She had scarcely drawn breath before Christian's shirt was pulled over his head. He winced at the twinge to his injured ear. His chest was only barely visible in the milky moonlight, but what she *did* see was remarkable. Hair was scattered across his chest and around his small, dark nipples before it narrowed to a thin line down his abdomen.

The lighting of the small loft window particularly highlighted the contours of his muscles. He was remarkable. How did a man locked away in his estate maintain such a striking form? The beautiful, smooth skin of his side was marred by purple bruising and scabbing from their carriage accident. It looked rather painful, the poor man.

The thought swiftly fled as he reached for the buttons of his falls.

A line from *The Schoole of Venus* sprang to Violet's mind: *"The Thing with which a Man Pisseth is called a Prick…"* Did men *really* call their members 'pricks'? Would it appear as the book described? *"A Prick hath a fine soft loose skin, which though the Wench take it in her Hand, when it is loose and lank, will soon grow stiff and be filled…"*

Christian's was most certainly not loose at the moment, and his skin didn't *look* particularly fine or soft. It looked heavy, engorged, and impossibly hard.

He slid his trousers down his thighs before he lifted each knee to slide them off entirely, fighting unabashedly with his boots. His member jutted proudly from beneath a thatch of thick black hair, rousing her desire and curiosity.

"So you see me," he whispered, on his knees and fully displayed before her. Part of Vi wished that they had improved lighting so she might see him better.

The moment was short-lived, for he lowered himself atop of her. Their lips met, the passion between them frenzied and feverish. Violet wrapped her arms about his body, the heat of his skin on hers unlike anything she'd ever felt.

The insistent pressure of his erection on her *mons* was nigh unbearable. She wanted *more*. Her hips rose to rub against him, the material of her trousers and short pants an irksome barrier. She reached between them to the buttons.

"Allow me," Christian muttered, giving her another quick kiss before sliding down her body.

Violet stared at the dark wooden ceiling of the stables as Christian worked to remove her trousers. Soon, her boots, stockings, trousers, and short pants were gone, leaving her entirely nude, just as Christian was.

With a satisfied grin, Vi reached down toward him, eager to have his skin against hers once more. But he didn't return to her. Instead, he pressed her thighs apart and touched his hand to her *mons*.

She twitched, and a gasp was pulled into her throat.

His fingers slipped between her folds as he sidled up beside her, kissing a path up her body. Rising on one elbow, with one hand still caressing her intimately, he kissed her.

It was an onslaught of pleasure.

The combination of sensations had her writhing. Gasping.

"*Oh, hell*," Christian groaned. "Touch me… Please, Violet…touch me."

Violet stretched her uninjured hand across her body to touch him. The book explained that men enjoyed being touched in a particular way: "*which she by rubbing gently…makes the man spend in her hand.*"

She clasped his member. It was thick, and simultaneously hard and soft. A paradox, just like the man. Then she began to stroke, just as the book described. He moaned into her mouth, the movements of his tongue working in tandem with the movements of his hand.

He dipped a finger inside her passage and used his thumb to rub her pleasure centre. It was her turn to moan. She felt the need to burst, as though her skin could no longer contain her. Her pleasure was building, her heart veritably beating out of her chest.

Tightening her hold ever so slightly, Violet pumped her hand faster. Christian's movements grew uneven, and he thrust against her.

Suddenly it was more than she could take. The coil wound so tightly that it broke. A great explosion of delight burst through her body, and lights flashed behind her eyelids. Her passage throbbed and her body quivered with the aftershocks.

Christian cursed and his body jerked. His hand covered hers, stilling her movement as his member pulsed. Her hand and hip warmed with his seed. "*The seed of the man is of a thick white clammy substance…*"

He pressed his forehead to hers, their breaths coming fast. Vi's senses were filled with the scent of hay, horses, and *Christian*. Horses snuffled and shuffled in their stalls below them, remarkably unchanged after the magic that had just occurred in the hayloft.

With another passionate kiss, Christian turned away, reaching for something behind his back. He returned with a handkerchief, which he used to wipe his seed from her body before tossing it aside. Using her coat to cover them, Christian settled himself beside her and wrapped an arm about her shoulders to pull her close against him. Careful not to pull at her wound or the bandages on her neck, Vi put her ear to Christian's chest, listing to the gradually-normalising beat of his heart.

Chapter 20

Christian held Violet close, listening to her steady, deep breaths as she fell asleep. His mind was reeling. Had that truly just happened?

Part of him felt a cad for using her in such a despicable way, but his baser side leapt for joy. Having her hands on him had felt better than any illicit liaison he'd ever engaged in. He'd wanted to take her fully, to be sheathed inside her warmth and bring them both to heights heretofore unknown—

He shook himself. What a devil of a time to begin a seduction. Additionally, sex was impossible; he couldn't risk a pregnancy, couldn't let what happened to his mother happen with her. He hadn't any cundums, after all.

Violet sighed in sleep, her breath ruffling the hairs on his chest. He tightened his hold on her shoulders. Damn him if he didn't want to let her go.

There were more pressing matters at hand, however.

What was he to do about the issue of Violet? Bristol was to be taken to the school for questioning in order to assess his potential guilt in his father's treasonous activities, then brought to London to face trial. There was the possibility, however, that the students had failed—which was why he and Violet had taken precautions that evening.

Christ, but Violet had said how lovely her parents were, which he didn't doubt, but how the devil could they be so lovely and yet have relations such as Hale and Bristol?

He sighed, tightening his hold on the slumbering woman at his side.

Violet had said that her cousin claimed to want to *break* her, which Christian assumed meant that he wished to break her spirit. Violet had also said that her cousin and uncle wished to marry her off to one of their friends. That, in itself, was terrifying. To live with a man who desired naught more than to abuse you until nothing was left of you but a shell, was nothing short of perdition. And if Chris and his fellows succeeded in taking the Chaisty family down, what of the man to which Violet was promised? Would *he* come in search of her?

Hell, if it would help, Chris would marry her himself.

His heart hiccoughed, and he frowned.

'Tis a ludicrous thought, his mind baulked. But something in him—instinct?—felt differently. Truthfully, Christian had never before considered marriage. When his father was alive, Chris had let the man believe he would beget an heir, but he had never intended to follow through. He preferred his staid, yet cryptologically active, solitude to a life filled with obligations and an unfulfilled wife.

He wanted to reject the notion, to think of another way to save Miss Violet Wilkinson. But, God help him, the idea of marrying her wouldn't be dismissed.

Giving Violet his name would safeguard her from a non-life with whomever Bristol deemed worthy. Chris could alter their course from Violet's grandparents' estate—after stopping in Gretna, of course—to his own home.

Bristol would not expect them to head to Gretna after returning to Carlisle. He would anticipate them perhaps to travel east to Brampton, northwest to Dumfries, or even directly north to Violet's grandparents' estate in Glasgow. Christian *could* take her to his estate in Falkirk, but, undoubtedly, Bristol knew that Violet was travelling with Chris, and would anticipate that as a possible destination. Chris would have to take her outside the realm of predictable routes.

His heart raced and his palms grew damp. What was he thinking? Was he *truly* considering marrying Violet? The maddening woman with the spirited temperament, confoundedly skilled hands, and soft, alluring lips? They would certainly fit well in the physical sense, but would she be content to live her life with a man who did not believe in love? A life without children?

He nearly scoffed at the absurdity of the question. She would certainly be pleased to have a life of comfort and safety over what Bristol would give her: an early grave.

After their coupling, then the removal of their immediate threat and the subsequent questioning and detainment of Hale and Bristol, Christian could return to his estate in Eastbourne to enjoy his solitude. Surely Violet would not require more than the occasional visit and a healthy stipend to do with as she pleased. She would have his name, his money, and freedom to rule a home as she saw fit. Indeed, it would be an ideal situation for them both.

* * *

Violet sprinted as fast as she was physically able, but it was not fast enough. The corridor stretched out before her, growing in length even as she ran.

Male laughter and Rose's disembodied cries echoed around Violet, forcing her feet ever faster. Her heart galloped frantically against her ribs, her breath coming in deep, rapid puffs.

She burst into the belowstairs room where she drew to a stop, terror lancing through her. Lord Hale held Rose by her half-fallen coiffure, a bloody dagger in his hand and unearthly hatred burning in his eyes.

"Rose!" Violet gasped.

Her sister wore only her shift and was covered in blood, her skin ashen and her eyes closed, as though in sleep.

Vi screamed, terror slicing through her. "No!"

She dashed toward her sister, but suddenly she was gone. The room turned dark.

"Now it's time to have some fun with you," her cousin's voice somehow surrounded her.

Violet spun, trying to see him through the gloom. Suddenly, he was there in a cloak of milky moonlight. She stared at him, her eyes wide as the minimal light glinted on the pistol he carried.

"You will not escape me this time, Violet." He stepped toward her, slow and menacing.

Violet bit her lips together to keep them from trembling. She would not let him see her fear.

She could smell him, then feel the waft of air as he came within arm's reach.

Dragging the barrel of the pistol across her jaw, Americus grinned cruelly. "Do you recall the first days after your parents' death? How much fun we had together!" He traced the barrel over her collar. "I intend to make good on my promises..."

Her throat began to close.

"Have you seen them?" Americus demanded.

"P-pardon?"

"Have you seen her?"

Violet came abruptly awake, her body throbbing with each rapid beat her of heart. She gazed at a rough wooden ceiling, the bright light of day shining through the cracks.

"Damn it, man! I am looking for a man with grey hair and blue eyes, and a woman with brown hair, blue eyes, both of average height and weight, and the man's got a limp, wot? *Have you seen them?*" the furious voice emanated through the stable's walls, striking fear in Violet's heart.

There was a mumbled response before the man grunted.

"Righ' this way, sir. I'll show ye te their room meself," a voice replied.

Footsteps shuffled away, followed by the ominous *clip* of booted heels.

Vi sat up, entirely unmindful of her nakedness. This was not the time for modesty.

"*Christian,*" she hissed.

He draped an arm lazily across her hips, trying to drag her back to their makeshift bed.

Violet growled—terror and impatience riding her—and shoved him. "*Christian!*"

In one great movement, he stood, nude and glorious. Despite their desperate hurry, Violet could not help but stare at his impressive appendage. Had she truly held that in her hand last eve?

"What's happened?" he asked urgently.

Vi internally shook herself and stood to face him. "Americus is here," she whispered. "He's been led inside to our room."

* * *

With a vile curse, Chris took charge. "Dress as quickly as you are able. Are you certain that it was him?"

She shook her head. "No, but he gave the stable hand our description. Perhaps it was a comrade of my cousin? I'm not certain."

With a grunt and a deep sense of foreboding, Chris found his trousers strewn upon the mounds of hay and tugged them on. Turning, he searched for his shirt, but caught sight of Violet's bared back instead. He stopped. *Was that…?*

"Just a moment," he muttered, clasping her shoulders to keep her from moving.

Layers of scars lined her back, some angled downward from her left shoulder, and some from her right, stretching toward her hips. Many of the marks were recent, red and puckering as they healed.

Christian pressed his fingertips tenderly to her back. How many years, how many lashings would it take to create such a design? Nary a patch of unmarred skin remained.

His emotions were in turmoil. Hate and rage battled with his desire to comfort her, to take away her years of pain. But above all he wanted to see Hale and Bristol hanging from the end of a rope.

Chris had spent years away from active duty. No longer pining for adventure, he was content to remain distant from violence. But damn it, seeing further evidence of these blackguards' perversions and perfidy had him seeing red.

Violet lightly pulled away from his touch and dragged her bloodstained man's shirt over her head, blocking his view of her mutilated back.

He cleared his throat as he found his own shirt. "We will need to change your bandages. Perhaps when we stop for a meal."

She nodded, but said nothing.

They dressed in silence, resuming their urgency. Chris hastily returned Violet's book to his coat pocket, hauled the saddlebags over one shoulder, and motioned for her to follow him toward the ladder.

Careful to balance the saddlebags and hold the rungs, Christian grit his teeth as he led the way down. He hadn't noticed the pain in his knee until he'd taken the first step. Rain was undoubtedly on its way. It was fitting weather for his dour mood.

Reaching the ground floor of the stables, Chris extended one hand to aid Violet in the last steps of her descent. His gaze caught on the dried blood on her shirt and the bandage around her neck, and he resolutely closed himself off to his anger.

He was an out-of-practice spy but a spy nonetheless, damn it! Now was the time to wall away his emotions and get Violet and him away from danger.

Christian inhaled deeply, breathing in the scent of horse, leather, and old hay.

The stables were cool and clean, with enough stable hands to cause Chris and Violet a great deal of trouble. Turning, Chris reached behind him to grip Violet's hand. He strode toward the first stall on his right and peered inside. *Empty.*

Voices murmured several stalls down, followed by a laugh outside.

Movement to his left caught his eye, and he turned to see a calico cat flick its tail at him, its green eyes narrowed with menacing indifference.

The next stable held a grey mare, and Chris was grateful for their luck. The pretty mount would do well for Violet. He released her hand and quietly opened the stable door. The mare nudged at him curiously, sniffing at his coat and bumping his arm.

"I haven't any treats for you, girl," he murmured quietly. "You're a sweet one, aren't you? How would you like to go for a run today?" He patted her down and scratched at her jaw. "Yes, that's a good girl."

Chris turned to whisper to Violet over his shoulder. "If I get the tack from the tack room, will you know how to saddle her?"

"Yes."

Chris couldn't help but admire her confidence and determination. "Excellent." He swept in to press his lips briefly to hers, the tingle of their contact sending a jolt of desire through him. *Bloody hell, this woman!* "I will return directly."

Chapter 21

Her stomach ill with nerves, Violet tightened the straps on her mare's saddle. It had been years since she'd saddled a horse, but she recalled the basics.

When he'd returned, Christian had dashed into the stall, lifted the saddle upon her horse and was away directly again. He'd chosen the horse in the stall next to Vi's mare and had given her direct orders: *"Make no sound. Saddle her as quickly as possible. Mount her, and wait for my signal before we ride out of the stalls."*

Oh, hell. Vi was certain her stomach could not twist any further. She had butterflies, bees, and bloody badgers racing around in there.

She fastened the final strap of the saddle, and had begun to work on settling her crownpiece, when a commotion erupted at the entrance to the stables.

"I'm right sorry, I am, sir. But like 'ey said, we dunno wot's 'appened te them!" a man exclaimed.

There was a growl, and Violet's heart clenched.

"They were *here*, eh, wot. Where are they *now*?" a man snarled. "Did anyone see them leave? Were they spotted on the grounds?"

Violet wanted to abandon her purpose and hide, to cower in the corner and pray she wouldn't be found. But what sort of weak, snivelling coward would she be if she gave in to such atrocious desires? As much as she now trusted that Christian would do his all to protect her, she was the hero of her own damned story, and she'd best start thinking like it!

Forcing herself faster, Violet nimbly worked the crown piece onto the mare and began to fasten it.

"Please, sir," the other man's beseeching voice seeped through the walls of the stables, "do come in fer a fine glass o' whisky."

"I haven't the time." He cursed soundly. "Has anyone checked the stables? Have you all your mounts?"

Blast the man! Violet tugged on the last strap and brought the reins over the pommel, preparing to mount.

"The stables 'aven't been checked, but we would've heard 'em if'n they stole a mount."

"*Check them*," the voice growled.

Dash it all! If the stable hands searched the stables, she and Christian would be discovered for certain! What could she do? What would create a commotion enough for her and Christian to escape? If she had her pistol on her person, she might be able to spook the horses, but it would also spook her mount. *Foolish.*

Then it came to her. *Aha!*

"I will be but a moment," she whispered to the pretty grey mare.

Voices came from the entry to the stables as Vi crept out of the stall. With a quick glance down the aisle, she dashed to the stalls across from hers and began to unhook the latches and open the doors. Three horses stepped curiously out of their confinement.

"What the devil?" exclaimed a stable hand leading a small party of men into the aisle.

"*There!*" a man exclaimed, his eyes narrowed on her.

With her heart in her throat and her eyes wide with fear, Violet slapped the last horse on the rear. It rose up on its hind legs and gave a fearful whinny, spooking the other two horses.

Violet dashed back to her stall, giving nary a glance toward the men. She hopped upon a stool and awkwardly mounted the mare astride.

Suddenly, a great *bang* rent the air, sending splintering wood flying about. Violet cried out, her mare agitated beneath her. The remaining horses in their stalls neighed and bumped at their confining walls.

Christian rode his large gelding out of the neighbouring stall, the door having been kicked down by the beast. He sat tall in his seat, a pistol held high in his hand.

"Pardon me, sirs, but we must be on our w-way," Christian said imperiously, faltering on the last word.

Feeling a burst of bravery—or perhaps foolishness—Violet rode her mare out, ducking through the stall's door, to halt next to Christian. He sent her a conspiratorial wink and she felt a jolt of something—anticipation? Excitement?—travel through her. But the expression on his face told her something was wrong. It was in the dulled colour of his eyes, the worry creasing his brow.

She took in the men at the end of the aisle, and one of them had eyes only for Christian. The man reached beneath his coat, withdrew a pistol, aimed, and pulled the trigger.

Crack!

The stable hands shouted and the mounts reared up, but, gratefully, the shot didn't appear to have hit its target. The man cursed.

Reaching into his coat's pocket, Christian retrieved several pound notes and tossed them to the ground before nodding to the stable hands. "Your master's payment for the horses, and some for your trouble."

The click of a pistol's hammer being pulled back echoed alarmingly around them.

"I won't allow you to leave!" the man shouted, aiming another pistol at them.

Christian lowered his voice. "You do not have a choice."

His complexion growing slightly green, Chris took aim and shot the strange man in the arm. Their horses reared once more, and Vi grabbed for purchase around her mare's neck.

"*Go!*" Christian hollered, nudging his horse into a gallop, forcing their pursuer and the stable hands to retreat.

Violet followed close behind him.

The man cursed foully. "*Fetch me my horse and a bandage, damn you!*"

They dashed through the stable's main doors and into the innyard. The grey sky mocked them with the prospect of rain, the warm wind blowing hard as they ran. Shouts rose up behind them, but Violet dared not look. She knew that whoever that man was would ride after them, but she held out hope that they could put enough distance between them that he might lose their trail.

Vi felt as though her heart galloped as quickly as the horses ran, each beat thudding against her ribs. Escape was exhilarating.

* * *

Christian pulled his mount to a halt as the first drop of rain hit his face. His breath came nearly as heavily as the horse's; the poor beast had been running for quite some time.

His attention was diverted as a dog barked wildly from its position by the inn's main door, his tail wagging swiftly in its excitement. The inn at which they'd stopped had crumbling, cream-coloured plaster and dark wooden beams that gave the exterior walls definition. Stables stood off to the left, the structure seemingly leaning to one side.

A stable hand dashed out to grab Chris' reins as he dismounted. His aching knee buckled, but he caught himself before he fell. Damn, but the hours of riding had taken a toll on him.

He turned to watch as another stable hand aided Violet in her dismount. As much as Chris wanted to do it himself, he knew he would embarrass himself by collapsing under the strain to his knee.

Clearing his throat, he called to the lad, "We require two fresh mounts. Ours have been exhausted." Indeed, they gleamed with sweat, their nostrils flared, and their eyes were wild.

The young man nodded. "O' course, sir."

Chris didn't bother correcting the stable hand's assumption.

"Would ye care fer anythin' from inside? Me mam is th' cook, and she makes a mighty fine biscuit. It'll be a few ticks afore we get th' fresh mounts saddled an' yer saddlebags transferred."

Inclining his head, Chris thanked the lad then turned to Violet. She looped her arm through his as they walked haltingly toward the inn's front door. Chris' limp was heavily pronounced, the lightly falling rain an early symptom of what was to come.

Christ above, they were in trouble. The man from which they'd just fled was Mr. James Piper, one of Hale's associates and a suspected spy for Napoleon Bonaparte. Chris had seen the man around Eastbourne, and... Damn, but he ought to have known better. He'd become complacent, too confident in his ability to outrun and outwit a man ruled only by anger and desire like Bristol. Early in their journey, Chris had considered the possibility of someone coming in search of him, as his identity had been compromised. But after seeing only Lord Bristol, he'd simply assumed...

It was a lesson learned.

"We mustn't tarry," Violet whispered.

"No," Chris agreed. "I did what I could to take unpredictable turns and kept away from long stretches of road, but I daresay you are correct. If you've a need to avail yourself of the facilities, now is an opportune time. I am quite taken with the thought of those biscuits, so I will arrange for some to be wrapped up for us."

Violet smiled thinly. "Thank you, Christian." She released his arm and walked into the inn ahead of him.

Something flipped over inside him as she disappeared from his sight. He'd had a terrible feeling gnawing at him since they'd ridden from the inn that morning. Piper was in pursuit, of course, but Chris knew that wasn't it. The sight of her scars had remained with him, haunting him. If those were her visible scars, how many did she possess that *weren't* visible to the naked eye? What sort of internal scars had she incurred at the hands of her despicable relations? Was that why she hadn't trusted him, why she'd felt the need to use force as a means to garner his compliance?

Christian grit his teeth and entered the inn's small foyer. He quickly located the innkeeper and requested a half-dozen biscuits, some water, and a bottle of claret.

They were mere hours from Gretna, though there were fewer hours until nightfall. Chris would have Violet wed and bedded before midnight, so long as she agreed to his plan.

His heart leapt and his cock twitched at the thought. There was no doubt that he wanted her. If last night's encounter was any indication, they would suit well in the marriage bed.

His body ached, and his mind was tormented. Evening couldn't come soon enough.

* * *

The driving rain had long since soaked Violet through. Her fallen hair hung in wet, stringy strands, some stuck to her slicked skin. The sky was darkening with the coming night, and the horses had slowed to an exhausted walk. Pain sliced through her with every movement, but she kept her head held high. Any number of aches was worth her freedom.

Chris cursed as he shifted in his saddle, and Vi cut a sideways glance at him. He'd kept quiet since their last stop, scarcely uttering a sound. His limp had been rather heavy; she imagined it smarted. What was he thinking?

It was unaccountably irritating. They'd not discussed their plans, but every stop they'd made since that morning had been a part of her latest mapped plan. She was grateful that he trusted her enough to choose their route, his—

Her thoughts halted as she caught sight of an estate surrounded by rolling hills on three sides. That was not on their route!

"Did we make a wrong turn?" she asked over the din of the falling rain.

He pulled his mount up short, shaking his head. "No."

She blinked, halting her horse as well. "Then where are we going? This road is not part of the planned route."

Raking a hand through his wet hair, he replied, "We are going to Gretna."

Chapter 22

Violet nearly swallowed her tongue, her heart thudding rapidly. "I beg your pardon?"

"You require protection." His pragmatic tone was grating. "Lord Bristol will not stop until he has seen you married. If you already have my name, there is a good likelihood that he will leave you be."

Indignation and hurt swept through her at his imperious presumption.

"Of course, there are other merits to our union," he continued, undeterred by her lack of a response. "Marrying me would beget you the title of Lady Leeds. We would fit well in the physical sense—"

"That is quite enough, Lord Leeds!" Violet interrupted him.

He watched her in confusion, rain sluicing down his face.

"This is preposterous!" she exclaimed.

He scowled. "I beg your—"

"You seem to be under the impression that I am a willing participant in this mad scheme, that somehow I would happily imprison myself in an affectionless marriage just to avoid another distasteful union." An arranged marriage was the final threat that had induced her and her twin to finally make good on their plan to escape Willow Hall from the start.

Christian scoffed. "I hardly think that a marriage to *me* would be as distasteful as—"

"Did it never occur to you that you might *ask* for my hand in marriage? That you might offer your protection in a manner that would induce me to accept? That perhaps *my* opinion on the matter was just as important as yours? Your high-handed, arrogant haughtiness—"

"I thank you," he drawled. "Your point has quite made its mark."

The drawn and hurt expression on his face belied the dismissive nature of his words.

Guilt swamped her. She had gone too far.

"I apologise," she said above the rain.

His lips thinned. "You have every right to your opinion, naturally." He cleared his throat. "It is I who should apologise. Had I realised your dislike of me, I would have never considered a union between us."

"I do not dislike you." It was quite the opposite, in fact. She liked him rather more than she would have expected. "I oughtn't have said what I did. While I don't care for others planning my life on my behalf, I needn't have been so unkind."

While she *was* angry with Christian for planning their wedding without first consulting her, the majority of her anger stemmed from hurt. Before the fever that had claimed the life of three members of her family, Violet had dreamt of a grand wedding with lace and flowers, ribbons and bows…and a man whom she loved—or at the very least a man who had courted her properly. She knew that that would not happen now, not with the state of her scars, her crude vocabulary, and her simple desire for freedom, so this non-proposal came as a painful reminder of what she'd lost hope of attaining.

Deep down, Violet had hoped that Christian felt something for her; even friendship would suffice. But his rational and unemotional proposition for their future left her feeling wounded.

With a softly uttered curse, Christian smoothly dismounted, then limped toward her mare, leading his horse behind him. He aided her to the ground, her legs trembling slightly as she stood before him.

A flash of light streaked the sky, followed by the distant *boom* of thunder rumbling through the dark clouds. Thick, heavy droplets of water cascaded down upon them, further soaking her men's suit of clothes.

Christian's silver hair was matted to his head, and the bandage on his ear sagged sadly.

"I'm a cad," he said over the tumultuous rain. "You are unequivocally correct. My behaviour was unpardonable."

Clasping her hand with his, he caught her gaze through the torrent, his eyes earnest. "Neither one of us can claim that this is a love match," he began. "But a relationship based on esteem, mutual attraction, and friendship is certainly a respectable union. I hold you in high regard, Violet, and I believe that we would make a suitable match." He lowered himself to one knee, dunking his trousers in a shallow puddle of mud. "Please, Violet. Will you do me the honour of becoming my wife?"

The mare shifted behind her, possibly agitated by Vi's nervousness. Her stomach fluttered, and her heart all but leapt from her chest.

It was very like Christian to not extol her virtues or deluge her with flowery praise. He was genuine and sober. But could she marry him?

"Yes." *Oh, Lord. Did I just say that aloud?*

Christian stood shakily, a rare smile on his lips forcing the corners of his eyes to crinkle. He put a hand to the back of her neck and leaned close so he could kiss her.

It was passionate, but brief. The contact sent a jolt of awareness through her, warming her despite the wet chill to her skin.

He helped her mount and pressed a hot kiss to the back of her cool hand before pulling away and mounting his gelding.

"Are you ready?"

She nodded and guided her mare into motion. Had that truly just happened? Was she engaged to be married? The thought was too much to be borne. Only moments ago she had been furious with the man for his haughtiness, for goodness' sake! But he had apologised. He'd expressed himself honestly and respectfully. And she couldn't regret it.

Rose would be disappointed to have missed her wedding, but once the difficulties with their relations were settled, Violet would have Rose visit her. And perhaps her handsome footman, as well!

Unless… Did Christian intend for them to have a "fashionable" marriage? Surely he intended for them to be intimate? Did he wish to have children? Where would they live? Would he sequester her away at some estate while he went off to London for months at a time?

Vi almost groaned. She ought to have inquired after his intentions. Though, she would grant, it was a far sight more appealing than marrying one of her uncle's acquaintances, which was Hale's and Americus' aim.

Her anxious curiosity got the better of her. Violet cleared her throat. "Will we have a *true* marriage, Christian?"

* * *

Chris' brow puzzled as he thought. After the long hours of riding, he feared that his mind was a mite foggy. They certainly weren't going to engage in a *faux* marriage. If Violet thought they were merely going to fool her dastardly cousin into *thinking* they were married, then she was labouring under a misapprehension. "Of course," he replied, casting her a sideways glance. "Did you *want* a true marriage?"

"Y-yes, that is what I assumed. I merely wanted to be sure we were in accord."

"Naturally," he muttered.

Silence filled the space between them. Rain fell heavily, the noise drowning out the *sloshing* of the horses' hooves in the mud. At one time Chris had rather enjoyed rain; it was beautiful, tranquil…but now it pained his knee something fierce.

"I intend that we should stop at the next inn," he said. "We require fresh mounts, and our bandages require redressing."

"Could we not request a carriage?" Violet returned.

Chris shook his head. "A carriage would be too slow, unfortunately. From now until we reach Gretna, it would be safest to keep to riding." He glanced at her. "If you wish to change your attire, you may. I would not wish for you to catch a chill."

She laughed derisively. "How gracious of you, Christian. While I would enjoy a change of clothes, what would be the purpose of doing so if they were to become ruined, as well?"

"Very well," he drawled. *Feisty woman.*

* * *

Christian straightened his waistcoat and tugged on his coat sleeves. He considered himself in the mirror, his sky-blue eyes reflecting his conflicting trepidation and anticipation. He was mad, surely, for concocting this scheme, but, Lord help him, he was also very much looking forward to the novelty of it.

He raked a hand through his freshly washed hair, vainly attempting to tame a lock that stood on end. He'd wanted to get on with the wedding, but he could not have Violet standing at the anvil in a sopping wet, bloodstained men's suit of clothes. They therefore took rooms and completed a cursory wash before donning fresh attire. He'd been tempted to peek while Violet dressed, but he'd respected her privacy and remained behind the screen, redressing the bandage on his ear.

His body continued to ache, both from the accident several days before—the bruising was atrocious—and from riding all day.

The pale blue walls of the inn at Gretna surrounded him in the mirror's frame, firelight from the hearth and two candelabras flickering about the room. White-painted trim edged the walls and adorned every wooden surface of the room, from the white bedposts and side tables to the fireplace's mantel. It was a quaint bedchamber, suited to a couple on the verge of eloping…and for their first night together.

Chris' stomach clenched. He very much looked forward to that aspect of marriage to Violet.

"I've unfastened this bandage while arranging my frock," she said from behind him. "Might you help me re-wrap it, Christian?"

"Of course." He strode toward her, his limp still pronounced even though the rain had abated.

She eyed him as he moved. "The last miles of our journey were difficult, to say the least. Are you well?"

Despite the sting to his pride, Christian nodded. "I will manage."

He re-wrapped the last bit of the bandage around her neck and tied it off, but instead of pulling away, his hands lingered. Her skin was warm and smooth. Caving to temptation, Christian trailed a finger over her collar then down the centre of her chest and along the modest décolletage of her mint-green frock.

Violet's breath hitched, sending a sharp pang of need through Christian.

The sound of carriage wheels and a bark of laughter drifted up through their window and broke the spell. If they were to be wed before Piper followed their trail and found them, they mustn't tarry any longer than they already had.

Taking a deep breath, he stepped away. "Are you ready to go down?"

Violet's chest rose and fell rapidly as she blinked the dazed look from her eyes. It fired Christian's blood to know that he affected her, for the feeling was most certainly reciprocated.

"Yes, but I mustn't forget my reticule."

Christian sat on the bed's edge while she fluttered about the room, gathering her pistol and her devilishly naughty book and putting them in her absurdly large reticule. She paused.

"Whatever is the matter?" Christian asked.

She made a face. "The luncheon from our last stop has made my reticule smell of beef. It's a dreadful odour to have linger in one's bag."

Laughter bubbled up from within Christian. It was part amusement, part nerves, but the peals of laughter could not be helped.

Violet grinned at him, a hand fluttering to her still-damp, slightly loose chignon. At what point had he become used to…no, *used to* was not the correct term. He *anticipated* the feelings that she brought out in him. It was only days ago that he'd determinedly reminded himself that he was *never* affected by women in such a way. Violet was spectacularly different.

Holding his elbow out to her, he sent her an uncharacteristic wink. "Are you ready to get married?"

Chapter 23

"You're supposed to tie them like this," one halfwit was saying as he attempted to tighten the bindings at Americus' wrists.

"No," someone else said. "This is meant to loop around—like this."

Americus couldn't see past the cravat with which they'd covered his eyes, but he assumed from the scent of yeast and musty dampness that he was in a cellar, and on a very uncomfortable wooden chair as well. His wrists were tied behind his back, and his ankles to the legs of the chair.

These bastards had set upon him at the inn, tied him up, and brought him...wherever the hell he was. But he wouldn't be there for long, damn it.

"I have the need to relieve my bladder," he said to whoever was in the room.

There was silence before someone said, "Fetch the chamber pot."

"I can't piss in a chamber pot without the use of my hands, nor while I'm tied to this bloody chair, unless you'd like to hold my cock or mop up a mess."

The bastards grumbled and mumbled to each other before they came to an agreement. "We'll untie you and allow you to use the chamber pot without your blindfold. But someone will remain in the room with you."

Ah, the halfwits! It was his time to escape.

* * *

Violet's palms were damp, and a bead of sweat was slowly trickling between her breasts. The urge to itch it was overwhelming. How had the last hours moved so quickly? How had she come to the present moment? Just that morning she had been fleeing a strange man in the stables, and now she was marrying Christian.

Oh, Lord! The smithy was speaking solemnly, but Violet could scarcely make out a word. Her pulse thudded in her ears, drowning out the man's speech.

His calm brown eyes turned to her expectantly. *Ballocks.* Had he asked her a question? She could sense Christian watching her as well. What had the smithy asked? How should she answer?

"I do," she offered.

With a nod, the smithy returned his gaze to his small, worn book, and Violet sighed in relief. Damn, but she was nervous! Her stomach was so twisted she felt ill. Perhaps the beef from the last inn had turned.

Christian's deep, firm voice rumbled beside her, "I do."

Violet's gaze lowered to the anvil between them. Its surface was worn and smooth, although some spots along the edges were dented with little divots. The stone floor beneath their feet was swept clean. Barrels stood nearby, one filled with water and another with bits of excess metal. Tools hung on the walls and sat on tables at the edges of the room, there was an inglenook in the corner, and an enormous fireplace graced the wall behind the blacksmith.

The room was warm, the air still and scented with coal and metal. Firelight flickered over the walls, battling with the darkness coming from the windows.

Forcing herself to return her attention to the smithy's words, she followed along, repeating what required repeating, though scarcely aware of what she said. Then, suddenly, she was facing Christian, his eyes the colour of a bright summer's sky watching her intently.

His lips moved as she gazed into his bewitching irises, but she heard nary a bit. He clasped her hand in his, warm and comforting, as he slipped a ring onto her finger.

Even past the heartbeat filling her ears, the smithy's next words were unerringly clear. "Ye may noo seal yer marriage weth a kess."

Vi's nervous stomach trembled.

Christian's lips quirked as he cupped her jaw in one hand, stepping closer. His lips were hot on hers, slow, luxurious. His mouth opened just enough to flick his tongue over Vi's, the touch banishing her nervousness and firing something decidedly more lascivious within her.

There was something remarkable about his ability to so alter her mood. All at once her worry fled. No matter the circumstances of their wedding, Violet felt certain she'd made the right choice in marrying Christian.

"Ye are noo husban' an' wife."

* * *

The moment he'd signed the registry, Christian felt absurdly lighter. He was a married man, now and forever more. It was an entirely foreign feeling, but one he was bound to become accustomed to.

His gaze sought Violet where she sat to his right at the table. Apparently, late evening elopements were commonplace in Gretna Green, for there were two other couples enjoying their wedding supper at their *private* dining table.

The food was adequate, though Christian scarcely noticed its taste. He knew he was hungry, but his nerves disguised the feeling. Regardless, he ate because he knew he must.

Chris was too busy thinking about their wedding night. He'd gotten a taste for what she was like the night before, and damn it, he wanted more. Much more.

There were certain acts that one performed only with mistresses and lightskirts; wives were meant for producing heirs—which he would never allow to happen. But Violet had *pornographia* and had expressed her desire to learn more about the acts within the book…

His pulse sped, and his cock began to swell as he thought of the possibilities.

"Cor! A real lord and lady," the woman across the table said around a mouthful of food.

Chris shifted in his seat, wishing he hadn't encouraged his body's reaction to Violet at such an inopportune time.

He cleared his throat. "Yes."

She fanned herself, her fork still in her hand, the motion sending a small chunk of potato soaring across the room. Her rosy cheeks glistened as she spoke with animation. "My friend Martha will not believe her ears when I tell her I dined with such fine company! Will she, Percy, dearest?"

Her new husband, "Percy," turned to her with disinterest. "Not at all, my lovely."

"What I can't understand," the other new husband said from his position beside Violet, "is what a lord like you needs to elope for. We all got our reasons, o' course, but couldn't you just post the banns and wait the expected time?"

Christian clasped Violet's hand above the table and gazed into her blue eyes, putting as much feeling into the look as possible for the benefit of their audience. "I simply could not wait to marry her."

Violet smiled at him, and the other two ladies sighed.

"Have you finished eating, my love?" he asked. "I fear I'm rather fatigued."

* * *

The stairs creaked as Vi and Christian ascended the second staircase to their bedchamber. As she had never before experienced a wedding night, and her mother had not lived long enough to explain it, she did not know what to expect. She knew they would make love, of course, but how did one *start*?

Did he carry her across the room's threshold? Would he bring her to the bed? Would he undress her, or ought she to disrobe behind the privacy screen and get beneath the bedclothes first? Would they perform the acts they had last night before he put his cock inside her?

She abruptly wished that her naughty book had explained what to do on one's wedding night. Perhaps then she might have been prepared.

They stopped before their bedchamber door, and Christian slid the key in the hole and turned. The door swung inward, and Christian watched her expectantly.

"After you," he murmured.

Vi's stomach flipped over as she strode forward. The room had been entirely prepared while they were belowstairs. The scent of cinnamon drifted along the air, luring her further into the room.

A steaming bath sat in the middle of the bedchamber, the water's surface sprinkled with her favourite spice. The fireplace burned high, lighting the room with its warm glow. The bedclothes were turned down, and a tray of port, champagne, and fruits sat on their writing table.

I'm married! She turned her gaze down to her wedding ring. It was Christian's gold signet ring, engraved in an elaborate design. Vines swirled up the sides, spiralling into the initials T. S., while a lion held a shield with the Leeds crest on the top.

The *snick* of the lock being turned into place brought her out of her reverie and sent a frisson of anxiousness through her.

Christian strode unevenly toward her. "I intend to commission you a proper wedding band once I am able; my signet ring will have to do for the moment."

Vi turned her face up to him. "It is lovely."

He watched her, his light-blue gaze boring into hers.

Silence stretched out between them, the only noises that of the crackle of the fire and their soft breathing. Did he expect her to move first? Ought she to say something? She didn't know what to do with her hands.

She grit her teeth in frustration. She was never so indecisive and unsure of herself; why was she at sixes and sevens when it came to these moments with Christian? *I am the hero of my own story*, she reminded herself.

His lips curved upward in one corner, and he stepped closer. The air between them was thick with intent and desire. Chris curved his palm at the back of her neck, his lips inches from hers.

"Are you nervous?" he inquired softly.

In answer to his question, Violet closed the space between them, taking his lips with hers.

Chapter 24

Violet's nervousness fled, as it had the last time she'd kissed Christian. Something about his heat and the softness of his lips cleared her mind and expelled her ill feelings immediately.

Pulling back enough to look into his heavy-lidded eyes, Violet slid her arms about his shoulders. "No, I'm not nervous," she answered, before pressing her lips to his once more.

With a growl, Christian wrapped his arms around her waist, hauling her against him as he ravished her mouth. He ground his hips against hers, the insistent firmness of his arousal rubbing her *mons* through her skirts and making her throb with need.

She impatiently tugged at his coat, needing to see him nude in the light of the fire. He released her, his lips still intent on hers as he began to disrobe.

Violet unfastened her walking dress and slid it from her shoulders. The material gathered on the floor alongside Christian's coat and waistcoat. He pulled at his cravat while Violet removed her petticoat and began working on the buttons of her chemise.

Several heart-pounding moments later, Christian stood nude, his erection proudly bobbing before him, while Violet wore only her garters and stockings. She reached to unfasten them, but Christian stopped her.

"No," he said gruffly. "Keep them on."

Desire pumped through her veins, fast and addictive. Despite having never before made love, Violet felt in her element. She'd spent years reading her naughty book, learning about the act. Now was the time to put her knowledge to good use.

Christian's body was glorious. He looked especially broad while unclothed; the muscles of his shoulders were generous, his arms thick, and his stomach defined. His cock protruded from springy silver hair, blue veins running over its surface toward the rosy head. His thighs were corded with muscle, though one narrowed quickly toward his knee, the skin rippled with scar tissue. She wondered briefly what had injured him, but she put the thought aside for another time.

Confidence, and a wild need to consummate their marriage, urged her on. She wrapped her hand around his shaft, gently stroking him.

He shook his head. "Not tonight." His voice was rough, deep. "Tonight we do this properly."

She grinned at him. "I'd rather hoped we would do this *im*properly."

Something dark and wicked swept across his face, and a resultant shiver travelled down her spine.

"To the devil with propriety and expectations," she murmured, the burning arousal in her voice foreign even to her own ears. "I want wild abandon and untamed lust!"

With a groan, Christian lifted her in his arms, encouraging her to wrap her legs about his waist. "Then, by God, you shall have it."

His mouth claimed hers as he carried her to the foot of the bed. He laid her on her back as he leaned over her. With his feet still firmly planted on the ground, Christian reached between them, using the head of his erection to wet himself with her dew.

Violet gasped. It felt entirely different from his fingers, both soft and hard with enough pressure to have her moaning.

Encouraged by her reaction, Christian continued, quickly moving the tip of his erection back and forth over her slick, sensitive skin. Her orgasm built quickly. She found herself pulling him closer by pushing the heels of her stocking-clad feet to his rear.

She lightly fisted his hair in her hands, massaging his scalp as she grew nearer and nearer to her release.

Then it hit. Her head pressed back against the counterpane, the exultant pulsing and surging of ecstasy rushing through her.

"*Bloody hell*, Violet!" Christian growled. "I can't hold back."

Her immense joy still coursing through her, he slid himself inside. The pressure was not as bad as she'd expected, and not at all painful. His questioning gaze caught hers, and she nodded.

With one great thrust, Christian fully sheathed himself within her. Violet gritted her teeth, expecting a burst of pain. She felt filled, certainly, but not at all injured.

Christian hissed a breath. "Are you well?"

"Very." She hooked her ankles together over his back.

"I can't go slow," he confessed.

She shook her head. "Then don't."

He kissed her, grunting into her mouth as he sped his pace. The slap of their skin, the thumping bed, and their gasping breaths echoed through the room.

Pressure began building once more, but somehow different...*deeper*. She brought her knees higher, clasping Christian about his waist. The changed position somehow allowed him to reach a different part of her, causing her to break their kiss on a gasp.

He pumped his hips faster, the new friction almost too much for her to bear. But she needed something...more. As though sensing her need, Christian reached his hand between them and swirled his fingers around her pleasure centre. *Yes!* The tightening coil of her release wound tighter and tighter, getting ready to release.

Then she burst. The force of it rushed through her, far more powerful than before. She cried out, clinging to Christian as the waves of pleasure rocked her.

With a curse and a grimace, Christian stilled, spilling his seed inside her.

* * *

Chris rolled to his back, his legs hanging over the edge of the bed as his chest heaved. By God, tupping Violet was far better than he'd hoped for.

He would find great joy in making love to her for the remainder of his life. They would—*Oh, bloody hell.*

Terror struck his heart, the lingering pleasure still coursing through him notwithstanding. He hadn't procured French letters and didn't withdraw from her body when he'd spent. What if Violet were to become pregnant? He couldn't bear to be responsible for her death. The entire purpose of their journey was to protect her, for God's sake!

His stomach abruptly in knots, Christian rose and strode to the washstand.

"Is everything all right?" Violet's soft voice came from behind him.

Damnation. What if this first encounter had impregnated her? What if she was, even now, carrying his child?

He felt ill.

"Everything is well," he replied without turning. "Please, avail yourself of the bath."

There was silence as Christian dunked a cloth in the washbasin water and lathered it with soap. He should have taken precautions when becoming intimate with Violet. She'd felt so damned good, though.

To the devil with propriety and expectations. I want wild abandon and untamed lust! Her words repeated in his mind. It was too much to be borne.

His stomach lurched.

It would be prudent to put some distance between them. Now that they were wed, their original intention—to bring Violet to her grandparents—no longer mattered. He could take Violet to his own estate, ensure her safety with a guard, then return to question Bristol and conduct a search for Hale. Once their interrogation had concluded and the men were on their way to London, he would return to Brampton to aid in the search for Richards. He had funds on him for their morning meal and two horses, enough until he could acquire more at his estate. It was an adequate plan.

Chris used the wet, soapy cloth to wash himself, shame and fear riding him.

The shifting of fabric and soft footsteps alerted him to Violet's movement. The bathing tub's water sloshed as she entered, the action releasing more cinnamon scent into the air.

Not for the first time since they'd embarked on this journey, Chris deeply regretted requesting the scent for her bath. His heart beat faster, his breath quickened. Despite his efforts, he could not control the primitive reaction. He silently vowed that he would never again allow his staff to keep cinnamon at any of his homes.

His wash and ablutions concluded, Chris opened his saddlebags and withdrew a pair of breeches to don. He hastily drew them on and buttoned the falls.

"Where will we go on the morrow?" Violet asked.

He turned to face her, and his throat closed. She sat in the tub, the water lapping at the tips of her breasts as she ran a cloth along her skin, leaving little bubbles behind. Firelight reflected off the droplets clinging to her skin, her face half in shadow from her long, dark, sopping wet locks.

She was temptation incarnate—a siren calling him, luring him.

Confound it! The woman had far too much power over him. He lost his senses when she was near, and it was unacceptable. He was a member of the Secret bloody Service! He'd never lost control of his wits around a woman before, and he'd be damned if he allowed it to continue now.

He stood straighter, his arms crossed over his bared chest. "Come dawn, we will ride out to my estate in Falkirk. There you will reside while I leave to summon the magistrate—"

"You intend to leave me?" She sat straighter in the tub.

You mustn't allow her to sway you, old boy. Stand firm! Chris' inner voice whispered. It was for the best that they live contented and apart while he lived his life as a spy. Violet would certainly be pleased to shop and visit with friends and acquaintances, while Christian would decode cryptic messages by Bonaparte's cohorts. At least until the war was over.

* * *

Violet's heart thudded nauseatingly, and her stomach sank. *Lofty* Leeds had returned in full form. His demeanour reeked of arrogance and superiority.

"It is for the best that I see you safe and deal with Lord Bristol on my own. Your accompanying me would be far too dangerous."

Desperation pounded through her. "I have lived with Lord Bristol for years, Christian. I know the man and of what he is capable. Surely I could be of some help. If you leave me to the staff at your estate, does that not put me in *greater* danger?"

He dismissed her words with the shake of his head. "You are my wife now. It is my duty to do what is in your best interest."

"Would that not include remaining by my side?"

He scoffed. "Come now, Violet, you cannot be so naïve. A great many marriages of the *ton* contain similar arrangements."

Violet's stomach sank further. She was surprised at the sting of his words. Her foolish heart had hoped that he *wanted* to be with her. "You mean to say a 'fashionable' marriage." The sort of marriage that Violet had vowed never to enter into, in which the husband and wife were allowed to engage in trysts as long as they were discreet, in which the couple spent much of their time apart, even living in separate homes…

"I suppose you could call it that," he agreed. "Does not our circumstance warrant additional precaution?"

"And in order to protect me, you intend to hide me away to cower like a goose awaiting the hunt?"

Christian's jaw clenched and his gaze darkened. "That is quite enough."

"I'm not nearly through! I did not agree to—"

"But you *did*, Violet," he growled, uncrossing his arms to step toward her. "You agreed to a marriage—"

Vi stood, water splashing over the rim of the tub. "I agreed to a *true* marriage!" She reached for a towel, wrapped it around herself, and stepped from the brass tub. "You said it would be true! Have you lied to me, Christian? Have you tricked me into marriage?"

He scowled, his neck growing red. "We *were* married in truth!" He put his hands imperiously on his hips. "What had you expected? I made clear my intentions from the start, damn it. I told you that this would not be a love match; I don't even believe in the damned emotion!"

Her eyes widened. "Pray, tell me that I have heard you incorrectly," she said cautiously. "Did you say that you do not *believe* in love?"

Christian's arms and chest were distressingly distracting as they tensed with his agitation. "Love does not exist," he asserted. "It is a fantastical, *fictional* emotion that only fools and little children believe in. I can safely assure you that ours will *never* be a union of love!"

Violet's heart all but stopped beating. She felt frozen with shock and...Lord, was it pain? *No, no, no!* What had she done? She had begun to feel something for the blasted man. She must endeavour to stop that now.

Part of her must have hoped that while they hadn't begun as a love match, they would grow into those emotions. Knowing now that Christian would never feel anything but indifference or companionship for her sent pangs of hurt through her chest.

The sharp sting of tears prickled behind her eyelids, but she tamped down the feeling. She would not weep in front of the loveless man.

Shadows wavered over his incensed features, his silver hair glowing orange in the firelight. Violet's chest ached as she looked at him. What more was there to say? How could one convince another that there was such a thing as love?

Without a word, Violet gathered her chemise and disappeared behind the privacy screen. She quickly dried herself and donned her chemise. Christian had managed to acquire tooth powder, which Violet gratefully used to brush her teeth. She re-dressed the wounds on her neck and hand with fresh bandages, pleased with their progress in healing.

She sent him nary a glance as she strode to the bed and settled herself beneath the counterpane. Exhaustion weighed heavily on her. She closed her eyes, but her mind continued to churn.

Violet knew with certainty that she loved her twin, Rose, just as she had loved her mother, father, and sister Helen. Had Christian never felt familial love? It was a rather lowering thought. In fact, she pitied him such a tremendous loss.

While she had never loved a man in the romantic sense—as her sister had before her fiancé had perished in battle—Vi knew that it was possible if one found the right person. Evidently Christian was not that man.

He *was* her husband, however. Whatever her feelings on the matter, no matter how much it might hurt, she would stand by her vows. She merely wished she'd known the truth before she had agreed to the union.

* * *

Chris drew a shirt over his head, his gaze on Violet's still form in the bed and guilt sitting like a stone in his stomach. He'd never intended to quarrel with Violet, most particularly on their wedding night.

It occurred to him—very briefly, of course—that he might tell her the truth about himself, give her a reason for his desire to live separately. Naturally, the notion was absurd. She was already under the watchful eye of his enemies and would require constant observation and protection by someone he trusted until every one of Bonaparte's spies with knowledge of his identity had been taken down.

Nonetheless, he felt remorseful for having furthered the argument. Despite her fiery personality and penchant for quickening his blood, Violet was a tortured soul and did not deserve additional grief.

Careful not to disturb her, Christian slid into the bed beside her and closed his eyes. They had a long ride on the morrow.

Chapter 25

"If there be anythin' else, yer ladyship, I'm right 'appy to 'elp."

Violet was so entirely unused to being addressed as a lady that it was a moment before she realised that the maid had spoken to *her*. Vi smiled in response and accepted the box through the narrow opening of the door. "Thank you. Perhaps some tea?"

The petite maid's dimples deepened. "O' course, milady!" With a curtsey, she turned and trod down the hall.

Vi quietly closed the door and returned to the writing table. She quickly placed her burden down and opened the lid. Within sat sheets of parchment, an inkpot, pen, blotter, and wax. She sat in the nearby chair, arranging her Pomona-green paisley skirts about her, and began to pen a letter to Rose.

My dearest sister,

So much has happened, I scarcely know where to begin. Our journey north has been long and arduous. Suffice it to say my plan did not particularly go as intended. Rest assured I am still in the company of Lord Leeds.

Vi paused, her pen hovering over the parchment as she carefully considered her words.

I despair of not giving my written word enough feeling, for at the moment I am overwhelmed with conflicting emotions. I promise to give more detail in the future, but I fear I do not have the luxury of time to explain. Americus was in pursuit of us, and is determined to see me ruined before he returns me to our uncle for the arranged marriage. It is for that reason that I consented to marry Lord Leeds. I sit, now, in our room in Gretna Green, as the Viscountess Leeds.

It quite boggles the mind, does it not? I confess, however, that I have ill feelings about the union. I will reserve that explanation for another letter.

Violet's attention was drawn away by a light snore emanating from the bed's occupant. With a shake of her head, she continued writing.

He is not at all what I expected him to be, Rose. You will learn this upon meeting him, I daresay.

I miss you dreadfully, my sister, and think of you often. I dearly hope that your journey has been far milder than mine! Have you reached London? How fares your handsome footman?

Once we reach Leeds' estate, I shall write you the direction. By my troth, I will be more frequent in my letters.

Affectionately,
V

She pressed the blotter to the parchment, then folded it and melted the wax with a tallow candle for the seal. Sliding the loosely-fitting ring from her finger, Violet pressed it into the wax then carefully peeled it back, leaving a perfect indentation of the Leeds seal. She hastily returned her ring to her finger and wrote the direction of her aunt's home in London.

It was not as comforting as a discussion with her sister, but Violet certainly felt better after having written. They had never been apart for so long before. Being away from Rose left something empty and aching within her. She hadn't anticipated such strong feelings when she had orchestrated their escape.

Waving the letter in her hand, Violet stood, retrieving her reticule and carefully inserting the parchment between the pages of her naughty book.

The door burst open, and Violet yelped, frozen in fear as a resounding crash shook the room. Splinters from the door's frame soared through the air while Christian leapt from the bed, his frosty eyes wide and his bared chest heaving.

His limp notwithstanding, Americus strutted across the threshold, malevolence resonating from the sneer on his otherwise handsome face.

"How did you escape?" To Violet's embarrassment, her voice trembled.

"Halfwits, the lot of them!" he shouted, eyes narrowed on Violet. "Think you that your wedded state would deter me? Fleeing to Gretna was a foolhardy plan." His gaze turned to malicious delight. "I merely need to make you a widow."

Violet caught the gleam of her cousin's pistol as he raised his arm toward Christian.

"No!" Vi screeched.

With a roar, Christian lunged toward her cousin just as Americus' pistol discharged with a *bang*. Vi's ears rang, and gunpowder smoke filled the air.

Her heart stopped. Her new husband lay on the floor, blood covering his chest and splashed across the floor. *"Christian!"*

"Don't move," Americus warned, his voice low and ominous as he withdrew another pistol from his breast pocket.

Vi's chest constricted as she laboured for breath. She couldn't fight Americus again, and she certainly couldn't leave Christian to die on the floor!

Instinct driving her, Violet withdrew the pistol from the reticule clutched in her hand, just as Christian had taught her, and aimed it at Americus. She didn't need to kill him to stop him.

He laughed. "You won't shoot me," he jeered. "You're weak. You don't have it—"

The firing of her pistol cut off his words. The force of the discharge knocked her hand back, nearly throwing her off balance. She caught herself, waving the smoke away, in time to see Americus fall to the ground with a startled howl.

Still unable to hear anything beyond her rapid pulse and the ringing in her ears, Violet ran to Christian. Blood seeped from the wound on his left side, flowing over the hand he pressed against it.

A growl arose from her cousin's slumped form. "I will come for you, Violet. Wherever you are..." He sighed, his face pressed awkwardly to the wooden floor, as he lost consciousness.

Christian's pained gaze met hers, his irises shockingly pale. "You must...take me...to Grimsbury Manor." His voice was weak and broken by grunts of agony.

"You require a doctor, Christian! A lengthy ride will only further your injury."

He shook his head, adamant. "*No*. There...is a doctor at...the school. You...*must* bring me there."

Violet nodded. She wanted to question why, but it was rather an inopportune moment. "Of course."

He visibly sagged with relief. "Load your pistol…but be…careful, as it…will be hot." His throat worked. "And…my daggers. Keep…them…close."

Her fingers trembling, she withdrew the shot, rod, and gunpowder and loaded her pistol, using a cloth to protect her hands from the heat.

"Piper…" Christian said.

"I beg your pardon?" she asked over her shoulder.

"The man…from the stables. He'll…be here, too."

"*What in blazes?*" The innkeeper and two of his servants rushed into the bedchamber, shock suffusing their features as they took in the aftermath of the events that had just unfolded.

"*Arrah now!*" one of the servants cursed vulgarly, only to receive a rap to the back of the head by the innkeeper.

"Keep yer tongue in yer mouth, boy! There's a lady present."

The young man's cheeks reddened.

"This man attacked us!" Violet cried, ignoring the exchange. "Please… Please help me dress my husband."

The innkeeper turned to the maid behind him. "Have the magistrate summoned!"

She curtseyed and dashed off down the hall.

One of the young men pointed at Christian. "But 'e needs a doctor!"

"We live but a few short miles from here," Violet lied. "A surgeon awaits us there. If you help me get him dressed and on a horse, I can ride us home."

The man might have offered a carriage, but the determined set to his jaw confirmed that they both knew a horse would be quicker.

"O' course, yer ladyship. Come, lads." The innkeeper and the young men took over.

* * *

Violet caught one of the young men staring at her bit of exposed leg, and she attempted to arrange her green skirts over it. It was fruitless, of course, for being mounted astride in a frock afforded very little modesty. She'd had no choice, however, for the inn had only one large mount left, and no sidesaddles.

"The others 'ave become sick," the innkeeper had said. "I cannae explain it!"

With their time so urgent, Violet had left her own clothing in their bedchamber at the inn. She had put her reticule in Christian's saddlebags, but while dressing that morning she had withdrawn her own clothes and hadn't bothered to return them due to their constrained timing. Her frocks and her men's suit of clothes were ruined by mud, rain, and blood, so the loss meant little to her.

"Are you ready for him, Lady Leeds?" the innkeeper asked, one of his arms wrapped about Christian's waist.

The innkeeper and his men prepared a temporary bandage in an effort to stem the blood flow. They then could fit only Christian's boots, shirt, and coat—with his daggers in one pocket—on him, eschewing the use of his cravat and waistcoat. He appeared rumpled, pale, and blood-soaked. The sight of him churned Violet's stomach.

"Yes," she replied, carefully holding the gelding still for the men to seat Christian behind her.

With a great deal of effort and a few muttered curses, the men had Christian in the saddle with her. He weakly wrapped his arms about her waist, his chest pressed firmly to her back. She might have felt a thrill at the intimate contact, but Lord knew she felt far too much fear and trepidation to allow any sort of warm feelings to arise.

"Thank you, sirs," she said to the innkeeper and his young men.

They bowed, creating an odd sort of wave. A gust of chill wind ruffled their coarse coats, the grey sky briefly darkening. There was precious little time before the rain began to fall. Vi wished to cover as much land as possible before the dirt roads became mud.

"'Tis our pleasure, your ladyship," the innkeeper replied.

Her lips thinned. "I promise to return with payment once my husband has seen a doctor."

The innkeeper shook his head. "We 'elped you out of the goodness of our 'earts, I assure you."

Violet sent the kind man a sad smile. "I vow to return nonetheless." She turned to look at Christian over her shoulder. "Hold on tightly."

With one last nod at the innkeeper and his men, she nudged the enormous horse into motion.

Chapter 26

His cheek pressed to Violet's shoulder, Chris closed his eyes. Her voice rumbled through her body, and he relished the sensation, focusing on the good rather than the agonising pain coursing through him.

"Why the devil would you wish to return to the school in Brampton when a doctor could easily be had somewhere nearby?" she asked him, her voice vibrating against his cheek. "You could have been treated at the inn, and we could have ensured my cousin's encounter with the magistrate took place." She sighed audibly. "Foolish, stubborn man."

Chris smiled weakly against her shoulder. They had slowed, briefly, to a canter while Violet and their mount caught their respective breaths.

"You ought to be grateful I didn't force it upon you, you know." She was silent a moment. "If you die from your own foolishness, I shall never forgive you."

They rode for another half mile in silence before Violet spoke. "I rather wonder at your state of mind when you requested that I bring you to Grimsbury Manor. What an odd sort of school it is to have a doctor—oh, ballocks. I hadn't even asked, I'd only assumed. Do they have a surgeon there, Christian?"

He grunted in response.

"I should hope so." She was quiet for another moment. "When I was a young girl, my elder sister broke her arm. Rose and I were quite young at the time, but I recall the horrid angle of Helen's bone, and the rather owl-like doctor who came to set it…"

Violet's nervous chatter faded from Christian's awareness. He distantly felt himself press more weight onto her back, entirely unable to hold himself off of her. His breathing deepened, and, gradually, his vision went dark as he slipped from consciousness.

* * *

Christian's body slumped fully onto Violet's back, and her worry heightened. They were scarcely half way to the school!

The brightness of the grey clouds soon gave way to the darkness of the evening storm. Rain cascaded down, long since soaking through their attire and muddying the roads. The squelch of their mount's hooves broke through the rapid thrum of her pulse in her ears.

No. Not just her mount; there was another set of hoofbeats coming up the lane to her right. She drew nearer, and her pulse sped faster.

It is likely just another traveller, Vi, not a threat. But Christian had warned her to keep vigil.

Keeping one hand on the reins and ensuring that Christian remained balanced upon her back, Violet reached back with her right hand toward his coat pocket and the daggers within. The pistol would not work in the rain with the gunpowder wet, as it very likely was, so the small blades would have to suffice.

In a burst of movement, a rider charged from the nearby lane as she passed, his sword drawn and impatience on his features.

Violet veered her mount to the side, only just keeping Christian steady behind her. It was the man from the stables—Piper?

"Surrender Leeds to me, and I shan't kill you, wot?" he called over the din of rain as he drew up beside her.

"No!" Without warning, she threw a dagger at him.

"Argh!"

The blade sliced weakly at his thigh before falling to the ground. She gripped another.

His scowl darkened. "If you don't surrender him, I shall take him by force."

The man swerved toward her until their legs and their mounts were practically touching. She fought to keep control, even as he reached out for her reins.

"Give them to me!" he grumbled.

"I'll never let you have him!"

The man—Piper—brandished his sword and swung it toward her. She couldn't—simply *couldn't*—allow this man to have them. She knew what would happen, and she and Christian had been through far too much together to simply give up now. And to surrender to this man, whose motives were entirely lost on Vi, was unthinkable.

The man had a vague acquaintance with her uncle, but that didn't explain his fixation on Christian. She needed to convince the man that her husband was useless to him.

Her heart squeezed and her stomach trembled, but she mustered her courage and strength and clenched her fist around another of Christian's daggers.

"Stop your mount and surren—*argh*!" Piper hollered as Violet thrust the small blade between the ribs at his side.

"Christian was shot!" she shouted at him through the rain and his groans. "Do you not see him? He has died; I am merely returning his body to his home." *Please don't die, Christian.*

Piper's wild eyes looked them over before he withdrew, slowing his mount and letting her ride past.

A combination of relief and fear warred within her, but she hadn't the time or the capacity in her mind to focus on her feelings. She must get Christian to a surgeon.

* * *

"Not much further," Violet said to the silence. "You're not going to die; I have you."

Christian's weight was heavy at her back, and her muscles trembled and ached as she attempted to remain straight in her seat. His hitched breaths warming the nape of her neck were her only assurance that he still lived. Lord knew what hours of riding had done to aggravate his injury.

Their enormous mount laboured for each step, grunting with every breath. Violet pitied for the poor beast. She would have begun to walk but feared Christian would fall from the horse should she dismount.

The reassuring light from distant windows shone through the wet and dreary darkness. They were not far from their destination!

Violet patted the gelding and uttered soothing words. "Very good, you handsome fellow. You will soon rest."

Her stomach rumbled loud and long. She had not taken care of any of her needs for the entirety of the day. She might very well faint from hunger.

As though their mount could sense the conclusion of their journey, he began to weakly run.

"That's it, boy! Very good," she urged him.

Wet gravel crunched beneath the horse's hooves as they trotted up the drive. The windows became brighter, and the building grander, as they neared.

"*Help!*" Violet shouted, desperately hoping someone would hear. "Help! Lord Leeds has been shot!"

Silence greeted her, and she shouted again. "*Help!* Lord Leeds is in need of a surgeon!"

Relief flooded her as the front doors opened, the shaft of light reaching her as they drew nearer. The footman named Milford emerged, his hand shielding his squinting eyes. Awareness dawned, and he shouted something unintelligible over his shoulder before dashing out to meet her on the drive.

"Thank goodness," Vi breathed. "Lord Leeds is unconscious. He has been shot."

"We'll 'ave 'im fixed up directly, Miss Wilkinson," Milford said, giving her a reassuring smile.

"Actually, it's Lady Leeds now," she gently corrected him.

The man's dark brown eyes lit with surprise before he muttered an apology.

"Are *you* well, my lady? 'Ave you been injured?" He eyed the drooping bandage at her neck.

"My injuries are not paramount. Lord Leeds is presently the one in need of care."

Milford nodded, taking the horse's reins from her. He kept the beast still as two other young men dashed out of the front doors holding two planks of wood with tightly woven wicker between them. It appeared to be a makeshift, mobile bed of some kind.

"It is I, Ferris," one of the men said to Christian. "If you can hear me, your lordship, we are going to put you on this stretcher and carry you to a bedchamber within."

Without further preamble, the men worked to lay Christian upon the wicker mat. He groaned faintly as they moved him, the blood staining his shirtfront growing darker with the fresh flow. He was deathly pale, his face all but entirely grey.

Violet's stomach flipped over. Had he lost too much blood? Would he survive the night? *Oh, Lord.* What if he survived the night only to catch the fever...?

"Might I aid your descent?" Milford stood before her, his hands outstretched.

Vi nodded. "I fear that I mightn't be able to do so on my own at the moment."

Another man came to hold the horse's reins, tipping his sopping hat to Vi as he did.

She twisted sideways to put her hands upon Milford's shoulders as he put his hands on her waist. But her muscles rebelled. "I cannot lift my leg," she confessed.

He nodded. "Lean into me, and I shall pull you from the 'orse."

Doing as he suggested, Vi awkwardly fell upon him, her legs limply dropping from the horse's back.

"Come," he said over the din of the rain. "Let us get you inside."

* * *

The school was bustling with people while the man Violet presumed to be the school's headmaster, Mr. MacLean, barked orders. His neck and cheeks were red with the force of his shouts, his green eyes filled with worry.

Violet's stomach knotted. Christian was taken into a bedchamber off the upper landing while she slowly followed on Milford's arm. Her legs were stiff, her body protesting every movement.

Milford uttered reassurances, but the disquiet in his warm brown eyes told her that she had much to fret over. Her instincts told her that she needed to help. She couldn't be his doctor, but she'd nursed Rose after her injuries inflicted by their relations, and she had cared for her family while they were ill. Surely she could be of some use to her husband.

"You." She pointed at a young footman. "Fetch cloths and fresh water. And you two, help me remove his soiled clothing."

"Yes, of course, my lady." The men did as they were bade, one dashing out the door and two others joining her at Christian's bedside.

Together, they carefully removed her husband's coat and blood-soaked shirt, setting them aside to be destroyed. They'd just bared his chest and exposed his wound when a tall man darted into the room, a large leather bag in his hand. His long face and crooked nose gave him the appearance of a hawk, but his kind brown eyes encouraged trust.

"This is the surgeon, Lady Leeds," Milford said in hushed tones.

The surgeon nodded, set his bag upon the bedside table, then examined Christian's wound. "The shot didn't go all the way through. Milford, please fetch a leather strap for his teeth. We need to retrieve the ball," he said.

Her rescuer darted away as she clutched Christian's hand, scarcely able to move as she watched the action unfold. Horror gripped her and didn't let go. She'd done all that she could; now, she must let the doctor do his part in saving her husband's life. But she couldn't—wouldn't—leave his side.

Milford returned and leaned across the bed, forcing the leather strap between Christian's teeth as the doctor commenced the procedure. The moment he began, her husband tensed, a soul-deep growl of agony muffled behind the strap and his clenched teeth.

"Hold him down," the surgeon urged.

Violet and two other men held down each of Christian's limbs, and Milford held his head.

Her husband's pale, sweat-soaked body raged as the doctor dug deeply for the ball. Violet wanted to close her eyes. She wanted to cry as Christian did, tears streaming down his temples and into his hair. His jaw was shadowed with a day-and-a-half's growth of beard, but she still saw the muscles flexing beneath.

Violet wanted to be weak, to give in to the desire to release her dread and panic. She wanted to scream and curse, to the devil with anyone who heard. But she didn't. She *couldn't*. Christian needed her to be strong.

At last, the surgeon held the ball betwixt forefinger and thumb before he set it aside, his hand doused in Christian's blood. He silently returned his gaze to the wound and began setting it to rights.

She could not say how many minutes had passed, for she felt that time had stopped. Christian's wound was sutured, and the doctor prepared a poultice and bandages. Beads of sweat covered Christian's ghostly skin, his chest rising and falling rapidly.

Several of the men helping the doctor sent her remorseful glances as they departed, their presence no longer required.

Mr. MacLean appeared at Violet's side. "Our seamstress has offered these for your use, Miss Wilkinson."

She turned her tired gaze to meet his, too exhausted to correct him. "Pardon?"

He gestured to the garments hanging over his arm. "We employ a seamstress at Grimsbury Manor. She had several items that had been set aside, which she thought you might enjoy."

Vi blinked. "How generous of her! I am much obliged."

A brief smile replaced the worry etched on his lips. "Of course. Would you care for some comforts yourself? A bath, something to eat? Or perhaps you would prefer some help to dress?"

His kindness was almost too much for her to bear. Tears threatened once more, but she kept them safely at bay. "I thank you, Mr. MacLean, but I am rather tired, and I would like to stay here with Christian. I am uncertain if I could eat a bite, despite my hunger; however, I believe a change of clothes is in order." She leaned away from the bed, though she still clutched Christian's hand, and looked down at her ruined green frock.

He smiled reassuringly. "I will fetch a maid to help you dress. We will also have the doctor redress your bandage." He eyed her neck.

"Thank you."

"Of course." His lips thinned in thought. "Might we speak on the morrow about what happened to Lord Leeds?"

She nodded silently, grateful that he did not press her.

He bowed, his bright copper hair flopping forward. "Good night."

Chapter 27

Violet gazed at herself in the mirror while the young maid, Eleanor, buttoned the back of her frock. It was a pretty, pale-blue, striped walking dress with a cream underlay and, though it was slightly overlong and quite taut over her bosom, Vi thought it rather handsome on her.

The fire crackled in the hearth, its light putting the drawn lines on her features in full relief. Rain rapped against the windows, the wind howling in a haunting, lonesome way. Vi suspected it was merely a reflection of how she felt inside. *How maudlin.*

"There we are, my lady." Eleanor smiled at Vi's reflection. "Very pretty, indeed. I will see about fetching a *fichu* for you in the morning, as I promised. Will that be all for this evening?" The maid clasped her hands before her. *The dear girl must be exhausted.*

Vi attempted a smile, though she feared it was rather sad. "I thank you, Eleanor; I am well satisfied. You are free to go."

The maid dipped in a deep curtsey before she slipped from the room.

Then Vi was alone. Her gaze slid to the ghostly form on the bed. Even with the deep warmth of the bedchamber, Christian's complexion was as pale as death.

Her heart squeezed, and she strode to his bedside. Pulling a chair over, she sat, clasping his hand in hers. The silver of his hair and eyebrows appeared darker, somehow, against his pallid skin. The blanket had been pulled up his torso, and his arms lay atop the bedclothes at his sides.

Despite her efforts to withhold it, a choked sob forced its way out, and she covered her mouth with the back of her hand. Hot tears slid, unbidden, down her cheeks in a steady stream.

She had always been the pillar of strength, the image of hope whenever her sister required it. Vi had taken the brunt of her uncle's and cousin's punishments in an effort to shield her twin from the emotional and physical burden. She had borne it and remained positive. This was her moment to be weak.

Witnessing Christian's surgery had been far more difficult than she would ever have imagined.

She whispered, "I am so very sorry. I do not have words enough to express my sorrow and regret for having put you in this situation." She swiped at the twin paths of tears on her cheeks, a damp laugh escaping her. "Despite your being a curmudgeon whose every word begs to be contradicted, I..." Her brief mirth disappeared, and shame and grief swiftly returned. "I am fond of you, husband. You do not deserve what has befallen you. I...I want you to live, Christian."

Vi leaned forward in her seat to press her forehead to their linked hands, her tears making them damp.

"*Please* live."

* * *

"Are you certain our location is correct?" Bramwell Stevens asked, a bead of sweat dripping down his temple as he searched the study's desk.

Christian's lips thinned with impatience. "I know how to decode a damned letter, Stevens. His lordship will return on the morrow. This is our only chance to look for the documents."

The man raised his hands in a gesture of surrender. "I concede, Samuels. You are the superior cryptologist; I bow to your expertise."

Chris sent a glare his comrade's way before continuing his search of the study's bookcase. The document he had decoded implied that the proof of this man's treachery was somewhere in his home. They simply needed to find it.

Sun shone in through the windows lining the far wall, lighting the dust motes as they floated through the air. Christian slid books out of their places on the shelf, flipping through the pages for any hidden bits of parchment.

Something scraped against the floor behind him, and he frowned. "Hush, Stevens. We needn't alert the servants."

"That wasn't—Samuels!"

A thick arm wrapped around his neck, pulling him against a solid chest. Bloody hell! *Chris elbowed the man in the gut, fighting to be free, but instead of releasing him, the arm tightened, cutting off his air supply.*

He reached behind his head, aiming for the man's face, and poked something soft and wet.

The man roared and released his hold on Christian. Chris spun around, pulling a dagger from within the sheath in his coat, and entered the ready position.

Stevens fought another broad and burly man across the room, their grunts and the thump *of each strike reverberating off the walls.*

How the devil had this happened? How had these men known he and Stevens would be there?

The behemoth of a man swung his meaty fist at Chris, but he evaded it, planting his own fist in his opponent's ribs.

Damnation. *The possibilities were numerous, but Chris suspected one of two options. Either this had been a trap, the letter being deliberately allowed to pass into the hands of the Secret Service as a lure, or, heaven forfend, Christian had made an error in decoding the missive.*

He felt ill.

The man charged him, slamming Chris against the bookshelf and knocking the dagger from his hand. He clenched his teeth on a growl, pain slicing through him. He retaliated, hitting the man's ears with his fists until he retreated.

Christian pulled a pistol from the holster at his back, aiming it at the blackguard.

"Hold!" Chris shouted.

The man stopped, his small grey eyes narrowed venomously. They stood thusly for several heartbeats, tension and vitriol heavy between them. Ignoring Chris' warning, his opponent reached for a sword displayed on the nearby wall and wielded it.

Chris aimed for the man's thigh and pulled the trigger. Bang! *Gunpowder smoke filled the air around his face, briefly obscuring his vision. The bastard took advantage of Chris' distraction and lunged, plunging the sword into his knee.*

A howl of agony was torn from his throat as he fell to the ground...

* * *

Violet was pulled from sleep by something moving beneath her cheek. She blinked, stretching the stiffness from her neck and back, before she realised what had awoken her.

Horror rushed through her anew. Christian thrashed, sweat beading on his pale brow, his cheeks flushed. She rose from her seat, ignoring the tautness in her back.

No, no, no!

She placed her lips to his damp forehead, confirming her fears. Her heart in her throat, Vi dashed to the bell pull and gave it three hard tugs. She then hurried to the washbasin and dampened a cloth with the cool water before returning to Christian's bedside.

His brows were drawn together in a frown, his limbs moving agitatedly against the bedclothes.

Violet pressed the cloth to his forehead and patted him comfortingly on his shoulder. "Hush now, Christian," she uttered softly. "You will be well."

The door burst open, and Mr. MacLean and the doctor rushed in.

"He has developed the fever," Violet said, nervously twisting Christian's signet ring around her finger.

The doctor turned urgently to Mr. MacLean. "I need fresh cloths for cold compresses, and items for re-dressing his wound."

With a tense nod, Mr. MacLean quit the room.

Violet strode to one of the windows and opened the sash, hoping that the fresh air would help.

Christian began to mumble, his thrashing worsening. "The code..." he muttered weakly. "The key was...incorrect."

The doctor sent Violet an oddly guarded glance before he began removing Christian's bandages.

She might have given more thought to the oddness of her husband's mumbling, but one in the throes of a fever was wont to utter any number of odd things. Even her family members had rambled incoherently during the fever that took so very much from her...

Returning to Christian's bedside, she clutched his hand and watched the doctor work, a sense of helplessness grabbing hold of her. Mr. MacLean returned with the requested items, then came to Violet's side.

Christian groaned. "*Damned Bonaparte*! The men are missing!"

Mr. MacLean stiffened beside her then cleared his throat. "We have an adjoining bedchamber, should you wish to rest." He followed her gaze to Christian's pale, restless form. "He is in Doctor Stainton's capable hands. There is not much to do but wait and pray."

Chapter 28

Dearest Rose,

It has been nearly a sennight since my new husband has been consumed with the fever. I fear for him. My stomach twists and my heart aches to see him in such a state. Doctor Stainton comes to see him twice per day, and I have not yet left our rooms. Gratefully, Christian's wound appears to be healing adequately. But, my dear sister, I cannot yet find joy from it.

I am too often reminded of our previous dire circumstance, which only serves to frighten me further.

Violet's gaze wandered across the bedchamber to where Christian lay sleeping, a heavy sweat beading on his brow. Her eyes filled with tears, and she hastily blinked them away.

Though I have not mentioned it in my previous correspondence, I must inform you that I am not with child, as you might hope. My current cycle has propelled me into a state of nigh constant weeping. I am both embarrassed and ashamed, dear sister. You would not recognise me! Gratefully, my courses have nearly concluded, for I despair of continuing on in this mien.

There are many things I wish to impart in my letters, but I fear I oughtn't tell you more until we meet again.

I miss you fiercely. I have sent you my current direction. Are you well?

Affectionately,
V

She folded and sealed the envelope, pressing the wax with the Leeds signet ring before returning it to her finger.

The room had begun to darken with the coming night, leaving the fire in the hearth and the strategically placed candles to light the room. A hazy rain fell outside the opened window, the sound of it hitting the earth below a melody to Violet's ears. It was a peaceful sound, though she felt anything but peaceful inside.

Rising, she strode to Christian's bedside and resumed her oft-used seat.

"Damn it..." Christian mumbled, his movements agitated.

Vi was no longer shocked by her husband's nonsensical ramblings. Neither the doctor nor any of the school's staff or students who had come to pay their respects to Christian had seemed put off by his ramblings, so Violet felt that neither should she be.

It had brought one disturbing thing to the forefront of her mind, however. She did not know the man she had married. Of course, she knew him to be the sort of gentleman who would take a bullet for her, who wanted to protect her, who was brave, maddening, gentle, and courageous. She knew his father's name was Theophilus Samuels and his mother died in childbirth, that his father took in urchins from the streets of St. Giles to raise as his own, and that Christian was often scolded as a rambunctious child. But, his attributes and small facts aside, she did not *know* him.

Some might argue that she knew more about her husband than did many women who entered into marriages of convenience, but Violet had not *wanted* that sort of union. Their quarrel at the inn, however, suggested that that was precisely what she had.

Love does not exist. His words repeated in her mind. *It is a fantastical, fictional emotion that only fools and little children believe in. I can safely assure you that ours will never be a union of love!* He intended to sequester her at his estate while she mouldered and pined for another life.

Her gaze travelled over his drawn and pained features. She'd had time enough to consider her circumstances in the last days, and while she was still hurt and cross, her fondness for him had not changed. In fact, the terror she felt for his health rather told her that her feelings were stronger than she had believed. Perish the thought!

Christian groaned, his limbs moving restlessly against the bedclothes. Violet retrieved the damp cloth that sat in a dish on the table at his bedside, and applied it to his forehead.

She clasped his hand in hers. "You *will* be well, Christian..."

* * *

Light shone beyond Christian's eyelids, and somewhere without, a bird called. A gentle breeze swept through the warm room, cooling his skin.

He felt like death. Everywhere, his body ached. His head and side throbbed, his stomach felt ill with disuse, and his muscles were simultaneously stiff and weak.

Something cold and wet slid from his forehead, and he cringed. Where was he?

With effort, his eyes slowly crept open, drawn toward the light from the window. He was in a bedchamber, and it was early morning, judging from the dew upon the branches of the trees outside.

What the devil had happened?

Memories caught up with him: his impulsive wedding to Violet, their first blissful—then disastrous—wedding night…and their even worse morning. Damn Bristol to hell. The scurrilous bastard had shot him!

Something brushed across his hand, and he craned his neck to examine it.

Violet.

She sat hunched in a chair at his bedside, her head resting upon the bed beside his hand and her dark mass of fallen hair in tangles. Something clutched in his chest at the sight of her. How long had she remained with him in this room? Had she worried for him?

As though sensing his consciousness, Violet stirred, inhaling deeply as she stretched the stiffness from her neck.

Despite a desire to remain present, his eyes slid closed of their own accord. He wanted to tell her that he had awakened, but the words just wouldn't form.

Fabric rustled, and then there was silence. Violet's breath hitched before she vaulted forward to place her hand upon his forehead.

She gasped. "*Oh!*"

Surprise surged through him as she replaced her hand with her lips, pressing a quick kiss to his cool skin.

"*Thank you for not dying,*" she whispered, a sob in her voice.

Chris' chest clutched again, the foreign feeling alarming him with its intensity. This was new. How long had he been lying in this bed? How severe had his injury been? He thought to open his eyes, but now that he'd closed them again, they refused to open. His body was clearly exhausted and would not cooperate.

Violet quickly bustled away with a *swish* of her skirts. Within moments, the bedchamber door opened.

"What has happened?" Chris recognised Lachlan MacLean's voice.

"His fever has broken!" Violet replied breathlessly.

Lachlan cursed under his breath, a deep sigh escaping him.

Footsteps approached.

"I came as soon as I heard the call," Dr. Stainton said.

Violet relayed the happy news before they gathered around his bed. Despite wanting to speak, to open his eyes once more, his face remained impassive as the doctor checked his wound and changed his bandage. The bloody thing hurt something fierce.

It was pleasing, however, to simply listen to his wife and his friends, even if he could not interact with them just yet.

* * *

The splash of water echoed through the bedchamber as Violet wrung out the soapy cloth. Poor Christian would feel dreadful if he awoke in his current state. She wished for him to feel clean and refreshed on unsoiled bedclothes.

With a great deal of effort and some additional help, Violet had managed to change the bedclothes on Christian's sickbed. Now, she must clean *him*.

The water was warm and the soap was foamy. The room was filled with the scent of soap and fresh air, though she had mostly closed the window so as not to give Christian an undue chill.

She began with his arms, gently massaging the muscles as she cleaned. Little bubbles coated his skin with each wipe.

"I have had many hours to contemplate the events at the inn," she uttered softly. "I wonder if Americus survived. Would they have brought a doctor in to see to him, do you think?"

Vi dipped the cloth in the soapy water and wrung it out once more. She moved it along the breadth of his chest and around his neck.

"My cousin is strong," she continued. "I daresay he has already fully recovered and is in search of us, even now. Mr. Piper, as well.

"He believes you to be dead, so you shall have to resolve whatever issue you have with him before he discovers the truth. But we can discuss that more when you've awoken."

She shook her head, moving on to wash below the bandage across his abdomen.

"I wish that we'd had more of an occasion to converse, you and I," she confessed. "You will now regain your health and leave me at your estate to do...whatever it is that you intend." A deep sigh escaped her. "I wish I had the courage to tell you—"

A knock sounded at the door, and Violet hastily covered Christian to his neck with the bedclothes before calling entry.

Mr. MacLean strode in. "How is our patient doing?"

Violet smiled openly at him. "He is still in slumber, but his fever has not returned. The doctor is optimistic that he will recover fully."

Mr. MacLean nodded as he moved to her side. He sent Christian a critical stare before turning to Violet. "We have taken the liberty of drawing a bath and preparing tea for you in the adjoining room, Lady Leeds."

Her gaze was pulled longingly toward the door leading to her guest bedchamber, but she forced it away. Christian might awaken while she was gone! "I thank you, Mr. MacLean, but—"

"Indeed, I will brook no refusal. You must be exhausted! You haven't yet left this bedchamber since you brought him in. Do take care of your needs. Christian will be here when you return."

She sighed, giving in to the deep temptation of a bath and a cup of hot tea. "Very well; I concede. Thank you, Mr. MacLean, for your generous hospitality."

He sketched a bow. "Of course, your ladyship."

With a long glance at Christian, Violet quit the room, silently closing the door behind her.

Immediately, she was enveloped by the warm humidity from the bath's cinnamon-scented steam, and the alluring aroma of teacakes. It was almost enough to make her weep. Again.

With a grateful grin, Vi began to undress.

Chapter 29

Chris listened as Violet closed the door to her adjoining room.

"You're a right bastard, Samuels," Lachlan grumbled. "You were about to let that woman wash your cock for you without the slightest protest, weren't you?"

Despite himself, Christian felt the urge to laugh, the sudden tensing of his muscles as he huffed a breath paining his injury. He groaned, and struggled to form words.

"Can you speak?"

His eyelids were weighed down, but he made the attempt to force them open, another groan forming deep in his throat. For a brief moment, his vision blurred, but he blinked heavily, finally focusing on his friend.

Lachlan shook his head, a grin on his dry lips. "How do you feel?"

Christian took stock of his body, then licked at his dry lips, forcing out the words. "Remarkably well. I...have either healed...fast, or...I have been unconscious for...several days." He raised an eyebrow at Lachlan in question.

"Six days."

Chris cursed internally. Now he understood Violet's disquiet. Six days was plenty of time for her cousin to recover from a minor injury and resume his search of her.

"What...news have you? How is...security?" he asked. Despite his weakness, Christian moved to sit up, and Lachlan hurried forward to help him.

"We are well enough. Do not trouble yourself about the school, Samuels. Focus on your recovery and that lovely wife of yours." Lachlan raised a bushy eyebrow at him.

Something akin to nervousness rippled through Christian. "I—"

Lachlan raised a hand. "I cannot fault your desire of her. She is an extraordinary woman." He sat at Christian's bedside, crossing his arms over his chest and extending his legs before him. "I did not come to question you about your abrupt marriage, however. I have news."

Chris waited expectantly for his comrade to speak.

"Hydra has made the journey to Carlisle from London. He sent word that he would be arriving directly."

"Did he give a reason?" Christian sat straighter against his pillow backrest, his eyes and mouth at last cooperating. "Has something untoward occurred?"

Lachlan shook his head. "He did not specify a reason, I'm afraid. We shall have to practise patience and inquire when he arrives."

"When who arrives?"

Hydra—Sir Charles Bradley himself—strode through the open doorway, his blond hair windswept, his buckskin riding breeches dusted with dirt, and an unrepentant grin on his lips. The man closed the door behind himself then came toward them, taking stock of the room's furnishings.

Lachlan rose to shake Hydra's hand. "Damned good of you to join us."

"Of course! I'd already intended to make the journey to Brampton, but notice of Samuels' condition sped my departure." His gaze landed on Christian. "How do you fare, old friend?"

"Much improved, thank you." He looked down at the bandage across his abdomen before meeting Hydra's brown gaze once more. "I am rather stymied by how rapidly I've healed, all things considered."

"I am pleased to hear it." Hydra selected another chair and brought it to Christian's bedside, sitting next to Lachlan. "Now, I imagine you do not have a report readied, but I should like to hear of your journey all the same."

Stifling his urge to question the man about his fellows' wellbeing, Chris took a deep breath before concisely recounting the events of the past weeks. An array of emotions ranging from mirth, to outrage, to shock…to worry played over Hydra's and Lachlan's features as Christian spoke.

"Damnation, Samuels," Hydra muttered at the tale's conclusion. "I scarcely know where to begin. Your journey is not unfamiliar, though I confess to being shocked to learn of your elopement. You are not ordinarily so impulsive."

Chris nodded once. "You are correct, of course. It was an artless and curiously precipitous decision; however, I cannot regret it."

"I do not ask it of you, Samuels." His superior's lips thinned in thought. "I have heard much about her through her sister, Rose."

Christian was filled with the strong desire to request further details. It was hardly necessary, for he already knew his wife—how odd to think of her as such!—was incredible. Violet was brave in the face of danger; she fought off her abusive cousin with aplomb; she was capable, strong, fiery...and also kind-hearted. She had remained with him during his fever and had cared for him. *Hell.* She was far more than he had first imagined. Chris was fortunate to call her wife.

Hydra raked his fingers through his mass of blond hair, further dishevelling it. "I believe it would please you to learn that Lord Hale has been apprehended on charges of treason. He sits in the Tower, awaiting trial."

A grin tugged at Chris' lips. "That is fine news, indeed!"

Hydra's eyebrows rose in mirth, his mouth quirked. "Your wife's twin sister is to be credited for Hale's capture."

Chris's own brows rose in surprise, though part of him was greatly relieved that she and Stevens had safely concluded their journey to London. "Truly?"

Hydra raised his hands in a gesture of innocence. "By my troth, the woman beat the devil out of Hale with the butt of a spent pistol. Knocked the man senseless. I had to remove the damned thing from her hand so she didn't kill the blackguard."

A laugh escaped Christian before a twinge to his side made him stop.

The mirth faded slightly from Hydra's countenance. "My apologies."

"I very much look forward to meeting this Rose." Chris notched his chin toward his superior, his curiosity getting the better of him. "Tell me, Hydra, how fares the search for Hugh and Richards?"

* * *

With a sigh of regret, Violet stepped from the cooled water of her bath. How she wished that she could have remained in the soothing heat for hours! The pleasing scent of cinnamon filled the air, wafting around her as she dried herself with a towel.

It was very thoughtful of Mr. MacLean to provide her with such a luxury. She stepped, nude, toward the tea service and sipped at her chilled tea. She had enjoyed a satisfying repast and a lovely bath, but now she must see to Christian.

Had he awoken? Had his fever returned? How were his bandages?

Her thoughts consuming her, Violet perfunctorily dressed in the frock she had been gifted and donned her new slippers. As a last thought, Vi skipped to the tea service and prepared a plate of cakes and sandwiches in the event that Christian awoke and felt inclined to eat something other than broth.

With a smile on her lips, she sped toward the adjoining door. She reached toward the handle, but a barked laugh stopped her from gripping it.

A keen sense of ambivalence struck her. She was elated at the thought of Christian being awake, but something held her emotions at bay.

After a moment's hesitation, Violet internally shook herself. Christian would not be pleased to know that she listened in on his conversation. It would be better to have her presence known.

She reached for the door's handle.

"Richards and Hugh's disappearance is greatly troubling."

Violet did not recognise the voice.

"The bloody, rotten cur, Reddington, confessed within Stevens' hearing to holding Hugh at his estate in Leicester." There was a gusty sigh from beyond the door. "We found the small hovel in which he'd been held captive, but he was nowhere to be seen. We have yet to find him. I left the others in Leicester to continue their search while I rode on with Thomson to learn more of Richards' disappearance and to see to you, old friend."

There was a quiet mumble that Violet couldn't quite understand, and she pressed her ear to the door.

"Poor Barrows still lies unconscious at the house in town…"

There was another series of mumbles, and Vi strained to hear.

"…might wish to tell your wife that her aunt, Maureen Bolton, is no longer in town. Her whereabouts are unknown, but Rose has a forwarding address."

Swift relief flowed through her. *Rose is safe! That man knows Aunt Maureen and referred to Rose by her given name. Who is he?* Violet continued to listen, her chest aching with the force of her heart's beating.

"Indeed, I shall think of a way to tell Violet," Christian responded. "What is her sister's direction?"

"She resides with Stevens at his house in town. They are to be wed at the end of the month."

Vi covered her gasp with the palm of her hand. *Rose is to be married! But who is 'Stevens'? She left Eastbourne with Mr. Smithe.*

Christian laughed, the gravelly sound warming Vi's blood.

"I knew the man fancied himself enamoured of Miss Rose Wilkinson," Christian said succinctly.

Her husband knew Rose's intended?

There was a groan. "We all know your opinion on matters of the heart, Samuels. And while I would relish a debate on the subject— for I am deeply in love with my own wife—I haven't the time or the patience. It is simply something one must learn on their own."

Vi was certain that Christian scoffed. The sound cut deeply, reopening the emotional wound caused by their argument at the inn.

"…With the war over, the battle with Bonaparte's spies ought to come to an end."

Even as Vi jumped back on a gasp, she could hear Christian's exclamation.

The war is over! She could scarcely believe it. How had it ended? She pressed her ear to the dark wood of the door once more.

"…Battle of Waterloo on the eighteenth of June was the Frenchman's great downfall. We—and Bonaparte's other enemies— took staggering losses, but we won in the end," the voice continued. "Napoleon Bonaparte abdicated on the twenty-second of June, likely just before your arrival to the school, Samuels."

"Bloody, *bloody* hell," Christian cursed. "It's finally over."

Vi put a hand to her chest, covering the ache that had settled there. *Those poor souls.*

"What will happen with your position? What of this school?" Christian asked.

"There will always be a need for our services, I fear. Though we mightn't be battling Bonaparte's spies, His Majesty's Secret Service will always have a purpose."

Violet staggered back from the door, grasping for purchase. Her fingertips bumped a chair, and she gratefully slumped onto it with an inelegant *thump*.

Spies… The Secret Service… Her pulse trundled through her veins as her mind worked. The pieces of the proverbial puzzle fell into place: Christian's adeptness in self-defence and the use of weaponry, his knowledge of how to cover one's carriage tracks and fool pursuers into following the wrong trail, and his nonsensical ramblings during his fever…they all pointed to one thing.

Her husband was a spy.

Chapter 30

Violet was lost. Her thoughts had gone so far beyond her comprehension, while her lungs laboured for breath. How could she not have seen the signs? She was foolish, impulsive, and reckless.

Had Christian ever intended to tell her the truth? Would he ever have confided in her?

"We will ride out to my estate in Falkirk. There you will reside..." His words travelled through her mind. *"You cannot be so naïve. A great many marriages of the* ton *contain similar arrangements."*

Vi's chest constricted. The man intended to hide her away for her own safety but thought nothing of her feelings on the matter. She knew with absolute certainty that he would never willingly tell her the truth.

Lord, but it pained her to think it. She placed her free hand over her chest, the rapid tattoo of her pulse thudding against her palm.

Despite her resolution to halt any emotional attachment she felt for the blasted man, the fresh wave of agony that seared through her veins confirmed that she had failed.

Another guffaw permeated the adjoining door, earning Violet's glare. The man thought to fool her, to keep her in the dark for the remainder of her life... She would not stand for such disrespect.

* * *

Christian grinned at his fellows, a bud of hope alight in his chest. It had begun to feel as though the war would never end, that Napoleon Bonaparte's spies would forever be attacking good men on English soil. Undoubtedly, blackguards unable to accept the truth would remain, but Chris was certain that, in time, he and his fellows could capture each and every traitor and hold them accountable for their crimes against the Crown.

When Hale, his son, Bristol, and their dastardly associates were charged with treason and strung up at Tyburn, Chris was certain that a great weight would lift from his shoulders.

His comrades continued to speak amiably, hovering at Christian's bedside.

Lachlan cleared his throat. "I shall summon Dr. Stainton and have him examine your—"

The door to the connecting room swung open with a *bang* as it hit the wall behind it. Violet strode in, anger, worry, and hurt etched in her fine features. Her gaze instantly sought him out, and his stomach sank. *What had she heard?*

"*You,*" she emphasised ominously as she strode forward. She pushed past Lachlan and Hydra, who had stood at her entrance, until her thighs all but touched his mattress.

"Good afternoon, dear wife." Christian flashed her a stiff smile, his teeth gnashed. "Have you met my good friend Sir Charles Bradley?" He watched her with his steely gaze.

She glared over her shoulder, and both men retreated a step. *Cowards.*

"Pleasure to make your acquaintance, Sir Bradley," she gritted out, dipping into a shallow curtsey before returning her blazing blue gaze to Christian.

Violet wagged her finger at him as she shouted, "You manipulative, deceitful, impudent, unscrupulous lout! You *lied* to me! How dare you have the gall to—"

"For God's sake, *hold*, woman!" Christian cut over her speech, a sudden and visceral anger charging through him. "I have had enough of your harping to last me a lifetime!"

Her eyes widened, and her jaw dropped on a gasp. "Harping! Of all the insufferable—" Her mouth snapped shut and her gaze narrowed. "You have not yet seen harping, by God!"

"Yes," he drawled, "and I imagine you intend to show me."

The click of the door closing alerted him to his fellows' exit. Lucky bastards.

Violet's lips pursed as she glared at him.

"Why did you not tell me the truth?" she demanded. "At least once you claimed that we were to become partners on our journey..." She trailed off with a shake of her head.

There was no sense in denying what she very clearly knew; evasion would only serve to postpone the inevitable. "How can you possibly assume that I *would* tell you the truth? My profession is clandestine for a reason."

She placed her fists on her waist, the motion pulling the material of her frock across her breasts. Damn him if it didn't catch his interest.

"I am your *wife*!" she yelled.

"Think you that every husband illuminates his wife to the many facets of his life? Consider the many women that meet their intendeds for the first time on the day of their wedding! Would they know more about their future spouse than his name and rank? I wager not."

Her lips thinned as she studied him angrily. "You promised—"

He scowled. "Yes, and we were wed for all but ten hours when your dastardly cousin burst into our room and *shot* me!"

She placed her hands theatrically over her chest. "Oh, my poor Lord *Spy*! I imagine you have been injured far worse. How foolish of me to feel worried."

Indeed he *had* been injured far worse, but Chris was not about to give her the satisfaction of his admitting she was correct. He opened his mouth to utter a cutting retort…but he saw the crack in her façade. Through her veneer of fury, he could see the pain.

It was her eyes. Narrowed though they were, hurt lurked there. Her lips came second. If he hadn't been looking for it, he might have missed the quiver to her bottom lip and chin as she attempted to suppress her misery.

His anger deflated. He was a cad. He should have seen that her anger was meant to disguise any other feelings.

Chris breathed a deep sigh and softened his tone. "Knowing my secret could have gotten you killed, Violet. I was doing my best to offer you my protection."

"I could have been killed, regardless, when the man in pursuit of you came after us!" She threw her hands up in the air with a grunt of exasperation. "You and your irrational notions of heroism!"

Christian's frown returned and his gut churned. "I beg your pardon?"

Violet began to pace, her slippered footsteps muffled on the room's burgundy brocade rug. "Is that what you and your fellows believe? That keeping your spy lives secret will protect those around you?" She shook her head, her movements agitated.

He waited for her to continue, annoyance, curiosity, and concern warring within him.

She spun to face him from the foot of his bed, a determined set to her brow. "Have you never considered that perhaps the people closest to you would benefit from the knowledge that their lives might be at risk? That mayhap *preparing* said individuals for a potential attack and training them to defend themselves could very well save their lives? That you mightn't only save their lives, but also your *own* life from dreary days and nights of worrying about their safety?" She shook her head with a faint scoff. "The notion that you were protecting me by keeping me ignorant is simply absurd."

Chris was stunned. He knew not how long he remained silent, but certainly it was above a minute. His heart galloped in his chest. How had he never considered that before? How many of his fellows had assumed the same, and had avoided romantic entanglements because of it?

He, and the others within the Secret Service, had been warned during their studies that they must protect those whom they loved from the darker side of their positions, but never had he considered the possibility that they could teach their loved ones to protect themselves. Indeed, the school could host a single class for family members of their agents. It would be the basics of self-defence and firearms usage, how to—

"After having time to contemplate the matter since our last disagreement, I am disinclined to dispute our living arrangements any further," Violet said, cutting off his thought. "I would prefer not to remain close to a man who is so willing to be rid of me. Your decision for us to live apart is for the best."

Despite the fact that he had previously come to the same conclusion, Violet's words hit him squarely in the chest. Shock and disappointment throbbed through his veins.

"Once you are well enough recovered," she continued, "if you would give the direction to one of Mr. MacLean's coachmen, I will journey to your estate, leaving you free to fulfil your duties."

Her jaw twitched as she strode purposefully toward the adjoining door.

Christian's injuries notwithstanding, he tossed the counterpane aside and swung his feet over the edge of the bed.

"What in heaven's name—?" Violet exclaimed, her eyes wide with alarm as she rushed to his side. "Return to bed at once! You mustn't stand; allow yourself to heal."

He resisted the urge to glower, warmed by her concern and put off by his own inability to move about as he wished. "I have healed adequately through my unconscious state. I assure you, I am capable of determining my own limitations."

His stubborn wife set her jaw, and Christian clasped her hand in his. With one fist holding the sheet to his nether regions, he carefully stood. He used Violet's grip as support but refused to return to the bed. A dull, pulsing pain beat across his abdomen, and a bead of perspiration trickled over his temple.

"Do not go," he gritted out.

A combination of worry, despondency, and resolve filled her features. "I *must*. I shan't condemn myself to a life with a man who does not believe in love."

She shook her head haltingly when he opened his mouth to protest. Protest *what*, he wasn't certain, for he most definitely did not believe in that fanciful emotion.

"I intend to be a wife in the basic sense of the word," she assured him, the firelight wavering over her profile. "You needn't fear that I will be unwelcoming when you return to the estate, or that I will not perform my wifely duties when necessary. But I *cannot* allow myself to feel more for you than you are willing to return. It would…damage me."

Christian was caught in her gaze. There, her opposing emotions were laid plain. Her raw honesty touched something deep inside of him, but what, he didn't know. He wanted to tell her that he would be a proper husband to her, that he would father her children and dote on her. But he couldn't. Lord knew that siring an heir was both enjoyable and his duty, but *damnation*, the thought of witnessing his wife perish in childbirth curdled his blood.

Instead, he kissed her. She gasped in surprise but recovered quickly from the shock, her lips slowly melting against his. Chris placed his palm to the base of Violet's head, kneading his thumb along the column of her neck. He took his time, leisurely flicking his tongue against hers, enjoying the slide of her lips on his.

A fire ignited within him, heating him until he was nigh boiling with desire. He continued unhurriedly, showing with his actions what he could not put into words.

Chris wanted this woman, *his wife*. But his own conflicting emotions perplexed him. Even if threatened with torture, he was positive that he would still be unable to put voice to his feelings. He simply needed *her*.

Chapter 31

Warmth swirled up Violet's spine. It had not been many days since she had kissed Christian, but the moment their lips met, it felt like an eternity had elapsed. In addition to desire, his lips brought a feeling of comfort, of calm.

Their undeniable passion would not alter her opinion on living with a man incapable of love, but she could not repudiate the physical connection they shared. She must accept that she had entered into the marriage state ignorant of his true feelings on life and love, and his role in His Majesty's Secret Service. There was no sense in being displeased, for it would only perpetuate her dissatisfaction. She would make the most of her life and enjoy it as it was: full of desire.

On a groan, Christian deepened their kiss. He brought his arm around her, the bedclothes he'd held to his nether regions falling to the floor as he gently pulled her against him.

Vi baulked at causing him more pain and broke their embrace. "Your wound… And you just awoke from your fever, perhaps it is best if we don't—"

Christian shook his head. "It does not pain me. I assure you, I'm aware of my limitations; I will not injure myself further."

"But surely it will open if you move too…er…vigorously."

One of his silver eyebrows arched high. "Then perhaps you should move for the both of us."

Writings from within *The Schoole of Venus* skittered through Violet's mind, and her stomach flipped over in nervous anticipation. She knew precisely what Christian meant. He intended that she mount him astride and take him inside her.

Her abdomen quivered and her feminine core throbbed. *Blimey.* Even the mere thought of performing such an act had her aching.

"Lie down," she demanded, her voice unintentionally sultry.

Christian's eyelids lowered, his desire coming from him in waves as he did as she bade. With care, he eased back down on the mattress, his erection thick and stiff as it rested upward toward his navel.

With what she hoped was a seductive smile, Violet unfastened her gown, letting the fine material fall to the floor at her feet. Her petticoat and shift were next, both landing in a pile next to her frock. Her nipples tightened as they were exposed to the warm air of the room, her breasts heavy with need.

She reached for her garters and stockings.

"Keep them on," Christian ground out.

"As you desire," she purred. Vi could scarcely recognise her own voice.

Her body sang with the need to feel him within her, to feel him pulse as he reached his peak. If he did, in fact, leave her at his estate, she must have memories of his lovemaking to sustain her. And, perhaps, a babe in her belly to love.

Nervousness fluttered in her abdomen, mingling with anticipation and desire. She'd read about the particular act, but was unsure if she could put the motions into practice.

"Come, wife," Christian urged in a guttural voice.

Careful not to cause Christian any undue injury, Violet slid onto the bed. His hands immediately found her skin, the contact causing gooseflesh to spread over her. She drew one leg over his hips, settling herself comfortably astride him. The heat of his body radiated outward, settling deep in her bones…and melting her core ever further.

She sighed and trembled as Christian's hands slid reverently over her thighs, hips, and waist, his callused palms gently abrading her. She took a quavering breath as she sank her pelvis lower to rub herself over the hard ridge of his erection. Pleasure surged through her, and Christian groaned.

"Take me inside you," he said hoarsely.

Vi rose up on her knees, giving herself room to guide his thickness to her folds. She spread her dampness over him, using his ruddy tip.

A low, rumbling growl came from deep within Christian's chest, and he slowly glided his hands upward over her ribs to cup her aching breasts. Violet keened in delight and sank down, taking Christian fully within her.

It was like coming home. He filled her, body and soul; it was a feeling she was loath to be without. But heaven knew she craved the euphoric release that came from lovemaking with Christian.

His thumbs passed over the taut buds of her nipples, teasing them with his light touch. Vi gasped as he satisfied her ache with a pinch between his forefinger and thumb.

"Move," he groaned. "Please, Violet."

She leaned forward to brace her hands on either side of his shoulders, the new angle enabling the pleasure centre among her feminine folds to rub deliciously against him. "Call me Vi." Her voice was low, sultry.

Christian grunted, his hands returning to her hips as he guided her untutored movements. "Then you must..." he gasped, "call me...Chris."

The intimacy of his abbreviated name sent a tremor through her.

Then Violet began to move. She started out slow, tilting her hips in a rocking motion, back and forth. But she quickened her pace, desperate to appease the aching force of her need.

Chris' fingertips bit into the flesh of her hips, the pleasure-pain adding to the riot of sensations. She rode faster, her breaths coming in rapid gasps. Chris' lips pulled back in an erotic snarl as his hands urged her on.

Her pleasure hit in a burst of light behind her eyelids, the waves of bliss crashing through her.

* * *

Christian cursed. "Damnation, Vi. You make me—" He broke off his words, his mind delirious with lust.

Seeing his wife come apart was almost more than he could handle. Violet rode her pleasure, her head tipped backward, her eyes closed... She was enrapturing.

He couldn't hold back. With one last rock to her hips, Chris simultaneously lifted her up and tilted his pelvis away. Sliding himself from her slick folds, he spilled his seed on his stomach.

Violet hovered for a moment, before she nestled herself at his uninjured side. Entirely satisfied, Chris wrapped one arm about her shoulders.

"Have you any pistachios?" Violet's sweet voice sounded loud over their heavy breathing.

Chris frowned. "Pardon?"

His handsomely tousled wife rose up on one elbow to look down at him. "Pistachios," she repeated. "As a restorative after bed sport."

He snorted in surprise. "*Bed sport*? Where the devil did you—?" Awareness dawned, and he shook his head with a laugh. "I'll have to read that damned book so that I might teach you the truth of things."

Violet scowled in affront, the expression strangely rousing his blood. "I will have you know that it is because of that 'damned book' that I knew what to do at all in our lovemaking."

Chris did have to admit that her knowledge had a supplementary erotic benefit. "Indeed you are correct, sweetheart." He winked, then lifted up to exchange a passionate kiss, ignoring the twinge to his injury.

It was several moments before he finally returned his head to his pillow, the fire of her embrace still alight in his blood. He absently stroked the backs of his fingers over her arm, his eyes sliding closed.

Violet broke the silence once more. "May I ask you a question that is personal in nature, Chris?"

His pulse spiked at the sound his abbreviated name on her lips, and he opened his eyes to watch her curiously.

"What caused the injury to your leg?" she asked quietly, as though it would take away some of the pain at the reminder.

Chris was silent for several long heartbeats, unsure what he should say. He despised the thought of lying to her again. He'd already faced the consequences of deceit with his wife; God help him if he did so again. His pride would simply have to take a blow.

It was easier for him to follow this topic rather than revert to the matter of their argument, for he was at sixes and sevens as to how to resolve it.

I shan't condemn myself to a life with a man who does not believe in love, she'd said. *I cannot allow myself to feel more for you than you are willing to return. It would…damage me.*

Christian cleared his throat. "It was not many years ago that I was still active in the field, doing both reconnaissance and sabotage in addition to my cryptology—that is to say, decoding documents. We were learning about a gentleman with sensitive information in his possession, and I had decoded the documents. Ultimately, I made a critical error that nearly cost us the mission, and our lives. A quarrel ensued, and I took a sword to the knee."

"Oh, how awful," she breathed.

Chris shook his head, his hair brushing against his pillow. It was his punishment, and he'd deserved it. "It is better that than a lost life. I thank you, though, wife."

With a hand to his bandaged side, he sat up and gave Vi a quick kiss before sliding from the bed. His limp heavily pronounced, Chris walked to the washbasin and cleaned himself of his seed. He ought to explain himself to Violet, but she would not be pleased with his reasoning.

While he was desirous to have children, he could never bring himself to risk Violet's life in such a way. He would hope that if he explained himself, she would be flattered that he was fond enough of her to care whether she lived through childbirth.

He was fooling himself, of course. He was dastardly for keeping this from her.

If they lived separately, he could certainly justify their not engaging in sex for the purposes of reproducing, but... *Aw, hell.* This was damned difficult. Of course, she had that book of *pornographia*; surely "bed sport" of other varieties and positions would interest her. There were plenty of acts they might attempt that would not result in children.

Chapter 32

Violet gazed at the ceiling of Christian's bedchamber, the combined light from the fire in the hearth and the midday sunlight from the opened window wavering over its surface.

Her husband slumbered peacefully beside her, one of his arms draped over his eyes and his chest slowly rising and falling. Birds chirped gaily beyond the window, the sound at odds with the tumult growing within her.

Vi was conflicted. She was still in a state of euphoria from their lovemaking, and was rather heartened that Chris would confide in her a truth that would hurt his pride. But, ultimately, she felt dejected.

Christian evidently did not wish to father a child by her, otherwise he would have spilled his seed within her. Based on their previous argument regarding their living arrangements, he did not wish to spend an undue amount of time in her company, either. She would grant that he'd behaved sufficiently outraged when she'd agreed to their living apart—just enough, in fact, to give her the faintest glimmer of hope that he might enjoy her companionship. But his argument still remained.

Sex was not the problem between them; she could foresee many a lustful—and dare she hope, licentious—night for them. But no children, and no love.

Vi grit her teeth against the blow to her pride. Well, his notions of living apart could go to perdition. She might have wavered in her resolve when she'd learned of his clandestine activities, and she'd certainly put her determination on hold long enough to enjoy the intimacy of his touch, but she would dither no longer.

Violet was not a fainting flower; she was the blasted hero of her own story. The danger of her cousin finding their whereabouts and staging an attack became greater by the hour. Lord knew he could be approaching the rear entrance at that very moment. It would behove her to be prepared.

Careful not to wake Christian—*Chris*—Violet slid from the bed and gathered her attire. She slunk into the adjoining room, her arms laden with her burden, and closed the door gently behind her.

Vi draped her frock and undergarments over a chair and set to washing herself with the cold bath water.

She had long believed that she alone would be responsible for the quality of her future. Now, while she had a husband who ought to be perfectly capable of protecting her, Violet did not wish to rely so wholly on someone else for her safety. Most particularly when the man fully intended to abandon her at his estate.

Concluding her ablutions, Vi dressed in her serviceable lavender fustian walking dress, which had been gifted to her by the school's modiste, Miss Withers, and quit the room. She had been in residence for nearly a sennight, and she had not so much as left their chambers. Vi knew not where she went, but she was sure to happen upon someone willing to help her.

The corridor was brightly lit by wall sconces, and the air carried the odour of tallow wax, perspiration, and the faintest amount of gunpowder. *How odd.* What sort of a learning establishment would employ a modiste, a tailor, *and* a live-in physician?

The answer came to her in a startling moment of clarity. Violet shook her head in self-derision as she descended the grand staircase into the foyer. *Of course.* This was not an *ordinary* learning establishment.

It suited her plans for that afternoon well enough.

Her slippered footfalls were muffled on the marble tiled floor of the foyer. Her gaze darted about as she walked, curiously eyeing each room she passed, and all were peculiarly devoid of people.

Violet continued on through the hall when she heard a faint thudding. Her feet moved quickly toward the noise. It grew in volume and intensity as she drew near, the strange sound accompanied by indistinguishable voices. She turned a corner, drawn to warm, ambient light that shone from within opened double doors.

Someone grunted, and another laughed before the rapping resumed.

Undaunted, but admittedly nervous, Violet strode boldly into the grand ballroom. The eyes of every occupant instantly swung to rest on her, but Vi's attention was preoccupied.

"*Bloody hell*," she whispered in awe.

Though her experience was modest, the ballroom was one of the largest that Violet had ever seen. It wasn't, however, filled with dancing couples, simpering mamas, and gloating papas. Indeed, it was otherwise engaged.

Blimey.

Despite the wall of windows looking out onto the bright, sunlit gardens, chandeliers hung high overhead, their candles lit. Violet imagined it a spectacular sight in the evenings.

To her immediate left were figures made of wood and straw that appeared to have been sliced and stabbed several times over. The left wall was consumed by a display of wooden sticks, knives, axes, and other handheld weaponry. Hanging bows, arrows, and an array of pistols adorned the wall to her right, and a target range stretched the length of it. In the centre-left of the room, enormous mats that took up the majority of the floor space, and a man and a woman, both attired in white breeches and tunics, stood holding long sticks.

Vi must have interrupted a demonstration of some kind, for the mat was surrounded by onlookers...who were all watching Violet.

Undeterred by their curious stares, she gathered her courage and strode forward. "My sincere apologies for intruding. I am in need of some assistance."

The woman on the mat turned toward Violet. "What might we help you with, my lady?"

Violet blinked, her gaze drawn to the speaker. "*Eleanor*? Heavens, I hardly recognised you!" She gestured toward the woman's breeches. "I...er...find your attire quite dashing."

Eleanor dipped in a curtsey. "Thank you, Lady Leeds."

"Are ye in trouble, milady?" a tall, fair man asked from beyond Eleanor's sparring partner.

Emboldened by his inquiry, Violet straightened her shoulders and lifted her chin, addressing the group. "As a matter of fact, yes. I imagine that word of my husband's injury has reached all of you, as well as how it came to pass." Several among her audience nodded, so she continued. "The threat of my cousin and the mystifying Mr. Piper still haunts us, I fear, and while I am certain that Lord Leeds would protest this to his dying breath, he is not well enough at present to fight should my cousin or Mr. Piper decide once more to attack. I believe that I understand the nature of this school, and I had hoped that I might importune one of you for a lesson."

Violet's voice reverberated through the grand space, and for several heartbeats that was the only sound in the room.

"We offer our most sincere apologies on Lord Bristol's escape. We had apprehended him for questioning, but he...escaped. But are ye sure that is yer wish, milady?" a short, dark-haired fellow asked. "If ye remain here, we will protect ye."

Violet nodded. "Indeed, you are correct. I imagine, however, that my cousin will not strike when he knows we are among protectors. And while your offer is generous, I daresay that a life lived under a shield is rather dreary."

Eleanor's opponent finally broke his silence. "You are correct, of course, Lady Leeds. I believe your sister, Rose, would feel much the same."

Vi's gaze sharpened on the man. Awareness dawned as she recognised him as the gentleman with whom Christian had conversed in his bedchamber. *Of course.* He had spoken of Rose while she listened at the door. "You know my sister, Sir Charles Bradley," she stated.

He nodded, a lock of his tousled blond hair falling across his forehead. "Indeed I do," he confirmed. "We became acquainted in London."

"Pray tell me, how does she fare?"

"She was well the last that I saw her. I would be pleased to give you her direction so you might write her."

Violet smiled. "I would be much obliged, thank you."

He inclined his head again, then rapped his stick on the mat. "Now, would you care for that lesson?"

Vi's smile grew. "I would."

"Very good." He turned to his partner. "Eleanor, please fetch Lady Leeds a weapon."

The young woman bowed, then dashed toward the edge of the room where the weapons were mounted.

"Won't you join me on the mat, your ladyship?" Sir Bradley urged.

There was a murmur of encouragement and approval from the audience positioned around the mat. A frisson of nervousness rippled through Violet, but she determinedly squelched it. She would have to keep a clear mind should she encounter her cousin again.

She strode into the centre of the mat, facing Sir Bradley, acutely aware of the curious stares boring into her. Eleanor quickly returned with a stick just like the one in Sir Bradley's hands.

"This," he said, twirling the stick, "is a staff. This particular weapon might not be readily available if you are surprised by an assault, but there will always be something that one might turn *into* a staff. Likewise with many weapons, which you shall learn in time." One corner of his lips pulled upward in a grin, his eyes narrowed. "Now…*attack me.*"

* * *

Glasses rattled, and the taproom's patrons jumped as Americus slammed his palms on the table. "Tell me what you know," he growled.

"I-I swears it, I know nothin'! I ain't seen no toff or gel like ye describe." The innkeeper's pitiful snivelling grated on Americus' nerves.

His lip rose in a snarl. Every bloody innkeeper, ale house, gin house, coffee house, shopkeeper, nurse, and physician he'd questioned had said the very same thing. No one had seen Violet or her walking corpse of a husband. *Where have they gone?*

Lord Leeds must have sought a doctor's aid, for God knew Americus' shot had brought the bastard to his knees. He'd been brought to his own knees, and his *bitch* of a cousin had shot only his thigh; the pain had been bloody unbearable. It'd taken damned near a week for him to walk without too pronounced a limp.

He would simply have to travel to Leeds' estate—after a night of enjoyment, of course. If Leeds and Americus' whore of a cousin weren't in residence, he could most assuredly encourage them to show themselves. Servants were eager enough to send for their masters when the threat of death hung over their heads.

Americus clenched his jaw, his fury pumping hard and fast through his veins. The innkeeper squirmed in his seat as sweat formed at his temples.

Acting on instinct, Americus reached into his inner breast pocket and withdrew a banknote. The innkeeper cringed before he saw what was offered to him.

"Tell me," Americus drawled. "Do you happen to know where I might find some large men willing to do a lord's bidding?"

The innkeeper's small brown eyes narrowed in appreciation. "Now *tha'* I can cer'ainly 'elp ye with."

Chapter 33

Clack, clack, clack!

Each hit to her staff reverberated through Violet's hands and down her arms. Sir Bradley—or *Hydra*, as she had come to know him—swung his staff in the air, arcing high before connecting with her block.

It had been two days since she'd begun lessons, and every moment had been invaluable. Vi took her opportunities to learn while Christian lay abovestairs in slumber. Lord knew what he would do if he knew she was taking private lessons. As soon as his breaths deepened with sleep, Violet would return to the ballroom, where she would meet with Hydra, Eleanor, Mr. McKinnon, or one of the other capable spies.

How droll, she thought. That she should be learning to fight from members of His Majesty's Secret Service was quite unbelievable.

She caught a blow on her hip, and she winced. Returning her attention to their bout, Vi swung her staff with renewed vigour.

Clack, clack, clack! She blocked his blows and attempted some of her own. Sweat ran over her temple and down her spine, tickling the fine hairs there. She put her discomfort aside and made an oscillating attack.

Hydra paused, a grin on his lips. "Very good. Now, why do we not try the short staves?"

The sunlight from the grand windows created a fine halo around Hydra's blond locks, his features in dim shadow.

Violet thumped her staff on the practising mat with a nod. "Have you tired of my excellence already?" Her breath came rapidly after her exertion.

A snort escaped him. "Your confidence will do you well in intimidating your opponents, Violet, but you must ensure that it does not cause your downfall. You must always be vigilant. Pay close attention to your attacker's body language cues, and remember that when battling men, your swiftness is key. You are smaller, and he will be stronger. Avoid or deflect his blows rather than blocking. Keep out of arm's reach, or he might grab you. If he *does* grab you—"

"Yes." Vi nodded once more. "I recall the lesson, Hydra. Hit his weak spots and catch him unaware."

He inclined his head and handed his staff to her. "That is not quite all of it, but certainly *part* of it. Why do we not skip the short staves this afternoon, and resume our lesson on hand-to-hand combat, since you seem so self-assured?"

She resisted the urge to sigh. Her skills in hand-to-hand left much to be desired.

Violet strode quickly to the wall and returned the two long staffs to their proper place. She was by no means proficient in the art of combat, but she was beginning to understand how to defend herself should she be attacked.

She greeted a young gentleman as he withdrew a weapon from the rack. He smiled shyly in return before striding away to square off against a training figure.

Returning to the mat, she faced Hydra. He stood motionless, which made it rather difficult to watch him for any subtle nuances that would alert her to his first move.

Quick as a flash, he reached for her arm. Her heart pounding, she deflected it with the back of her wrist. He took advantage of her diverted attention and reached for her with both arms simultaneously. Violet leapt to the side, trying to remove herself from his reach.

He caught her. His hands curved around her forearms, squeezing slightly as he spun her. Hydra held her with his front pressed to her back, his arm coming around to wrap across her collar. Instinctively, Violet grasped at his elbow to keep him from choking her.

It frightfully reminded her of that moment at the inn with Americus, and her heart thudded mercilessly in her chest. At the inn, she'd had a dagger with which to stab her cousin in the leg, but now she had to extract herself from her opponent's hold with just her wits.

"What will you do?" Hydra whispered encouragingly in her ear. "What sensitive parts of me can you reach?"

Vi's mind was dragged back to the moment. A man's cods were sensitive, to be sure.

Bending her knee, Violet raised her foot behind her, attempting to reach high enough between his legs to injure him. He anticipated her move and pressed his knees together, holding her collar and shoulders more tightly with his arm.

She ground her teeth together in frustration.

"That was a good thought, Violet," Hydra murmured, "but it is one that any attacker will likely expect. *Think*," he urged.

Her mind worked furiously as Hydra's arms tightened. Christian's lesson and the hours of classes travelled through her thoughts until she came to her answer.

She stomped on Hydra's foot while also reaching behind her head with one arm, extending her fingers in an attempt to poke his eyes.

"Excellent," Hydra praised. "Now loop your ankle around my knee and pull forward with all of your strength."

Following his direction, Vi forced him off balance. His grasp on her tightened as he fell backward to the floor, dragging her down atop of him. Hydra's breath left him in a winded *oof*.

"Perfect," he wheezed. "If you elbowed my ribs after falling atop of me, I might release you from my grip."

An uneven tread of footsteps sounded beneath the clanging weaponry and the grunts of those practising.

"So this is where my wife has been spending her days..." Christian's low timbre cut through the room.

Hydra released her, and she scrambled inelegantly to her feet. Something inside her came to life at the sight of her husband. He wore chocolate-brown breeches and cutaway coat, a deep-green waistcoat, and cream stockings, shirt, and cravat. Something about the earthy tones brought out the blue of his eyes and the dashing silver in his hair.

She was reminded of their past two nights of passion, and the warmth in his gaze told her that he recalled their exploits as well. Her heart fluttered, and she cleared her throat.

* * *

Chris' gaze bore into his wife, something deep, dark, and entirely foreign pounding mercilessly through him. It should not have bothered him that Violet had sought the aid of his fellows to educate her on the art of defending oneself...but it did. He was her husband;

surely she ought to have asked *him* for his aid? And, *bloody hell*, what was she wearing?

His gaze heated as he took in her attire: cream-coloured, skin-hugging duelling breeches and an oddly curve-accentuating plastron. She was a vision. Finding her atop Hydra upon entering left an ill flavour in his mouth, however.

"What are you doing out of bed, Christian?" Violet—Vi—asked. "You ought to be abed, recovering."

Chris brushed the comment aside with a shake of his head. "I have had enough rest to last through my lifetime." Truthfully, he was rather remarkably healed, though still burdened with minimal throbbing pain. Mostly, he detested lying about when he knew there was work to be done. "I'm afraid that our time at Grimsbury Manor has come to an end; we must continue our journey to my estate. I expect to be on our way by nightfall."

Violet bristled. "Surely you do not intend to travel when you have not yet fully healed. And at night, no less!"

"Indeed I do." He strode forward, his deuced limp more pronounced than normal.

His wife's eyes softened, and she stepped forward as though to offer him help. Her pity was grating.

Hydra frowned. "Come now, Samuels. Allow yourself the time t—"

"*No!*" Christian sliced his hand through the air, silencing his superior and drawing the attention of the others present. He moderated his voice. "I appreciate and thank you for your hospitality, but the longer we remain, the greater the chances of Lord Bristol finding our location—and the very private school in which we keep the many secrets of our trade. Additionally, with the both of us in residence, the search for Hugh and Richards is put on hold. We must leave, both to draw Lord Bristol away from the school and to allow your imperative search for Hugh and Richards to resume."

Hydra and Violet watched him with opposing expressions of frustration and concern.

"If it is acceptable to Mr. MacLean," Chris continued, "we shall borrow a curricle and ride on to my estate directly."

His superior shook his head. "Should Lord Bristol still be in search of you, he will anticipate such a move. It is likely that he is already awaiting your arrival."

"All the more reason to go!" Chris exclaimed. "You must know what he will do to my staff if he does not glean the information he seeks…"

Hydra's lips thinned in distaste. "If you are so determined to leave, I cannot in good conscience allow you to travel on your own. We will arrange for a convoy. I will alert the kitchen staff of your plans and have a meal prepared for the journey."

* * *

Christian's boot heels clipped on the marble floor of the foyer. It had been three short hours since he had made the announcement of their departure, but it felt far longer. Something about his foreign mixture of emotions had set him on edge. It felt new, but he feared that it had been slowly growing stronger over the past weeks. Unfortunately, he could not put a name to the feeling.

"Are you certain this is the best course of action, Samuels?" Lachlan MacLean questioned from his position at Chris' side.

Christian shifted the burden of his saddlebags on his shoulder. "I have given my reasons, Lachlan."

Hydra came up on Chris' other side. "A curricle and pair of greys await you on the drive. The others have packed and are ready to follow."

"You have my thanks." Christian stopped and spun to face them. "Should Bristol find the school, please take him down and notify me directly."

Lachlan inclined his head. "Of course. It has been some time since we have had an occupant in the dungeon; I am rather eager to put it to use."

Violet's lilting laughter echoed from the corridor abovestairs. Chris' gaze was immediately drawn toward it. She emerged from the hall and descended the stairs, Ferris at her side holding her small, borrowed trunk. The unfamiliar stirring of emotion returned as he watched her. *What is wrong with me?*

He cleared his throat of its hoarseness. "Thank you both for your aid. Please extend my gratitude to Dr. Stainton again, and to Miss Withers for the supply of clothing to my wife and myself."

"Yes, please do," Violet added as she drew near. "Her gowns are lovely."

The scent of cinnamon surrounded him. It swirled about his senses, teasing him, luring him. His heart rate accelerated, and he had to resist the urge to tug at his cravat. His wife's impact on him was beyond perplexing.

He felt attraction for her, to be sure, but he'd thought those feelings would have waned since he'd sated his desires. Oddly enough, it felt as though the opposite was happening. The more he had of her, the more he needed her.

* * *

Violet sat stiffly against the motion of the curricle as it trundled down an old dirt road. The sky clouded over, darkening with both the coming night and the possibility of rain. It mirrored Christian's mood impeccably.

It seemed as though the further they drove from Brampton, the increasingly sour her husband's mien became. Something undoubtedly bothered him, but when she'd inquired about it, he'd brushed her off.

Could his wound be aching? Did his knee pain him? Perhaps the ache brought back troubling memories. Or, mayhap he was concerned about them possibly being set upon by Americus. They had a number of his fellows not far behind them, however, which had put *her* nerves considerably at ease.

She clutched her reticule closer to her stomach, the weight of her book and pistol a comfort to her. While she understood Christian's reasons for wanting to leave Brampton, she could not claim to agree with all of them.

A low rumble echoed along the trees, drawing Violet's gaze. Was a storm beginning? She watched the sky, waiting for a flash of light. None came.

The rumbling grew louder and her stomach sank. She turned to look around the edge of the curricle, and her heart nigh stopped.

"Christian," she hissed, spinning to face him. "There is a carriage approaching from behind us, and it isn't the one from the school."

His jaw tightened, but he otherwise showed no outward sign of distress. "It is likely that it is merely another road user, Violet. But we will exercise caution. There is an inn just up the road, and we require a change of horses; I propose we turn into the innyard and see if the carriage follows."

Anxiousness danced along Vi's nerves, but she nodded her acquiescence.

They came upon the inn swiftly and pulled into the drive, alert and aware of the carriage's direction. It followed closely behind them, stopping at their rear. Stable hands flocked to both equipages. Violet held her breath as the carriage door opened. A leg was extended, then a gloved hand...

But it was not Americus. Vi's breath left her in a *whoosh* of relief, and she smiled as the stable hand helped her to the ground.

Dusk had fallen, lending a blue hue to the quaint inn. Two large dogs slumbered near the front door. A heartbreaking pang clutched her chest at the sight; one of them closely resembled her sister's adoptive dog, and the reminder that she had not yet heard from Rose was decidedly painful.

"Shall we adjourn within for supper?" Christian's low timbre warmed her inside. "I imagine that the others are famished as well."

His lips curved upward, and her stomach wobbled. He was a sinfully attractive man. It was a shame he didn't wish for a true marriage. That was most certainly a topic that she must reopen for discussion once they reached his estate, for she had no intention of being left behind.

Christian reached past her to open the door of the inn, his other hand resting at the small of her back. The contact was brief, but entirely arousing.

With her mind and heart happily engaged in the heat of his touch, she entered the inn's taproom. The brightly lit room was bustling with patrons pausing in their travels for a hearty repast. The din of voices and clanking dishes filled the air, mingling with the alluring scent of spiced stew and buns. Vi breathed deeply of the aroma, a smile on her lips, as she took in the space.

All at once her smile faded, her skin turned cold and sticky, and her heart beat heavily against her ribs.

He was there. Sitting at a dining table with a large slice of venison rolling around in his mouth, laughing as he squeezed a taproom maid's bottom.

Hands clutched her shoulders and pulled her back through the door to the dim light of the evening. The odour of manure, hay, dirt, and leather brought her shockingly back to the moment.

"We must—"

"Have the curricle brought around," Violet cut across Christian's thought. "I've a plan to catch him."

Chapter 34

Christian bit back the desire to give orders. *His* plan was simple: hide Violet in the stables, storm the taproom once the others arrived, and take the blackguard by surprise. Unfortunately, his wife was exceedingly persuasive, for he'd immediately fallen in with her proposal.

He must grudgingly admit that his wife's plan was sound, if unnecessarily dangerous for her. He would remedy that.

Pulling on the horses' reins, he led them down an overgrown dirt road just off the throughfare north. Chris could only assume the direction Bristol was headed, but this was the most probable option.

Leaves and branches of the overhanging shrubbery tugged at their clothes. The horses tossed their heads in protest but pushed through, past the denseness and into a clear patch of road.

"This will do," Chris whispered as he pulled back on the horses' reins. "I've a feeling that we ought to have waited until the others caught up with us."

Vi clucked her tongue. "Americus could have left by then!"

The trees overhead blocked out the dim evening light, leaving them in near complete darkness.

Chris notched his head toward Violet's reticule. "Is your pistol loaded?"

"Yes," she returned.

"Excellent," he continued in an undertone. "Once we disembark, I must demand silence. Our voices would alert them to our presence, which is counterproductive to our plans."

Even though Violet was merely an opaque form against the darkness of the trees, Chris could still sense the thinning of her lips and frown of disapproval at his imperious tone. She would merely have to accept it for now, as his experience vastly outmeasured her own.

"We will hide among the shrubbery along the tree line and await Bristol's arrival," he continued. "Once I identify the mode of his transportation, I will step into the lane and hold him at the end of my pistol. You will—"

"Did you take that pistol from the school?"

Chris shook his head dismissively. "I always have a pistol. Listen carefully, Violet, this is of the utmost importance. *You* will remain in the shrubbery." He held up his hand to halt her protest. "You will *only* vacate the shrubbery if Bristol somehow manages to best me. I will then need you to hold him at pistol point so that I might relieve him of his weapons and bind him for travel. Are we understood?"

There was a moment of silence between them before Christian clasped his wife's hand. "*Are we understood?*"

* * *

Violet wanted to say no. She wanted to refuse to participate in his foolish adaptation of her plan. His haughty arrogance was too much to be borne. She supposed, however, that in this instance, he had turned into *Lofty* Leeds out of a desire to protect her. She *ought* to be flattered.

"Yes," she lied.

His clothing rustled as he descended from the perch. "Come," he whispered.

Vi followed the sound of his voice and let him aid her to the ground. Together, they wove through the trees and dense bushes until they reached the tree line. It was brighter there, out of the cover of the trees, though still dark enough to hide their forms from view.

Countless minutes passed while they hid, crouched low to the ground, the air thick with anticipation. Leaves rustled with the wind and the movement of forest creatures.

Despite her outward confidence and her overwhelming desire to see justice done, Violet's stomach was knotted with nervousness. She had only just begun to learn how to handle a weapon or escape an attack, and Lord knew that with this cover of darkness, she was more likely to run into a tree than to successfully defend herself against Americus. And she had but one weapon.

Hydra was an excellent instructor. She would use the darkness against her cousin and, with Christian's help, they would capture Americus.

The earth began to tremble beneath her feet, and her eyes widened as they focused intently down the road. Sound soon followed, growing louder in volume as the carriage neared.

Violet's heart echoed the pounding of horses' hooves, her chest rising and falling with each rapid breath.

An equipage rounded the corner, and Christian released a breath. "It's the others."

He stepped out onto the road and waved to them. The conveyance slowed, and Chris approached.

"Find a lane up ahead and leave your equipage. Come back on foot; we've a plan."

The driver nodded, and urged the horses on, and Chris returned to Violet's side.

"They'll return," he assured her.

Silence fell as they waited, but it was not long before the rumble of someone approaching sounded again.

A carriage came into view as it rounded the bend of trees, and the tightness knotting her insides eased. There was no crest emblazoned on the side of the carriage.

Christian's lips touched her ear, the sudden intimate contact sending heated awareness through her. "Would Lord Bristol travel in an unmarked carriage, or would he continue on horseback?" he whispered.

"Not if he could help it," she returned. "His vanity knows no bounds. He followed us on horseback before, but if he doesn't believe himself to be in pursuit, he might change to a carriage, particularly after being injured."

With that, he withdrew, the warmth of his body and his breath abruptly gone. She lamented the loss.

The carriage rumbled past, and Violet resumed her post.

Several more minutes passed in which the only audible sounds were those of the creatures of the night, and hers and Christian's soft, rhythmic breathing.

Faint vibrations once more alerted her to a coming equipage, and she trained her gaze down the road.

A carriage lamp swayed with the motion, lighting the driver's profile as it righted itself around the turn. The din of horses' hooves and rolling wheels grew louder, and Violet's breath hitched. There was a crest emblazoned on the side!

She squinted through the darkness, grateful for the carriage lamp that put light to the side of the carriage.

Her heart jolted. "That's his crest!"

Christian's hand found hers in the darkness, and she gave it a short squeeze. *This is it.*

Withdrawing a pistol from a holster he had hidden within his waistcoat, Christian stood and marched to the road.

"*Whoa!*" he called, aiming the pistol at the driver. "Hold!"

The horses whinnied and stomped their hooves as the driver pulled back hard on the reins. Before the wheels came to a complete stop, the door swung open with a *bang*, and a large man leapt out.

Violet's heart nigh jumped from her chest as the driver, another equally enormous man, jumped from his perch to land hard on the ground.

Everything happened in an instant.

The two imposing men charged at Christian, who pulled the trigger on his weapon. The loud *crack* echoed through the trees, frightening the carriage horses. One of the men roared and clasped his arm, anger alight in his shadowed features.

The other man charged faster, and Christian reached into this coat and withdrew four of his throwing knives. *Thwick, thwick, thwick!* He threw three in succession, hitting one man in both thighs and the other in his uninjured arm. The men howled, but continued toward him unabated.

His last blade still clutched in his hand, Christian began a series of attacks against the burly men, and while concern for his injury swept through Vi, her attention was diverted elsewhere.

Americus stepped confidently from the equipage, arrogance shown plainly in the set of his jaw and stiffness in his spine. He withdrew a pistol from his breast pocket and aimed it at Christian.

"*No!*" Violet's heart squeezed painfully as she withdrew her own pistol from her reticule and dashed from the copse of trees. "You will not harm him!"

The horses sidestepped. The carriage lamp swayed, creating an unearthly flicker of light that shone on her cousin's maliciously handsome features.

Christian continued his battle with her cousin's cohorts, while Americus came toward Violet with a slight limp.

"Do not come any further," she said. "I have no qualms about shooting you."

His lips curved upward in a vicious smile. "As I have learned once before. You cost me nearly a week in recovery, cousin. I shall make you pay for that."

Violet's hands tightened on the pistol, but before she could pull the trigger, Americus leapt at her. He gripped her hands, knocking them upward as his attack lifted her off her feet. They both fell to the ground, the weight of him landing on her chest forcing the wind from her lungs.

She gasped desperately for breath and struggled to keep a hold of her pistol, but Americus managed to toss the weapon away. Vi bucked and thrashed, trying to throw him off, but he remained.

Her lessons came rushing through her mind. She could not injure the man's kidneys with her thighs, for her skirts restricted her, but she was left with one excellent option.

* * *

A meaty hook swung toward Christian, and he dodged it, delivering a swift punch to the man's ribs. Aware of his other opponent, Chris leaned forward and extended his right leg in a rear kick, connecting with the man's gut. Winded, the man went down to his knees, leaving Chris to better focus on the challenger in front of him.

The man swore vilely and spat as he swung another fist. Chris blocked it, but once more cursed the pain slicing through his side. He'd overestimated how far he had healed, for it most certainly held him back. He was confident that he could have neutralised both men already if it hadn't been for their pointed attacks on his stomach. And his concern for Violet.

A shout rent the air, and Chris' gaze snapped toward his wife. His stomach dropped. She lay on the ground with damned Bristol atop of her. They struggled. Abruptly, Chris wished that he'd allowed Hydra to complete Violet's lesson that afternoon.

His opponent caught him distracted, punching him square in the jaw. Christian stumbled backward, then righted himself to deliver a series of punches back to the wretch.

With the heel of his palm, he struck upward, catching his adversary in the nose, breaking it instantly. The man shouted, blood squirting from his broken snout.

Chris dropped to the ground, sweeping his extended leg out in a wide circle, and catching the lumbering man at the ankle, knocking him to the ground. With the man down, Chris retrieved both of his daggers from the man's thighs and quickly stepped back.

Violet's scuffle drew his attention once more, his concern for her startling him in its intensity. "Vi—" His words were cut off when a body hit him from behind, thick arms squeezing his own to his body.

His gaze still on Violet, Chris swung his head back to knock the bastard in the face. Violet swung her hands together to clap Bristol in the ears. His scream coincided with that of the man gripping Chris.

Bending himself forward quickly, Chris flipped his opponent over his shoulder to land hard on the ground, the man's face a bloody mess and the wounds on his arms seeping. Chris retrieved his dagger from the man's arm and stepped back once more.

Violet managed to roll her cousin off of her, and she struggled to stand. Chris moved to come to her aid, but his adversary gripped his ankle and tugged, pulling him to the ground as well. He clawed at the gravel and dirt, his fingers and knees cut and stinging.

His wife stood menacingly over her cousin, a sneer and growl of hatred coming from deep within her as she raised her foot and stomped on the bastard's cods. Bristol howled, and Chris grimaced, though his chest filled with pride.

Violet broke into a run toward the tree line. *Damnation!*

"Violet!" he called.

Exploding pain radiated through his ribs as his other challenger kicked him. His mind still on Violet, Chris turned over and gripped the man's knee, throwing him off balance. He kicked his other opponent's face, and the villain released his ankle.

Finally free, Christian stood. He had to be done with this. With a swift *thwick, thwick*, he threw a dagger into each of his opponents' right knees, felling them both. He cringed, understanding the pain. *Now, where is Violet?*

Chapter 35

Violet's pulse sped as fear raced through her. Americus would only remain detained for a moment. As soon as he recovered, he would chase after her. She *must* find what she was looking for!

Her gaze scanned the dark forest floor just within the tree line.

While training with Hydra over the last days, her best weapon had been the staff. As she'd struggled beneath her cousin's weight, Hydra's words had come back to her. *This particular weapon might not be readily available if you are surprised by an assault, but there will always be something that one might turn* into *a staff…* And then she'd known her course of action.

Her foot bumped into something, and Vi bent down to feel it. *Aha!* It was a large branch, too thick for her to touch her fingers around its girth and just tall enough to reach her shoulders. It was perfect. She felt along the wood and broke off any excess twigs before she heard heavy breathing behind her.

"Where are you, filthy *bitch*?"

Vi's eyes widened and her stomach threatened to embarrass her as she pressed her back to a nearby tree. He would undoubtedly hear the movement, but that would be to her good fortune.

His footsteps neared, one slow *crunch* at a time.

Then he was upon her, a loud growl escaping him as he reached for her. She spun, swinging the branch high. It connected with his head with a hollow *thunk*.

A string of curses flowed from his lips as he lowered to one knee on the forest floor.

Violet ran—awkward though it was with a large stick in her hands—back to the road. Christian was there, retrieving his daggers from the two men whom Vi's cousin had obviously hired to aid him. His intense blue gaze lifted to meet hers, and relief filled his features.

Americus was close on her heels. She had but a moment to assess Christian's position before her cousin was at her back.

Recalling her lessons, Violet spun the stick overhead. She moved to hit Americus over the head again, drawing his defence, but she quickly altered her course and jabbed him in the stomach.

He grunted, fiery hatred blazing in his gaze, as he stumbled backward. He came at her again, making successful connections with her.

Panic began to rise up within her, replacing the confidence she'd felt. She swung and jabbed, only some of her attacks connecting with her bastard of a cousin.

She missed one swing and nearly toppled forward. "Ballocks!"

Americus laughed cruelly, and the heat of anger burned in her chest.

With a calculated hit, she aimed directly for the spot on his thigh that she'd stabbed over a sennight prior, and, to her gratification, he howled in pain.

* * *

All at once, the energy leached from Christian's body. He must aid Violet! But he very much feared that he could not.

Between the exchange of punches to his tiring and bloody foes, he'd caught glimpses of his wife fighting Bristol. She was a warrior. Even in two short days, she had learned a great deal about fighting in defence of herself. Her efforts were admirable, to be sure. But he'd be damned if it didn't look as though she was being dealt even more injury than her opponent.

Her lips were split and bleeding, there was an oozing wound at her temple… *Hell*, she looked thoroughly beaten.

Christ, but his stomach knotted, and he stumbled forward.

"*Huh*!" she grunted as she caught Bristol across the hip with her large stick.

The man grabbed the end of her makeshift staff, his lips pulled back to reveal his bloodied teeth in a snarl.

No!

Bristol tugged her forward, but she raised her foot and kicked him hard in the chest, forcing them apart.

Pride cut through Chris' pain as he watched his wife move. She was remarkable.

* * *

Americus stumbled with the force of Violet's kick, and she took advantage. She swung the stick and hit him with two hard swings: one in the side of the knee, and the other again to his previously injured thigh. He went down once more with a howl.

Vi abandoned her branch and ran in the direction that the discarded pistols had landed in the brush. Searching through the tall grass, she found Americus' and whirled around to aim it at him.

"Stop, cousin," she said firmly.

He had begun to rise from his downed position, but her words halted him. "We know how this ends, Violet."

Vi shook her head. "Not the way you envision it." She notched her chin at him. "Lie down on your stomach," she demanded.

She was acutely aware of her husband's weakened state. This mustn't take much longer. Christian required a physician. And where the devil were the others? Hadn't they said that they would join them?

Keeping her pistol trained on Americus, Violet knelt on the ground. She gripped the filthy bottom of her petticoats with one hand and brought it to her teeth. Suppressing a shiver of revulsion, she tore a long strip out of the material.

Americus lifted his head to watch her, a vile glint in his eye.

Violet gritted her teeth. "Keep down! You move, and I shoot."

"Could you live with my death on your hands, Violet?" he rumbled.

Her lips thinned. She was certain the man was attempting to distract her enough for her to lower her weapon. She would not fall for it! "Most assuredly," she lied.

Careful to keep the pistol aimed steadily on him, she rose and stepped cautiously toward him. He could easily reach his arms out, grip her ankles, and pull her to the ground. She mustn't allow him to take the upper hand again.

Scuffling and grunting came from Christian several yards away, and Vi resisted the impulse to see if he was well. Her gaze and pistol were fixed on her cousin, watching for any sign of movement.

She moved slowly and prudently, kneeling at his hip. Violet pressed the barrel of the pistol into the bastard's back, silently letting him know that she still had it trained on him.

"Put your wrists together," she demanded.

With a growl, he grudgingly did as he was told. Vi placed the cocked pistol in her lap and hastily tied his wrists together, ensuring the knot was tight.

Gripping the pistol once more, Violet rose. She watched Americus and inspected her knot. It was sound.

Now she would help Christian.

Despite the dreadful ache and fast, rhythmic throbbing throughout her body, Violet dashed to Christian's side. And her heart sank. He was pale and sweaty. He looked ill, indeed.

Americus' two men were no better, however. Their faces were drenched in blood and sweat, their noses bent at horrifying angles. Their attire was splashed with red and torn in several places.

Vi grimaced. "Both of you, roll to your stomachs and place your hands behind your back."

The two thugs rolled dutifully to their stomachs as Chris limped toward his own spent pistol, groaning as he picked it up.

Chapter 36

A bead of perspiration trickled down Violet's spine as she drove their equipage back toward Chris and the others. The horses swerved, and she struggled to regain control, her stomach abuzz with nerves and her body's aches and sores protested every movement.

Her cousin's brutes had already been loaded into another carriage, by the time she rolled to the stop.

Her heart in her throat, Violet hurried to her husband's side. His complexion was pallid, and a light sweat dampened his brow.

"What happened to him?" she asked, nodding toward where Americus lay prostrate on the dirt road.

Chris shrugged one shoulder, then winced. "He had an accident with the butt of my pistol." His voice was low and rough; the sound tightened the knot in Violet's stomach.

"Come along. Get in the curricle, and we'll get you to the surgeon."

Chris jerked his head in a nod, and the students helped him to his feet and walked with him to the equipage before aiding him onto the seat.

"I've not driven before tonight," she reminded Chris, climbing onto the seat beside him.

He held a hand to his ribs. "I have faith in your ability, sweetheart."

A tremor of untimely delight travelled through her at the term of endearment, but she quickly shook herself. Her husband required a doctor immediately.

"Drive slowly," he continued. "Be sure that you are able to see the road in front of you."

Violet nodded, her entire body alight with nerves. "Would you prefer it if I brought you back to the school, or might I return us to the inn down the road and seek help there?"

Christian's eyes slid closed, and his lips pursed white. "The school, if you please."

Vi murmured her response and loosely grasped the horses' lead.

"Good evening once again…er…ladies," Violet said softly to the horses. "We have an important matter at hand. I am a novice at driving, so please be kind."

Vi flicked the reins, pulling one side back and giving the other slack, urging the horses to turn the carriage. To her immense surprise and delight, they moved, making the tight turn just as she wished.

Soon, they were turned entirely around, facing the direction they had come.

"Wonderfully done, ladies," Vi praised. "Let us pick up some speed."

She flicked the reins, and the mares broke into a trot. A smile stole over Violet's lips. *I am driving! And Chris will soon be well.*

* * *

Pain radiated throughout Christian's body. He no longer merely *felt* it; he *was* the pain. Surprisingly, he did not believe that he had sustained any terribly serious injuries, simply a great many little ones. He must be purple and blue from head to foot with bruises, abrasions, and some deeper cuts. But none of those injuries held his concern. His side burned. He knew not if his mostly healed wound had reopened or if he suffered with some internal bleeding. Whatever the cause, he felt like death.

He braced himself as the curricle swayed in a turn. He watched the passing darkness, the wind blowing over his face and rapidly ruffling his hair, his thoughts reeling.

Strangely, the threat to his mortality was not what had his heart doing aching flips in his chest. As he had fought the two buggers, he had scarcely taken notice of *them*. His attention and concern had been entirely for Vi. He'd felt each of her blows, felt pride for each of her triumphs…

Chris had wanted to congratulate her on a job well done. He had wanted to pull her into his arms and kiss her, to fight side by side with her, to defend her.

The realisation had hit him suddenly... He didn't want to ever be without her.

Over the past weeks something had been building within him. Something that he hadn't, until now, been able to put into words. What he felt were always *unnameable*, enigmatic emotions, but the strength of them had been growing staggeringly strong. This evening, they were nigh virulent in their power.

Chris had heard and read about such "fictional" feelings from nauseating poetry, novels, and foolish friends and acquaintances. Never would he have ever considered that it was *he* who was wrong. *Never* could he have imagined that he would one day fancy himself *in love*. But that was the only word that could possibly describe what was happening to him.

I am in love.

He was ashamed that it had taken him so long to realise it. That it took them both being attacked, and him knocking at death's door, for him to accept the truth.

The curricle jolted slightly before being righted. A loudly exclaimed "*Ballocks!*" came from the woman beside him, and Chris laughed, gripping his side as pain sliced through him. His smile lingered on his lips. Violet was a delightfully spirited woman. He was going to enjoy spending his life with her.

The realisation that love was real was a terrifying one. While poetry certainly extolled the positive aspects of the emotion, they also rather horrifyingly detailed the negatives. Could one truly die of a broken heart? Was it as agonising as it was described on the page? How would *he* feel if something were to happen to Violet? It was too awful to contemplate.

His thoughts circled around his startling discovery as the gentle vibrations of the curricle lulled him into a fitful sleep.

* * *

Violet trembled with nervousness and fear as she guided the curricle down the dark road. Her knuckles had whitened considerably as her grip on the reins tightened. The chill wind had made most of her extremities numb, but she persisted.

Pride filled her to bursting. She had done it! Vi had proven to herself that she could defeat her vile cousin and that she would make a serviceable and practical wife to Christian. This evening, she felt truly accomplished; not in the sense that most women would be, with sewing, painting, or playing the pianoforte…but well and truly capable of being a part of the world. Her own hero.

Once the doctor had come and Christian was on his way to recovery, Violet would tell him. She would let him know that he would not be rid of her so easily. She knew his secret life, she had met his fellows, and she had fought alongside him…and *won*!

Christian did not believe in love, but Violet would make it her purpose to prove to him that it was real. She would allow her love for him to show in every kiss, every passionate embrace, and every gaze. For it was true: she loved the lofty man.

A wave of relief washed over her as the school came into view. She led the mares into the drive but couldn't get them to curve properly, so she pulled them to a halt in an awkward, skewed angle and shouted for help.

"Hello! Might we have some help, please?"

Two men ran out the front door and gawped at her in shock.

"My husband needs the doctor!"

One of the men nodded and dashed into the main doors. The other strode forward and aided her to the ground.

She thanked the man before turning to focus on Christian.

"Blimey!" the man breathed as he took in her husband's condition.

Bending forward, she gently tapped her husband's knee.

"Christian? We are at the school."

His eyes slowly opened and a grin formed on his lips. "Excellent," he said drowsily. "Very well done, sweetheart."

Hydra, Ferris, and Dr. Stainton burst through the front doors and sprinted toward them.

"What happened?" Hydra asked.

Vi shook her head. "I haven't the time to explain it in full. Suffice it to say that my cousin and two of his hired thugs are unconscious within the carriage that will arrive shortly."

The men watched her with wide eyes, taking in the state of her.

"I would very much like to hear more," Hydra began, "but time is most certainly running thin." He nodded at her, respect warming his gaze. "You have my utmost appreciation and admiration, Violet."

With that, he spun and began giving orders. "Ferris, look after the horses and put the curricle away."

The man sketched a short bow and stood aside, waiting for access to the curricle.

"Come." Dr. Stainton appeared at her side. "We must get Samuels indoors. He could very well be critically injured."

Vi's stomach sank further as they worked together to help her husband from the curricle's high seat and bring him indoors.

Chapter 37

"...For we do not [rut] like Beasts, who are only prompted thereto for Generations sake by nature, but with knowledg and for Love's sake..."

There was a knock at the bedchamber door, and Violet put her book aside. "Come," she called.

The door opened to reveal Chris. Her stomach fluttered at the sight of him. He wore an amusingly familiar cerulean banyan—though it couldn't possibly be the same one—that served to brighten his eyes. He appeared almost precisely as he had on the first night they'd met, though a little the worse for wear during his process of healing.

Vi beamed at him. "Good afternoon, husband."

He grinned back at her, his colour much improved from the evening before. "And you as well, wife." He eyed the book at her bedside table. "A bit of light reading, hmm?"

"It is the only book I own."

"We shall have to remedy that." He strode forward, his limp pronounced and requiring the use of a cane.

"How do you fare?" Her ever-present worry over his welfare churned in her stomach.

The moment they'd returned to Grimsbury Manor, he had been taken to his room to be cared for by Dr. Stainton. The doctor had then come to see Violet, though she'd only sustained scrapes, bruises, and fatigue.

Chris closed the door behind him then came to her bedside. "I fare well. My injuries were not as bad as I'd feared. I'm merely weak from the fever of last week."

"That is wonderful news!"

He nodded. "And you? How are you? Did you sleep well?"

Vi laughed. "I am bruised and rather sore in my muscles, but I shall recover. Dr. Stainton wishes for me to rest." She frowned at him. "You ought to be resting as well. Come, sit beside me."

His eyes crinkled in the corners, and Vi's heart skipped a beat. She'd nearly forgotten how much she loved his expressive eyes.

Chris perched his walking stick on a nearby chair and shuffled onto the bed beside her, arranging his banyan to cover him as modestly as possible.

"Lean forward," she demanded.

He dutifully followed her direction, and she placed a pillow at his back.

"There," she whispered, a smile on her lips. "Comfortable, yes?"

He returned her smile and took her hand in his.

"Now that I have a moment alone with you," she began, "I have something—"

Leaning sideways, Christian cut off her words with a short kiss. The brief contact sent a frisson of awareness through her body. It had felt like days since she'd last kissed the man, and it was a small piece of heaven.

"I have a letter for you." He reached into his banyan's pocket and withdrew a piece of vellum.

Her breath hitched as she recognised the handwriting on the direction.

"*Rose!*"

Nervousness fluttered in her stomach, and she spun her husband's signet ring on her finger. Vi tore the seal and began to read.

My dearest Vi,

I apologise for not writing to you sooner. I ought to have forwarded the mail from Aunt Maureen's apartments to my new address. When I thought of it, there were already letters from you!

Congratulations on your nuptials, dear sister! I must confess, I am sad to have not been there, but once reunited, we must celebrate. I very much look forward to meeting the Viscount Leeds; he sounds utterly fascinating!

What a harrowing journey, you poor dear. I do hope that our cousin is apprehended soon. And I do so hope that Lord Leeds' recovery is swift.

I know you are eager to learn what transpired in my own journey, and I am certainly desirous to tell you! One can only presume that you have learned of your companion's identity (and if you have not, then this letter will certainly prompt you to inquire!). Well, dear sister, as amazing as it is, my husband's true name *is Sir Bramwell Stevens. We were wed at a small church just outside of London. I dearly wish you could have been there with me, Violet. Perhaps we could celebrate for the both of us when we next meet!*

Bram works closely with Lord Leeds and their superior, Sir Charles Bradley. Imagine my surprise!

Our uncle had men follow me to London. We were chased on horseback through the forest, which was an entirely terrifying experience. There was an unfortunate fire in Bram's sister's house in town, but everyone escaped to safety.

Hale has been labelled as a traitor to the Crown and he, even now, sits in gaol awaiting his trial. The evidence they have suggests that Americus is also a traitor, which is not terribly surprising.

I shall save the remainder of my story for our next meeting. I do hope I will see you soon! Will you come to London once Americus is apprehended?

I love you and miss you, my dear sister!

All my love,

Rose

Post Script:
Dog is happy, and adjusting admirably to life in town.

Violet put the letter down and wiped at the moisture gathering in her eyes. There were no words strong enough to describe the bone-deep longing she had to see her sister once more.

"Is she well?" Christian asked softly.

"Rose is married!"

Her husband's silver eyebrows arched high. "To Stevens?"

She laughed. "Yes. She sounds joyful, and I am happy for her. It seems that Rose and Sir Stevens had quite the adventure as well."

Christian's gaze roamed her features, the crinkle at the corner of his eyes and the smile playing at his lips making her pulse speed.

"There is something I need to tell you, Violet."

She nodded, swallowing past the lump that had lodged itself deep in her throat.

"I wish to apologise for making a hash of our wedding night. I was certain that keeping you far from me would protect you from my life and somehow shelter you from danger. I am sorry, Violet, for not recognising your full potential as a woman, as a warrior, as a wife, and as a companion. I have come to realise how very much I need you in my life.

"You said to me that you did not wish to be in a marriage with one-sided affection, and you should not have to be. I know I said that I didn't believe in love and, at the time, I did not. I now can truthfully declare that love *is* real…" His sky-blue gaze met hers, deep and earnest. "For I love you, Violet. Deeply, and with my whole heart."

Despite herself, Violet's chin began to tremble and her eyes welled with tears, her heart bursting with joy.

Christian squeezed her hand. "You agreed to become my wife in the legal sense, as an impulsive solution to your troubles. I no longer wish for that sort of marriage. I propose partnership, friendship…and love. Will you be my *true* wife, Lady Violet Leeds?"

Her tears spilled over as she nodded. "Yes! I love you, too, Christian."

With a smile, Chris cupped her jaw and swept forward to take her lips with his.

Epilogue

Christian couldn't breathe. His throat was constricted, and his heart pumped a staccato beat in his chest. Panic overtook him, but he did his best to hide it.

A shrill scream rent the air and echoed in his very soul.

Sweet Lord in heaven! She's going to die, she's going to die, she's going to die! The horrible litany taunted its way through his mind.

"Truthfully, Lord Leeds, you are as white as a ghost. Why do you not await word belowstairs? Have a brandy. It will not be long now."

Christian swallowed past his fears and the dreadful emotion rising up in his throat. "I will not leave Violet's side."

The midwife shook her head in pity. His new sister by marriage, Rose, stood on Violet's other side, gripping her sister's hand. She smiled comfortingly at Christian, her other hand rubbing her own protruding belly, but it didn't ease his worry. His wife could very well die this morning!

"It is time to push again, my lady," the midwife urged.

Vi squeezed his hand, a deep growl coming from between her clenched teeth, her lips drawn back and her eyes squeezed shut. Chris wanted to do something. He wanted to help! Was this what it had been like when his mother had died in labour? Had she suffered as Violet was now suffering?

Her growl turned into another scream, her hand tightening on his.

Then it was over. A small cry filled the room, and Chris' heart nigh burst. Violet sank against the pillows upon their bed, sweat beading her brow and her chest heaving.

"Congratulations, Lord and Lady Leeds! You have a boy!"

Uncaring of what the women thought of him, Christian refused to hold back the tears that threatened. His eyes burned and his vision wavered as the midwife handed him his messy, pink, and squalling newborn son.

He was beautiful.

* * *

"What shall you name him?" Bramwell Stevens asked as he leaned a hip casually against the chest of drawers in Christian and Violet's bedchamber.

Chris' chest swelled with pride. *I have a son!* What a foolish man he was to believe that love did not exist. For there was no other word for the outpouring of emotion he had for his wife and new baby boy.

"His name is Alexander, after Grandpapa," Violet answered, her gaze on the little baby in her sister's arms.

Rose swayed back and forth. "It is a fitting name. He *looks* like an Alexander."

"I believe so as well." Violet smiled. "Tell me, what news is there from London? I have been so out of touch since my confinement began."

Bramwell cleared his throat. "The trial was over several weeks ago. Hale and Bristol spent some time in the Tower before the hanging. Mr. Piper took to the sea, and there is still no word on the whereabouts of Lady Hale and Lady Uriana. Our best assumption is that they fled to the continent or America."

Christian nodded. "Indeed, now that the war is over, I wager the continent is an appealing choice."

A frown touched Violet's brow. "What will happen to the Secret Service now that the war has ended?"

"Actually," Stevens began, "that is rather fascinating. His Majesty will always have need of those in the Secret Service, but the likelihood of him requiring so many new recruits is low. There is some appeal, however, in turning our band of spies into an entirely different profession."

"And what is that?" Vi asked.

"Do not keep her in suspense, Bram!" Rose laughed. "He loves theatrics."

Stevens lips drew sideways into an unrepentant grin. "A professional business as Bow Street Runners."

Violet's eyebrows rose. "Indeed?"

Christian nodded. "It promises to be very lucrative. But more importantly, it will help the citizens of England."

"I've heard tell," Stevens continued, "that Elizabeth—now Lucy—has chosen to change her name once more and begin a separate Bow Street business strictly for women. As I have come to understand it, many women feel more at ease hiring a woman to conduct their personal cases rather than relying on a man."

"How delightful for her." Christian grinned. "Women are damned impressive when they set their mind at something."

He locked gazes with his wife, his love for her growing stronger with each passing day. How different his existence had become in eleven short months. Never would he have thought that life could be so happy.

CPSIA information can be obtained
at www.ICGtesting.com
Printed in the USA
LVHW030007031221
705165LV00002B/151